B OSORIO POLGAR
7094 Spring Garden Dr.
#103
Springfield, VA 22150

DREAMERS

BELINDA OSORIO POLGAR

bosoriopolgar@aol.com
703-717-2301

Cover designed by Belinda Osorio Polgar
Printed in the United States of America
2019

Author page:
@dreamersbelindaosoriopolgar

Spanish and Yiddish Glossary In Back

For Lex,

a critical inspiration,

Adel, Michael,

and

Tom,

best husband, playmate, ever.

CONTENTS

4

Chapter 1

Bus 164

Settling itself like an oversized pig in a troth, snorting, squealing, spatting, spitting, dark fumes from its hind quarters, the engine quits, quivers, quiets. Bus 164 pulled up, two stops over, adjacent to murky greyish white exit doors. Exhaust gas fumes from incoming buses fills the bus terminal, making Kat and Rita more than a little nauseous. Bus 164 parked. This wasn't the visually spic and span clean decorative, double decker they'd taken earlier in the day from Washington, DC.

"Finally, came in, ova there. Holy shit."
"Hush mom."
"God damn. It's really late. It shuda pulled up here."
"Please mom, hush."

Tired. Spent. Journey, incomplete. Penn Station the halfway mark to wannabee central, the Izod Center, Meadowlands. Where *dreamers* were made or extinguished. Plausibility's, possibilities, *suenos*. Reality TV at its best. Such a long way to come, and yet the adventure hadn't begun. There'd be a surprise road trip ahead.

Rita looks past Kat, through expansive terminal windows, wondering how long the line is. Without noticing, it had gotten longer during their wait. Now it stretched down the interior hall and became two-fold.

Stoically, they step towards the bus. "We need to sit together." Wanting to find joined seats Kat decides to carry luggage onto the bus. Taking the suitcase, Kat, struggles up the stairs. Moving aside in the narrow aisle to let other passengers get past, offers "Sit here, mom, behind the driver." Lifting luggage overhead, finds it doesn't fit. "Don't think I can get the luggage down the aisle." Rita in first sits by the window. "I'll put it on my lap. Didn't think we'd make it out of town tonight, it's so late." "Time ta sit back, an' relax, sweetie. We made it. Didn't seem like tha cross-winds passage was blowin' in our fava, but here we are! On our way!" High-fiving, "Hooray! We'll be pullin' out."

Not on schedule, Bus 164 driver strives to move things along, to make up time, admonishing passengers on the loud speaker to "quickly find seats." Reminds, "headphones" must be worn. Finally, a Ticket Porter enters, walks up and down the aisle counting seats, heads. "O-kay, you're full, hav' plenty standing, but yew can move on out now." Removing pages from a clipboard, hands it to Bus Driver 164. "Okay, we'll roll." Business done, door closes, securely behind.

Overhead light turned off, air conditioner turned on, gingerly passengers finish moving articles in overhead bins, finally settling into seats. Noisy chatter, impatient rush of humanity entering a cramped space ends. Bus 164 becomes darkly, quiet. Backing out of parking spots, rounding squared column corners, leaving the terminal, enters street traffic.

Annoying electronic sound whirs through loud speakers, "Well now dat we're moving, let me, greet yew all. Ta night, like every night on my run, led me say welcome on board to Greyhound. We're on our way to tha Meadowlands. I will be makin' hotel stops. Traffic iz normal, sew, I don't see no problems. I lost some time gettin' into Manhattan, but we'll make it up. Sit back, relax an' 'njoy tha ride."

Sitting tightly, side by side, in seats made more comfortable, because they were so worn. Relaxing. Nothing pinched. At this point it wouldn't have mattered. Sitting, mattered. Getting to the Meadowlands, Izod Center, mattered.

Looking out the window Rita's tired eyes wandered. Settling on familiar sights. It was becoming more difficult to retrieve heartening memories. Old haunts egregiously missing. Sadness entered a layered heart chamber. Manhattan, gentrified too quickly. Rita, loved working class, old tenement shabbiness. Four, six, many storied tall. Walk ups. Clef shaped cornices. Slate chipped stoops showing wear, like a hard working woman's nail polish. Remembering, old decaying tenements, anchoring Broadway's Times Square larger than life 1920s, '30s, '40s electric neon lights. Neighborhoods, buildings, imagining *Papi* and *Tanya*, her parents, slowly walking. Holding, hands: children behind them. Secure in their salvation. Speakeasies, cafes, orchestral stages, nightclubs, concert halls *Papi* performed in.

Twentieth century dynamism. At the turn of the last century, Manhattan emoting new country wealth, exuberance. Streets smartly laid out, an urban planner's vision of sophisticated optimism. Technology, cusping with the precision of an architects compass, T-squares, templates, creating plazas, fountains, and parks.

Cohesive.

Uptown. Downtown. East Side. West Side. An island hugged by edifices reaching towards God. Capped by church-like steeples, antennas. Water towers, sustaining multitudes of life. Sweltering humid, in summer. Hydraulic steam rising from underground tunnels. Black, steel to gray metallic luster asphalt, melting underfoot, burning sole less feet, breathing during the summer. "Hades underfoot?" *Papi* asked his children. A sermon on Greek Gods followed. Autumn, cooled asphalt. Becoming, winter slick slippery hard. Dangerous underfoot, uncompromising, chilled, cracking, splitting under constant pounding of millions of unrelenting vehicles, populace.

Loving authentic, rugged humanity, her eyes continued to rove passing streets. Mid-town Manhattan, Dicksonian characters moved out, disappeared. East European languages, disappeared. Rita, child of the 50s, 60s, generation ushering in boisterously, a cultural schism, then explosively a social revolution.

Electric connectivity defined the mid-town relationship. Rita's cotillion to Manhattan's media, advertising, banking and cultural capital of these United States, was the result of an award. Earned. Seventy perfectly synchronized and executed minutes away from home, on a good day. Landing a coveted spot in a magnet high school. In 6th grade, older sisters sensing Rita needed an escape, offered, "*Bopkis*, you'll be outta 'ere, someday. Jist not now. Wait, mom understands. In, high school." They reassured, "Yew will love, high school." As a rising 7th grader, Rita had little awareness of the splendiferous magnitude, beguiling, intoxication, that was the adult Manhattan.

A new door would open. An *adventura*. Entry towards the adulthood Rita so wanted. Tanya, Rita's mother, understood a daughter's need to escape, recognizing familial DNA. On Rita's first high school day, to help without hesitation, Tanya, rose at 4 am, cleared the stove, warmed milk, and prepared a warm tea. Quietly in the early morning household, where Tanya took in newborns to six year olds, Tanya embraced the most important motherly task, preparing Rita for the sixteen hour day.

This was a household busy with early morning exits, and Tanya never failed with a *bendicion* at the door, waiting till the hard rubber, stiletto heal touched the last subway tile step, the heavy steel door opening then, closing shut. At 5:25 am, Rita left a third floor walk-up in *da Bronx*, walked ten blocks to the 'El' riding it to Forty-Second Street. The subway ride started elevated five stories, submerging underground past Yankee Stadium. Rita learned to sleep with eyes wide-open, subconsciously counted subway stops, never missing a stop while eyes shut when returning home late at night.

Like butterflies emerging from cocoons, walking through cavernous Grand Central Station bowels, Rita suddenly 'mid-town cool.' Five blocks later, arriving at high school, preferring to stand in front of the abutting Daily News building. *Tanya*, bought the paper each day for the wicked, illicit, *la Matrona* since arriving in the City.

Rita knew Tanya read it out loud, first page to last, practicing English while *la Matrona's* captive. Before school opened, Rita bought the paper at Grand

Central expansive sub-terranium newsstands, purposely arriving too early, walked across several streets, bought breakfast in the early morning Daily News café hot-spot, sitting beside reporters, editors and columnists ordering toast, English muffins, bitter orange marmalade, tea, pancakes with maple syrup, coffee, bacon and eggs.

Loud, intrusive electric chimes began the 7 am school day. It continued one school period after another. Its' sound resonating unto the already 42nd & Lexington, noisy busy street. The favorite, the last of the day, at noon, unleased hyperbolic energetic students onto unsuspecting passing business people. Rita skipped steps, running down three flights from home room, ninety-two pound frame heaving against heavy metal doors, robustly leaving the Romanesque early 20th Century building, melding, meshing forcefully into crowded unaware hurried streams of adult bodies.

The long frenetic walk in kick ass stilettoes, tight mini-skirts, teased hair, stiff, shellacked five coats hairspray, green eyeliner, blue shadow, layered mascara, pink lip gloss and fish net stockings, 'cross town' to a full time job, enjoyed. Paying. Doing that New Yawk walk, a pace frowned upon any place but 'tha City,' made her feel independent, adult like. The sixteen hour day, owned. Unchaperoned. This was the 'big time' no one the same age in that Bronx *shtetl* was privy to. Manhattan, the reward, for having studied hard.

Now, it was the same jolted energy, black cawfee over stimulated environment, as then, maybe more so. And yeah, sure, now it was Disneyland cleaned up. Litter had been conquered, gathered, hidden. Mice, rats didn't run past your feet while you stood waiting, in the subway, anywhere, deadbeat drunks, addicts chased away. Jailed. Moved. The City was now awash in post Giuliani police, so *tourista's* would be safe. Giuliani's dictatorial obsession with safety changed the City into an address so exclusive, Rita couldn't afford to come home.

Back in the good ole days, this part of town wasn't safe after 5 pm winter day light savings time. Gangs, miscreant looming characters filled its sidewalks, hid between alley ways, darkened poorly lite streets. Shysters, card players, hucksters, prostitutes, pan-handlers, pick-pockets, drug peddlers and rich white men, from Jersey, middle-class boys from New Rochelle, stopped by to buy drugs of choice, Long Island Five Town partiers, popping in and out of pulsating private dance clubs in oversized daddies Grand Marquis, moved up and down Broadway, looking for a good time. Certainly too scared to live in the City, but neva hesitating to take a snack of Times Square desserts. Women in tawdry, fishnets, semi-exposed breasts, vulgar outfits approached cars of every size and model in broad daylight, offering minutes, drugs, and longer fava's in a car or some shanty tenement hourly hotel, from another century.

Now everyone wore their comfortable gymnasium best, "under dressed." Gone were the day workers crisscrossing, trespassing night life boundaries, during the day when it was safe to reach real jobs, walking past them to the jewelry, fashion, newspaper, music, ad businesses in towering office buildings rimming Times Square. Gone were their tailored hand stitched, sophisticated uniforms; hair sprayed bee-hive bouffants, four inch high, stiletto Italian and Spanish leather shoes, men's fine fedora's with a tucked small feather, hand stitched white gloves, thick black false eye-lashes, conical hard bras that pierced the heart if you leaned into them, layered foundation, hiding pimples, acne, imperfect skin. Skin looking china doll polished. Smart theatrical make-up to die for, worn to a nine-ta-five office job.

Now caps, from everywhere in the world adorned, topped off Nikes, Pumas, Adidas, Avian and Reebok's. T-shirts, sweat pants, replaced tailored three piece suits, Italian silk ties, white stiffly starched shirts with gold pin lapels, men's neatly pressed, cornered square handkerchiefs in the left front pocket. Pleasantries, stiff polite formality. Gone. Flashing cameras and I-phones, tourists taking endless numbers of selfies, brushing against commuters, home boys and City dwellers.

Now there were, hedge-fund players, real estate moguls, out of town corporate executives, Senators, actresses, Congressmen, models, TV executives, billionaires and families treading water in the world's most exclusive real estate. Populace who had nothing to do with its industrial rust belt 19th and 20th Century embattled, rough and tumble, melting pot histories. Clueless. Its factories, its ship yards, its sweatshops. Had closed, moved on. These tourista's visited museums to be in touch with past histories, keeping their hands clean, finger tips uncalloused.

Demanding that only English is spoken here, in these United States. Forgetting their foreign language heritage. English standing last in line behind, German, Gaelic, Welsh, Yiddish, Italian, Spanish, Ladino, and Polish. Forgetting the mean-spirited melting pot that arose out of Five Points between the Irish and Blacks, rising up against the Protestant ruling class.

Exotic dining, settling in boutique size restaurants with magazine and television familiar famous chefs, shi-shi names. Gone, one by one were the one pound, New York steak, potato and ale joints beckoning, feeding a working class teenager, like Rita, with its $4.50 sign. One meal, feeding her, office refrigerated, over three work days. Gone where the white and red checkered table cloths with plastic flowers, fashion center seamstresses, jewelry piecemeal workers, Hell's Kitchen seniors, sitting next to push carts, filled with groceries, wrapping their one inch thick steaks into stolen napkins, eating the potato, and salad. Exchanging the dark ale for redeemable nickel bottled pop. Gone, like her Dresdenesque, Bronx *shtetl*.

Tho' late, there was ample human movement and traffic, but because they were so tired, Rita and Kat subconsciously wished they had stayed for a cozy visit with Manhattan cousins. Resting in a bed. Saving their arrival for the next day. Neither shared that thought.

Sacrificious.

Yes that was it, one had to sacrifice for one's art. Rita's musician father had taught that. Challenges, auditions, hope, desire, and wanting '*it*' was the life blood of an artist. Whichever kind of artist you became. And, *Idol-A-Try* could be the short ticket. While looking out the window, the second part of the journey began. Quietly adjusting themselves into seats, they relax.

Kat, found a shawl in the luggage case, pulling

it out. It was a tight squeeze in this common in-elegant bus, but finding a way to soften the experience, Kat made magic out of thin air. "So, here mom, this will make you warm. It's gonna get cold in here."

Rita accepted the kindness and indulgence. Kat had always been a world class child. So while they disagreed on most everything, 'it was generational.' Rita relished the warmth, the proximity, the reality of having Kat nearby. It wasn't about money. It wasn't about wealth, it was about proximity. It, proximity, was not forever as any mother knows, it was for now, now was in the moment, Rita basked in Kat's warm ephemeral glow.

"I love this view of Manhattan, mom, it's magical. Tonight's moon, is larger than anything I've ever seen in DC. Why's that?" Rita looks up towards the moon, smiles. "Don't know, yew cud almost touch it."

Turning, looking down the aisle, Kat observes, "Oh gosh, it's pretty crowded, people are standing. We got lucky. Barely lucky, but lucky." "Well, at least we're on our way. Secon' time ta-day, crossin' Manhattan ta Jersey. Luk, we jist passed all this. Shudda asked tha DC bus ta pull into tha Meadowlands."

The ride to the Meadowlands was direct, without stops. The *Idol-A-Try* website displayed a small map of the Meadowlands and the Izod Center. While the bus moved slowly, stopped and started because of city traffic, the ride was finally becoming uneventful. Kat played with the I-phone, texting friends while checking work schedules.

Rita looked down on passing traffic, sign posts, mile markers, metal skeletal gas cylinders, and towers, mentally slowly drifting towards pleasant thoughts of Kat singing beautifully, *exceptionally*. Imagining, Kat's voice soaring, touching hearts. The inner heart beat grew slower from sweet imagined notes, emanating from memories. Rita prayed asking God for support. Kindness. Prayed for a crack in that damn wall, called *Hollywood*. You know that place where wannabe musicians start, are used and abused. Few Hispanics made it past the security gate. And if there were, they usually wasted talented years in less heard, less successful cross-over markets. Kat would have to learn to sing in Spanish, maybe learn to speak it, sing music not cared for, to be sold to people she had very little in common. Kat was your typical American, speaking only English. For years' producers of commercial music generally ignored beautiful voices.

Exceptional voices.

This wasn't the old days when a beautiful voice, a singer had a chance of being produced. Now it wasn't about that. Rita raised an opera singer, expecting a classical world. The economic collapse created a short fall for Rita. So this was an unpleasant, rude short cut, and if Rita had to *finagle*, arm wrestle Kat to the Meadowlands to compete for a spot in the larger more lucrative mainstream market, and find a producer who respected voices, so be it.

Fifty minutes into the ride, as Kat was scrolling through e-mails while, Rita continued imagining Kat's voice, success, the bus driver announced, "We'll be makin' several stops ta-night, at dis time we dew not stop at tha Meadowlands."

16

Startled, disbelief, panic crosses Rita's face "Oh Jezus! Whad does that mean?" Jerking forward, cramped feet, pushing harshly against the driver's back seat. "Hell, no! No way! Aesk 'er, Kat, aesk, what's goin' on!"

"Why me? You ask."

"Well yur sittin' behind 'er! I can't reach 'er from this side. Aesk how close she stops to tha Meadowlands. This bus wuz supposed ta go there."

"No! Yoooou ask."

"You're closer. Damn Kat! Just lean forward and aesk."

"No, you ask you're better at it."

"Jist say, ... iz this Bus 164, Jesus, Kat! Tell 'er we bought a ticket tew tha Meadowlands."

Uncomfortably, moving luggage, shyly, quietly trying not to disturb sleeping passengers, moving forward, inquiring, "Mam, (hesitating) you don't stop at the Meadowlands?"

Kat, leaning, past the bus driver's seat, to be viewed, "Where do you stop?" Looking into the review mirror, the sista Bus driver remains unresponsive. Irritated, "Aesk, again how close tew tha Meadowlands, we'll havta walk tew it." Worried, Kat re-approaches the bus driver voice rising, "Miss, how close to the Meadowlands do you stop?"

Gruffly, this larger than driver seat woman looks up again into the mirror, looking right, finally replies, "I don't stop at no Meadowlands, I goez thru it. Uh, where yew wanna go?"

Diminished by the harsh combative bus driver's voice, Kat answers, "The Izod Center." Cautiously,

"The Meadowlands?"

"Well dis bus don't stop there. We pass thro' it. It's closed at dis hour. Yew see? We goez past tha Izod Center, into tha Meadowlands. But we don't pick up or drop off. What hotel yew staying at? I make hotel stops."

Turning to Rita, "Oh God, Mom, what hotel?"

"We're not stayin' atta hotel." Peeved, "We're sleepin' on tha sidewalk. Re-memmm-berrrrr." Kat confesses, "We're not staying at a hotel, Miss."

Brazenly, diva like, the bus driver shoots back, "Well, can't let yew off ta dew dat. It's closed. A bus driver," diffidently, "ME, yew kno' there's no way. I can't let yew off in the Meadowlands. Yew hav' ta hav a stop at a hotel. What hotel? It's all highway, after tha Izod Center, can't let passengers off on tha highway ... I hav' ta go through tha Meadowlands,"

Interrupting, Rita insists, "Name a hotel. Any friggin' hotel!" Angrily, "Make it up!" The bus driver continues, "Becuz of tha way tha highway lanes are. Yew tourist people don't realize it but, it's, all highway between hotels, ain't no City streets. It's like a belt roun' tha Meadowlands an' we goes thro' it 'cause that's tha way we gits to tha hotels."

"Sheraton, Ramada Inn, Motel Six, I don't know, who cares, what a freakin' *nudnik,* jist fishing." "Mom, shhh."

"Whad a pain in tha *tokhes.* Making us do the whole *shmeer.* We can't afford it. But name somethin'." Kat, pulls out a Blackberry, searches for a hotel. "You're too loud. We have to name something that's here mom, or she won't believe us. Uh, Ok," Leans forward re-engages the bus driver. "The Sheraton, that's it." Sweetly, "the Sheraton. Can you stop there? We need to get off there."

Tersely, combatively, the bus driver asks, "Are yew staying there?" Unprepared for the harsh tone, Kat answers apprehensively, "Uh, well, no ... not exactly." Firing back, "Den why shud I stop dere?" the bus driver disdainfully questions Kat. "Don't need ta make no needless stops. That's reckless, jus' plain reckless. And I'm not reckless. I can't leave yew off der, an' yew expecting ta catch n'otha bus tew tha Meadowlands. I'm tha las' bus tew-night. Yew shudda thought about dis before yew gots on. I've got scheduled hotel stops for tha other passengers."

"Well I asked the ticket master at the Port Authority for a ticket to the Meadowlands, and,' voice quivering, 'it says on the *Idol-A-Try* website, that, that, ... the number 164 bus stops at the Meadowlands. In the Meadows in front of the Izod Center to be exact. You're the only one saying, INSISTING, it doesn't."

Haughtily, "Well, I don't! Not at dis hour. Jist pass through. Git it? Why wud ya wanna go there in tha middle of tha night? See, we're passing it now. It's closed. Hotels are tha only place I stop at. An' hotels are all 'round it. ..."
Exasperated Kat scans the Blackberry, "So ... Ok, the Sheraton. Pleezzze!"

Cynically, "But yew sed, yew ain't stayin' ther'."

Condescendingly, "How cud yew git on a bus an' not know where ya goin' or stayin'? Tell me dat. Can't guess fer yew. No, I don't stop at no Meadowlands, an' I won't stop at tha Sheraton if yew ain't stayin' dere. Don't need no trouble from tha hotel people by havin' yew stand about in their lobby. Dewing what? Loitering? Looking ova the people? No dear! Not my pass'ngers. Hmmph! And, youse my passenger now." Interrupting, leaning forward, "Mam, mam. Pleezzzzz."

Steering the bus helm, navigating the circular asphalt ribbon that is the Meadowlands, derisively, repeats an angry rant to this demure, exhausted *wannabe contestant*, now captive of Bus 164, "Yew needta go back to tha Port Authority an' wait fer t'marra mornings' bus. Think tha first one's at 5:30 am. Dis is tha last 164 from New Yawk for tha night. And, I can't let ya off in tha middle of a highway. Jesus yew people shudda waited til t'marra at tha terminal."

Pleading, sinking into the seat "But, the ticket master said. Mam, he said, you would stop. And you're going through it now. Please stop, now. We paid for two tickets, for tonight's 164, so we could get on line early." Almost despondent watching the Izod Center lights grow smaller, and smaller in the distance. "We needed to be dropped off back there."

Young Black man, sitting across the aisle, leans forward into the aisle to his left, asks, "Uh, well, Miss bus driver ... (softly, lowering his voice) you said when I got on that you would let me off at the, the, the, at the Izod Center, Meadowlands. I asked you, you, remember? ... Before, I got on. It's pretty late, and this was supposed to be the last 164 to the Meadowlands. I can't go back to the City and buy another bus ticket tomorrow. That would be a problem."

"Well, it's not open now." Haughtily, "Anyways, I mean tha Izod Center. I was gonna drop you off before I got back on the highway ... and DEW YEW a fava. Jist, you bro, you kno' whad I mean? That gurl spoke up when I was planning to jist drop you off. I got interrupted and got past that spot."

"Uh, I need, need to, to get off around there. As close as possible, you, you said you could drop me off nearby. I remember now, you, you said that you don't stop at the Izod Center, but that you would let me off somewhere nearby. You go any, any further and it'll be a problem."

Looking towards the young man, acknowledging the question, bus driver 164's brashness softens becoming calmer, "Uh, huh, sure, uh, well dat wus jist yew and that sista in the back. A fava for you and the sista, yew kno. "

"But, but mam, you're going too far. We needed to get off back there, mam."

"They need ta kno' what hotel. That lady gotts luggage. I can't jist let 'er off on tha highway... I would have stopped for you. And what is she doing with luggage anyways if she's not staying at a hotel? An' tha shoes, she wearing sneakers? I don't know. I can't jist let ya off now, by tha side of tha road. Ya'all are giving me a,"

"Mam, you're making it really hard on us now, please mam, let us off ..."

"We're with him." Looking across the aisle, "We'll get off with him."

"But I wus gonna leave 'im off arounds near tha last area to the highway exit, I don't know if your mother, is, dat your mother?"
"Yeah."
"Don't know if she cud dew dat. We're past it all now. I mean the Meadowland and it's dangerous on tha highway. I mean yew kno'."
"Don't worry 'bout me. We're geddin' off wit' 'im."

"Can't believe yew people don't know whad yur doing. Well hell, ok, what are yew all comin' for anyway? Dere a few others in tha back of tha bus wantin' ta git off dere tew." Looking at Kat, Timothy says, "We're au-auditioning for *Idol-A-Try*. The line starts tonight to get tickets to audition. And this was supposed to be, be the last 164 to the Meadowlands. That's what the website posted." Timothy and Kat look in the direction of the back of the bus.

"Ok, but I won't drop ya off directly on tha highway. I'll dew it on a shoulda. Can't all of a sudden stop a large bus like dis on tha highway. It's not a scheduled stop and I hafta watch tha traffic. Cud git in trouble for leavin' ya on tha side of tha highway like dat. Yew understand! Don't git back tew ma' boss an' complain. Yew tha ones insistin' I'm breakin' all tha rules tew help ya."

Timothy feeling tautness in his chest release,

humbly, "Thank, thank you! Thank you mam, very much appreciated." The counter punching comes to an end. Relieved, Kat and Rita sit back into their chairs. "We appreciate it too."

Rita exhales. Staring at the passing Meadowlands offers, "Thank Gawd. Danken. Gracias. Grazie."

Minutes later,

"OK, I'm stoppin' now." Decelerating the bus. Loudly, on the overhead speaker announces, "Ok, anybody wanna go ta tha Izod Center dis is tha closest I can git ya. Yew hav-ta walk along tha highway an' go over tha bridge we just passed. I don't stop at no Izod Center dis time of night. Yew all can git off, I'm pulling' ova onto tha highway shoulder, gud luck!"

Door swings open.

Chapter 2

A Little Bit of Spice

At the end of an arduous ten hour work day, a twenty something white male drives down a two lane street lined with mature trees, manicured lawns and 1960s single level brick homes. Pulling midway onto the asphalt driveway, leaving space for the uncle he lives with. Checking around the littered cab, fingers search for a newspaper. Then, pushing aside tools, finds house keys. Leaving the truck, entering the simple brick, shingled house, through a side porch, throws keys onto the tiled kitchen counter.

It's warm inside the dark empty house. A northern Virginia summer arrived. Removing a uniform work jacket, placing it on the back of a kitchen chair walking through the foyer, towards the sofa, resets the thermostat, puts an overhead fan on. Moving his large thick body to the middle of the living room, slovenly hunkering into the sofa, placing soxed feet on a large square wood coffee table in front of the sofa, grabbing a remote, turns the television on, scans channels, looking through hundreds for anything remotely interesting. Grumbling, "Oh fuck, there's nothing on."

Finding a news channel, the news is carrying the usual local suburban crime story, a good deed, then, the weather. The weather man, the local celebrity guru talks to viewers as though family, offering up birthday greetings to some 101 year old grandmother sitting in a nursing home surrounded by equally loved, wrinkled grey haired residents, with a jocularity, you'd think it was *his* grandmother, wrapping with a wisp of a hand blown kiss.

"Okay, I shouldn't, but here goes. What Mr. Meteorologist, Mr. Science Man who reads all green screens and becomes all knowing," continues snickering, "what's the weather gonna be like for this weekend?" Like most weather people in the Mid Atlantic, whose batting average on forecasting summer rain storms is eighty-five percent wrong. "All wrong. I'm not payin' you no mind," Twenty-something shouts at the television. "YOU fuckin' messed up the barbeque last weekend. No rain, no rain, it rained." Harping continues talking derisively to the television, "Thank God we have that awning, Mr. Smiley Face Weatherman. Shit, would have lost all the food, if it weren't for that. Thanks teleprompter reader, I needed the outdoor shower. We don't have outdoor shower room plumbing. We're not part of the Trump billionaire yacht club yet. But, my times a cumin."

Bored, knowing it's time to get his game on to prepare for the four days of *Idol-A-Try* cattle call auditions, turns the intrusive television off. Walks to, opens the refrigerator, grabbing last night's leftovers, placing them on a plate, opening the basement door, steps down a slim, steep, narrow dark staircase. The basement is filled with wind instruments, percussion instruments; keyboards of various sizes, cymbals, the wood paneled walls are covered with R&B, heavy metal, country, folk and do-wop band posters.

Taking a quick look at one in particular; an *Idol-A-Try* poster, the poster he is most attached to. Scoping through national location calendars on its website, printing a paper copy, zeroing in on a small red calendar, taped to the downstairs, beer filled refrigerator, today, like yesterday and the day before that, and weeks before that, he counts days left. Hundreds of times checked the audition schedule, sites, marking, then circling Meadowlands, Izod Center. "Close enough to home. Meadowlands, is in driving distance. We could do it." The 'we' is he and his uncle Joe, the ever present male figure in his life. What hadn't his uncle participated in since he was a boy, left fatherless?

Like too many others who'd participate in the national prime time television talent show, Twenty-something had a story. A story needed telling. So, he scribbled his anguish, his fears, his loves, his happiness on blank lined music sheets. Day, after day, writing, hoping one of his songs would be heard, appreciated, applauded. So he could make it. Make it somehow in an industry where like the weather man, most musicians are not very good at getting it right or to the spotlight.

Moving about, switching on recording studio amps, adjusting the sound, playing with key boards, finally satisfied that everything electronic is working, Twenty-something picks up a favorite guitar. Lined up against the wall on the floor are eight acoustical wooden guitars. Rummaging through yard sales, they'd manage to find, collect good acoustical wooden specimens.

Guitars made of mahogany, with Indian or Brazilian rosewood, finely crafted were hard to find in the slim pickin's of yard sales and flea markets. But every now and again, Uncle Joe or mother would find something special. Excitedly giving a call, "Hey kid," the uncle cooed, "I think I found a right nice purty lady for you. You're gonna love this gurl I got for you. You're gonna hug this baby gurl right up tight against your chest. And, nestle 'er between your shoulder and neck. Then you gonna lean in, you're gonna stroke 'er. You're gonna stroke her lovingly. And, baby, gonna answer right back at you, make you smile."

Twenty-something's analogue heart beat pulsed across telephonic wires. No need to wait for a reply, feeling the love. Without a word between them, trading started. Especially good at this, his uncle, enjoyed dickering, bantering, the cajoling that went into the price. And his uncle always got his price.

Wondering whether or not to play Spanish classical music, checks his finger nails and callouses. Basement studio sessions were best started with Spanish classical music, forcing discipline, calm, dexterity, speed into stiff tired work day hands.

Seated with a guitar resting on his left leg, shifting, placing the left foot on a three legged sturdy footstool, "You have good hands for the guitar," Mr. Domingo, a slightly balding, aquiline nosed, retired public school music teacher, told him when first starting lessons. "Yes, nice long fingers," reassuring young, Twenty-somethings' mother. "Won't, have to work as hard as my students with small hands, or short fingers."

Mr. Domingo smiled, holding young Twenty-somethings' childish hands closely examining them. Pressing thin elegant calloused, long fingers on the palm side of the finger tips, "Of course, he'll have to work hard to get callouses. That's work my young musician." Young, Twenty-something glowed upon hearing these words. They were forever embedded in his gentle psyche. Beaming, looking up appreciatively at Mr. Domingo. He had become something at seven. He'd become a musician. The guitar became his first love.

Twenty-something was a right-handed player. Moving fingers from the top then downwards testing, adjusting pegs, polymer strings to make sure they were taut. Placing an ear near frets, adjusting, plucking up, and down strings, he listens carefully. Tuning, quietly listening, what he hears pleases. Starting, E-A-D-G-B-E, moving into a basic melody line on the treble strings.

In an effort to increase young Twenty-somethings world, Mr. Domingo set aside time, to share his personal vinyl collection, gifting a musical repertoire, large, varied. From behind a glass enclosed bookshelf, Mr. Domingo pulled early 20th century vinyl 78s. The collection included guitar masters; Segovia, Casals, Antonio Bossa, Miguel Llobert. Then moving towards Mid-century including; Julian Bream, John Williams, Christopher Parkening, and David Russell. Mr. Domingo lent him tapes and cd's to learn from, and finally to emulate. Twenty something, a talented gifted student, absorbed the vibrato of the grand master's guitars.

It was, "The best way to start learning music." Mr. Domingo said. "Spanish classical music will stay with you for the rest of your life. Into old age," he reassured. "You'll see, Albeniz, Granados, Tarrega, Rodrigo, Villa-Lobos, will come to you in the middle of the night, light your soul, fill your heart." He practiced patiently, every night in the quiet repose of his bedroom. It was physically, intellectually taxing. But he didn't know that then. Heart soaring, mastering, plucking strings in different positions, evening after evening. Learning, first position through twelfth.

Lessons with this old Spanish classical musician gave him another father figure. If it was singular attention needed, he certainly got it from the disciplined old man. An hour's worth, frequently more, twice a week he'd run down the street from home to Mr. Domingo's. The white lattice wooden screen door was never locked. Grabbing the rickety door handle, pushing it open with a thrust of energy saved for athletics, then abruptly running in. Sometimes, having to sit in the foyer eavesdropping on another student's lessons, quietly competitive, he measured his own worthiness.

While sitting, waiting, concentrating, continuing silently with alternations, moving fingers rapidly, never plucking a string twice in a row; the index finger, the middle finger, increasing rapidity each time, confidence grew. Mentally imagining the tonal qualities of notes, he'd practice over, and over in anticipation of the next lesson. The old man inspired him. Set high standards, established goals. The guitar challenged him. Through its timbre he learned to patiently, quietly listen to something other than a racing youthful mind and body. Calming, young Twenty-something.

After a time, growing musically, he moved onto other music genres. Welcoming impromptu visits, after long laborious work-a-day hours, Mr. Domingo guided Twenty-something's appetite whenever consulted. Never one to hinder a kindred spirit, Mr. Domingo warmly greeted his old student, after the childhood private lessons had come to an end.

Twenty-something practiced for a few hours, moving easily from classical music, to blues and finally to material he had written. Writing came too easily. Loaded with a bounty of songs ready for exposure, and production, knowing *Idol-A-Try* required selective choices, he picked four or five songs and worked through them. Standing in front of a mirror practicing movements, singing, standing, walking about with a guitar strapped to broad shoulders, comfortably he swayed hips, left, then right, then left again. Feeling the groove.

Tiring of practice, leaving the stool, moving his bulky frame to the floor, fingers rummage through the uncle's old 33's and 45's, stretching further, pulls from under a table, an old vinyl record player. It was late in the evening, just as thoughts of his uncle came to mind, a noise from the side door reaches the basement. The screen and kitchen doors are opened, there's familiar movement in the kitchen. The basement door creaks open, soft soled shoes managed the wooden stairs. Looking up, exchanging greetings, "hey," hands him a cold beer, then sits on the floor.

"Hey, Uncle Joe." Fist bumps, smiles exchanged, from under an arm, Uncle Joe pulls a plastic bag. "Let's look through these. Stopped at the library." Dust jackets slightly worn from love, use and study are handled delicately. Removing jackets, carefully brushing softened fingertips against the record player's delicate ancient needle, clearing it of lint or dust, nimbly fingers finally sets the needle down on the rapidly revolving black vinyl 33.

Side by side, pulling RPM Record label's star, B.B. King, Oscar Peterson's jazz duets with guitarists, Joe Pass, Irving Ashby, Herb Blis. Then King Crimson with guitarist Robert Fripp, Frank Zappa And the Mother of Invention's, 'We're only in it for the Money,' Santana, Led Zepplins' Jimmy Page, Hendrix, George Harrison, Eric Clapton and Yes.

Twenty-something was ready for his life to change.

Chapter 3

Papi

"But no, where are your people from?
Brooklyn."

Early on, "talent, check!" *Mami, siempre
Mami, Papi* recalled later.

Was it while in the womb? Voice, hypnotic,
seductive, harmonically-rich. Three, or was it two?
Two years, of age. *Mami, diminuendo,* spoke of gifts.
What was it? Even, before learning to speak. To put
words out there. Was it how he listened to *el radio*? Or,
the echo chamber that was her heart. Was it the *dolce*
heart beating? Hearing it back then?

A *forte* thump, thump, thump. Sometimes,
quiet, *pianissimo* rhythmic thumps. Then at times,
presto, thump, thump, whoosh, thump, whoosh.
Soothed by the thump, thump, but startled by skipped
beats. Even at two. Recognizing rhythms,
disconsonant notes of life. Strength, fear, weakness,
happiness, sorrow. Hearing it all, before speaking a
word. *Mami's adagio* heart beating cavity. Leaning in.
Hugged, surrounded by protective soft generous arms.

Was it because he smiled at those old classical
vinyl 78 rpm Stravinsky pieces, playing every Saturday
night, loudly emanating from opened living room
windows on hot, humid New York City nights? Or was
it the street vendor playing the violin *andante* and
singing *staccato*, 'gelato, gelato, of every flavor?" Or,
the Italian neighbor, next door, playing an accordion at

every family gathering? Maybe the Spanish guitar, mandolin player, always invited to melodically serenade a *senorita*? How exactly was it, when did *Mami* understand *musica* to be his soul?

But then, that's what *Mami's* are for.

What didn't *Mami* do for *familia*? What didn't she know about their wants, needs, desires, insecurities? A luminescent being. Never tiring. Ever. Always *trabajando*. *Siempre, dulce*. Always sweet.

Papi's socks as a young boy, never stood up. Having lost elasticity after a few days of wear, falling loosely nestled around boney thin ankles. Adding to pain felt, were ill fitted handmade leather shoes. They, the socks that is, were coarse, itchy, prickly. Wool. But they were his. To wash, hang on the open air roof metal laundry wire, every night. Or at least every night remembered. Steam radiators in winter best. Shrinking, warming the wool. Accepting they didn't always fit, weren't always the color wanted. These were little things noticed but never spoken of. Complaining wasn't part of their *familia's* nature. After all, *Mami* had lovingly knitted them. *Mami's* delicate hand, long, lovely hands, palms already deeply lined, yet to his mind, soft as chicken feathers plucked for meals, hands constantly at work, mending, repairing, bandaging. Artful hands. Finger tips calloused, prickled from factory sewing machine needle work. Never complaining, boasting of their dexterity. Boasting of their calloused hardness. Earned, *ganado,* like a fine Spanish guitarist.

He was thankful for such an angel. Friends at school whose mother's perished on journey's over from where ever to this bustling over crowded immigrant Red Hook section of Brooklyn, lived harsh motherless lives. Mothers, fathers, *familia*, wasn't a given, he'd learned, from an early age. Some had a *Mami*, some had not. Street urchins turned up at every street corner, begging, working, stealing, starving, dirty, abused, abandoned.

Orphaned.

Papi did not lead an orphaned life. *La familia* had a comfortable life. Mother's made life okay. *El mundo* was kinder. *Mami* made it *mas pacifico*. Made *Papa's* laugh, more thoughtful. Made *Abelito's* thank God for living longer. *Mami's* hug *Abuela's* keeping a place *en la familia entre ellos*.

Mami's.
Mama's.
Besos, mami.
Kisses, mama.
Que Dios te bendiga.
May God bless you.
Te Quiero.
I love you.
Mami.
Mama.
Con todo mi Corazon.
With all of my heart.
Mami.
Mama.
Bendicion.
Blessings.
Nunca te olvidare.
I will never forget you.

Mami.
Mama.

Mami's made all things possible. Heart strings soared when thinking of how lucky he was to have *Mami.*

Street noise, two flights below always woke him.   The long narrow single spring bed leaning against the papered wall, wasn't all too comfortable. Coiled metal springs pushed unevenly through cotton, against his thin boney angular body, the metal edge like a needle, finally waking him. Lingering, staring at the ceiling. "Too early to rise." Sunrise. "Yes, too early," to rise. Pressing down on the coil poking through thin white, blue cotton material, he moved a small thin pillow to the spot. "I'll have to fix this. Sew the opened area with *Abuelos'* needles."   Street noise increased as he laid out the day. Consternation rose from within because he hadn't noticed the break in material sooner, preferring to not wake till the very last moment. *Papi,* learned to sleep walk, eyes wide open on the way to school. Head draped over books, finally closing on late return, after the school day and private music lessons.

Down below, at dawn, noisy vendors pushed carts through streets. Another merchant voice added every minute. Melodious greetings, layered, voices rising above the din. Bellowing voices, a fugue developing, every minute adding depth to this American immigrant folk cluster. Wheels clacking, klit-ti-ty clack on cobble stone pavers. A vortex of European languages, sing songing wares provocatively, to formally dress a naked marketplace. Arriving, primping, propping their shoddily made vendor shacks.

Women, made come hither invitations, to anyone walking by to prowl through baskets of vegetables, and flowers. English not needed here.

Hardly eva.

Papi, studying yellow flowered wall paper, reaching the ceiling, imagined removing it. Dreamed of removing it. Painting walls a simple blue. Blue like the sky over Hudson waters at the Navy Pier on a hot breezeless summer's day. Blue like birds flying overhead, landing in shade less trees. Blue like morning glories awakening each passing day in late spring. Blue like cloudy *Abuelos* eyes. Rimmed with a murky white. Pulling a blanket closer to a thin angular chin, waiting for the street below to fill, his parents to exit, *Papi's* mind meandered a little longer, relapsing into a comfortable slumber.

"*Cafecito, papa,*" *Mami* offered *Papa* in the kitchen. Through the slightly opened door, the bitter fragrance aroma wafted over head. It painfully teased *Papi's* nostrils. The tin jar holding dark, thickly granulated *café*, sat on a painted wooden shelf over a deep porcelain wash sink. Sitting beside tea, salt, sugar, rice, saffron, pepper, vinegar, cheap paprika and flour. Not looking special. Or, royal.

El café.

But it was. It held qualifications, *Papi* hadn't yet met. The others were staples always replenished. Good dark roasted café metered out in careful doses. Never wasted, always appreciated. Shared with surprise visitors. But not immediately. Tea offered first to women in their company. Real café, not chick peas, were expensive. Finding its way from exotic shores to these Brooklyn navy yard merchants. Tea or café had to be carefully brewed to show respect for its heritage. A respectful brewing. Lorded over by *la senora de la casa*. A delicately painted *tasito* brought out from behind a glass cabinet, joined an equally lovely wiped clean matching saucer.

Brewed mornings, saved for hardworking adults. *Café con pan. Pan blanco.*

Never opening, that particular jar. Well not on his own. Holding *el cafe*, when *Abuelita* said, "*Ya pon lo aya.*' Put it over there." Or, when *Mami* shopping to replenish, *el café*, asked him to measure it, scooping it onto the scale. Using the stone weight, a smaller weight, a larger weight. Watching the tipping arrow go this way or that. Adding, or subtracting. Inhaling. Loving, inhaling that odiferous, adult drink before it was pulverized, its bountiful taste steamed into submission, reduced to liquid. Growing up couldn't come soon enough.

The aroma, lingered long enough for him to remember he wanted to join their table. Badly. Wanted to do more, to contribute more. But, they held back, asking him to study, study, study. *Papi* wanted to help. To give them relief, from their long hard days. *Abuelita* said, "*Espera.* Wait, your time will come. It comes to everyone. But not just yet, *amor.*"

Drinking that black malted, thick *café*, signaled arrival, *un hombre.* But he had to wait, to take a seat at *Papa's* morning table. *Abuelita*, reassured when alone, the turn *a la mesa* would come. So, waiting, he did as told. Studying, excelling at art, better at everything, than peers. Not arriving tired, like so many other students, sleeping in a small unshared room. Arriving rested, fed, on time, every day to a bustling, over crowded school. Excelling in music, he was offered a scholarship to the Conservatory for mastery of theory, violin, mandolin. *Papi* continued his musical study.

> *Exceptional.*
> *They had said, in the letter.*
> *Your son has multiple talents,*
> *which must be nurtured.*

Abuelita, knowing the hearts of men, of wanderers, recognizing seeds of dreamers, offered small tokens to keep him still. Groping his mind was, wanting more. *Abuela* offered, *café con mucho leche*, with A*buelito,* after *Mami* and *Papa* left for work. Happy for these moments with *Abuela*. Moments of recognition. *Abuelita* recognized dreamers, had seen this before in *Espana*. Young men pursuing dreams. Suenos. Dreamers leaving. Leaving *familia*. Leaving wives, mothers looking for a means of survival. Leaving everything in hopes of finding work. Survival.

> *Familia.*
> *Suenos.*
> *Dreamers.*

Readying for the cool September morning air. Contributing to the family order, *Papi* cleaned, work boots, placing them by the door, the night before, to avoid last minute worries.

"*Bendicion,*" *Mama*, asked *Abuelita*, the last rite, whenever anyone left home.

Papi waited for *Abuelita* to move away from the door. Both, waited for the click of the last step, the opening of the front door, and finally voices rising from the street. Moving to the kitchen window, hand rising from her side, *Abuela* made the sign of the cross. *Abuela*, offering an unseen *bendicion*. *Abuelita* prayed for their well being. Prayed they return, uninjured. The work at the navy ship yard dangerous, each day she worried. Theirs was hard work. *Mami's* sweatshop work needled her eyes. Tore at fingers, hammered down spine, back, cricked the neck bone, and weakened the body in small ways. *Papi*, wouldn't see them, till late in the evening. Sometimes for more income, *Mami* brought home piecemeal work. The work shared amongst them. On those days they toiled into the dark night, like most other immigrants.

Papi waited quietly in the bedroom for this final act of faith. This final act of love. *Abuela's* delivered, acts of love, of belief, acts of hope for the future. *Papi*, never stood in the way of these old ways. These *abuelitos*, hung onto their beliefs, no matter where. Maybe, just maybe it was because they were so faithful to their *Dios*, they survived, so much. Wars, famine, political strife, abuse, in their home land.

So, waiting, rustling through his mind were winds of change, dreams, and aspirations. *Abuelito*, opened the door quietly, "*Cafecito? Amor.*" "*Si*, I'll be right there."

Rising to prepare for school, *Papi* sat on the edge of his single spring bed, wrestling with shoes. These were shoes of his own making, he had not quite perfected the neat, exacting methods his *Abuelo* so deftly managed. *Abuelo* making sure *Papi* had a vocation, a way of making a living, *Abuelo* teased, so he would always, 'land on his feet,' eyes twinkling, with '*zapatos*.' *Abuelo* picked a spot near the kitchen window, for the triangular cobbler's bench. Fitting securely against the wall, *Abuelo*, shared his talents with his grandson. Lovingly. Teasingly. By example, *Abuelo*, taught, *Papi* learned.

Frugality was a consequence of life, along with knitting, sewing, cooking, laundry for a family of five. Everyone contributed. Papi's obligation was to study, learn, graduate from high school, becoming the first American high school graduate.

But on weekends to be by *Mami's* side, and steal away time from other family members, *Papi* volunteered to help grocery shop. *Mami* loved this duplicitous secret chatter, *rendezvous* into Manhattan. Taking street cars, ferries, sitting side by side, sharing on goings of the week, their talk was of school, art, music lessons. The day hot, *Mami* fanned cool whispers onto the childish face, with a delicate heavily sugar starched lace fan, of her own making. Coldness brought, soft hot blows unto woolen mittens. Elegant long fingers wrapped around small hands. Huddling together, pulling woolen hats, gloves and scarves around their exposed parts, sitting tightly, side by side in seats made more comfortable because of their physical proximity. They relished this time. Both knew, it was not forever.

Manhattan's small one room shops burrowed in aging tenement buildings, held trivial curiosities, only a teenager would notice. Buying knitting needles and wool from the same scruffy old Polish Jewish merchant, Mr. Ross, in the lower East Side whenever needing to refill supplies, was now a family tradition. Multi-layers of the same ill-fitting coat, clothed the old man whether temperatures were cold or hot. Mr. Ross always embraced *Mami* when returning. Good natured, easy going, passively aggressive made bantering a contest of jocularity, joviality. The room filled beyond the brim with skeins of wool, spinning and sewing machines, lace patterns, hemp, needles, pillow, bobbins, straight pins, thread with little room for their bodies was a testament to the old merchant's ability to collect and sell. Other darkened shops squeezed into 15 x 8 foot spaces, close to two stories high, windowless. Thick wooden planked floors creaked with every movement. Floor to ceiling ladders on wheels, leaning up, slanted against row, upon row of winter coats, men's clothing, women's dresses, children's items, hanging from ceiling hooks, the better to move them about.

The area smelled of workmen's sweat in hot summer, unbathed grimy humanity. Food stands in push carts filled with over ripened tomatoes, potatoes, sauerkraut, long thin sausages cooking, walked about over uneven cobblestone, by men and women too old to be doing anything but sitting at home. But need made them push on. Amongst them, peddlers cooking, selling heaping steamed portions to working class people, needing sustenance. Children spun heads stealing apples, strawberries, cabbage. Winter brought about a smell of smoldering, newspaper filled metal garbage cans, embers escaping helping to keep hands warm, layering everything with a coat of smoke. A cold vapor escaping from hoarse throats and larynx, chanting the language of exchanged pennies, nickels, dimes, quarters and George Washington's. Hamilton's in this austere time rarely seen. *Papi* celebrated these delicate beloved memories decades after *Mami's* passing from tuberculosis. Taken too soon.

There were many in the immigrant Brooklyn neighborhood, whose socks were worn beyond repair. Whose mothers, aunts, sisters, spent time repairing diligently, after long days of factory work, sweatshops. Everything repaired, salvaged. But after a time, one couldn't mend, worn, damaged holes. Like *familias*, sometimes the wear and tear of all of it, wore them down too. Sometimes migrations, losses, *sacrificios*, bigotries there, then here, the journeys being too arduous, resisted repair.

No curative bandages of repair.

Mami, first generation Brooklyn people, their family hailing from Bilbao, Spain, wending through one port of call after another, staying for a respite, first the Canary Islands, then St. Thomas, Puerto Rico, *las islas Virgenes*, and finally the great port city of New York, landing in Red Hook, Brooklyn. The trip took six months. Escaping economic hardship, war famine, along with Irish, Italians, Jewish, Norwegians, German and Slavic immigrants, *Papi's* family was thankful for this safehaven. Its streets crowded, bustling with merchants, workers, work, labor of all kinds.

The 1890s offered work, a chance to more than survive. Everyone worked. Including children. There were no child labor laws. Children were a commodity to be used, abused. Abandoned. Left to churches, streets, orphanages, criminals.

Papi's grandparent's family hunkered down starting with a cobbler's bench. *Abuelo* was able to finally own a small cobbler's shop, where two of the older sons toiled six days a week, saving Sunday as the day where they returned to God. Working in the basement of a small tenement building, piece meal work, *abuelo* hired as many *Espanoles* y *Italianos* as he could. Rising before dawn to handle repairs for factory shoes, his business became *la familia's* main breadwinning source until his blue eyes became clouded. Too clouded. But by then, his first generation *Americano* family, knew the lay of the land. His cobbler's shop taken over by older sons.

Along the way *la familia* became comfortable. At least, for a while. *Papi* understood going to school full time a privilege. Most children *Papi* knew, worked. Childhood, was often times a luxury in those small Brooklyn row houses and tenements. Cherishing *Mami's* gift, the music classes which made his heart soar, he felt forever indebted to her vision. *Mami* protected his childhood, providing time for the rudimentaries of early 20th century, education. *Papi* became the first *en la familia* to graduate from high school, and further. Second generation *American-o*.

Then the rest of the world interceded. Since their arrival, the family witnessed WWI, the stock market crash of 1929, bread lines, Salvation Army food lines, mass evictions, Hooverville's, unemployment, and WWII.

Papi, pursued on scholarship, the Academy of Music, Brooklyn a hub-bub of culture and mirror sister city to Manhattan. Within its border were two movie theaters, churches, synagogues, banks, clubs, ethnic restaurants, shops and a park. The area would see many changes while *la familia* lived there.

But after the death of his beloved *Mami*, armed with talent, good looks *Papi* crossed the bridge and found a new musical mecca.

Manhattan.
Mecca.
El Barrio.
Spanish Harlem.
Mecca.
Orquestras.
Conjuntos.
Chicago.
New Orleans.
Philadelphia.
Boston.
Cincinnati.
Los Angeles.
Miami.
Clubs.
Carnegie Hall.

While his family no longer traveled the four
   corners,
    he travelled these United State of America.

His homeland.
This was the place to be and to go.
The past was nestled in a memory pocket.
Of the Brooklyn Navy Ship Yards.
Red Hook.
Cobbler's bench.

Memories of his *musica*, his *familia, y por
supuesto …*
Mami …

Chapter 4

Da Bronx

"Holy *dreck* ..."

Rita's early 1950's northern Bronx neighborhood upbringing, rolls off her tongue with yews, doez, *schmuck*, cumon's, *schmo*, howboudit, *schlep,* and whaddayacalits. Making anyone exposed to mid-century segregated *"da Bronx,"* wonder how this happened. Pinched Streisand nasal d's, guttural, multi-truncated, hard consonant concentrated rapid fire speech punctuated with *Yiddish* emanated, made her ethnicity suspect. Rita was 'the gurl outta da Bronx,' but not 'tha Jewish accent outta tha *goy.'*

So, how exactly did Rita's *familia* get past the invisible obtrusively red lined 148th Street Grand Concourse border in segregated late 1930s, *'da Bronx?'*

In a diverse twentieth century *United States of America*, Rita, a white Hispanic, frequently judged by looks heard, 'but you don't look Hispanic,' all too frequently. The vowel ending Spanish surname didn't jive with the physical superficiality that had become America's favorite denied past time, profiling. She'd become accustomed to having features scrutinized like criminal fingerprints. Once the quixotic facial search ended, the inquisition type interrogation would start.

Even oh so many light years and miles from mainland birthplace. "So where are you from?" "Da Bronx." "But no, I mean where are you really from?" they begged. "Da Bronx," adamantly. "But no, where are your people from?" "Brooklyn."

But then nothing about the adult Rita was what you'd expect, that is if you practiced pre-1950s observations of New York City spic. Protestant, not Catholic. City smart. *Shiksa*. No Puerto Rican diaspora. English centric. Wasn't any bod's idea of spic-dom. Not even among *Caribenos*. No easy verbal rapid fire *Nuyorican*. No *Dominicana*. *Nuvo-Spanglish* spoken. Neva ever. Square peg, in Jewish princess land. Yet, despite all *their* cultural admonitions, ego intact.

Early 60s, civil rights righteousness, yes. Lyndon Baines Johnson, Great Society, yes. Anti-war movement, yes. Jacqueline Kennedy, photo-journalist, Eleanor Roosevelt feminist, yes. Individualist Ayn Rand, yes. *La Marqueta*, 116th street, *comida* shopping yeah. Oh sure. But this was an uptown gurl visit, dragged out of bed, pre-dawn Saturday's onto the 'El' to *El Barrio* by her "*No cosino de latas*. I don't cook from cans and TV dinners" mother. No ghetto *chica* here. Northern Bronx English language *perfectamundo*. The predominantly Jewish teachers, the language *gestapos* hoovering over the few Spanish kids who snuck into their classrooms and neighborhoods, under radar, couldn't *kvetch* about Rita.

As a 13 year old, the Seventeen Magazine wannabe Twiggy Bronx gurl, complained her mother was too conservative. Staring at *tuches* length hair in the mirror, "*Papi*, can I cut my hair?" "Not yet *hija*, it reminds me of your *Abuela's* beautiful hair." She envied the permanent ironed processed pixie styled straight hair of her classmates. Coveted their psychedelic colored purses filled with little psychedelic pink lipsticks, psychedelic blue eye shadow, psychedelic blue-green eyeliner. Older sisters offered, "*Bopkis*, you'll be mid-town cool someday. Jist not now. Wait, mom will let you." Rita studied the Jewish American princesses she met at middle school living in the neighborhood. "In high school." Sisters assured, "Mom will, in high school." Their ability to consume, acquire, accept entitlement so blithely, blindly, was something this church going *goy* couldn't exploit. An angel sat on her shoulder, watching every move, ready to pounce. Her Methodist Jesus *kulture* was about *humilidad*, fire and brim stone punishment.

Square peg, in Jewish princess land.

Shaking her head in dismay, disheartened, impatient, culling the local library with secret desires. Suffocating, Rita looked for a way out of this middle-class *shtetl*. Where her 'Spanish *goy*' identity somehow betrayed her as an accomplice of Holocaust horrors spoken, when five years old, over shared egg cream sodas, banana whipped ice cream sundaes, picking through colored penny Pegs stuck to white paper, at the candy store. Gently, quietly old men in guttural *Yiddish*, harsh broken, poor working class English reminisced on the tall metal stools, beside her.

How does one fit into a neighborhood where the elderly *bubbe* unbuttoned, then lifted their sleeves, to expose numbered tattoos, and fragile shattered histories of a past so horrid, Rita wondered if she wanted to be a card carrying member of the human race? Obscenities spoken, too soon, to a *goy* innocent. *Papi y Tanya* had no idea, what the sacrifice for a better education actually meant to Rita.

Guilt, *shmilt*.

Sacrificed, her parents did. *To live here*. Not far from the sacred *Yeshiva*. Early school mornings, encountering processions of pallid anemic looking young boys with shoe polish black hair, tightly woven ringlets, black *yarmulke* and coats, looking past her, never acknowledging her presence.

Invisible.

Not even once, though they shared the same address, lived on the same floors. Not too far behind, their thicket thick bearded fathers wrapped in deep thoughts, reading *haggadahs* equally oblivious to her being, walking past.

Invisible.

And finally, their diminutive *apple-kerchief* covered wives walking, pushing, three, four or five babies in carriages look cautiously away. Never an acknowledgement came her way.

Invisible.

And while all the wronged ghosts of *pogroms* past, swirled evil *banderas* of prejudice around their third floor six rooms oasis, *la familia* remained chivalrous. "*Dignidad*," the elegant silver haired most handsome in the entire neighborhood father would softly say. After all the "Spanish people are a proud people," Papi reassured. "They are the land where at one time *Judeos*, Muslims, *Espanoles* lived together. We are still a proud people. Like America."

Didn't her parents remind every day, to study, to work, set lofty goals? Books, pictures, classical music sheets, art, lined their walls. Didn't Rita squeeze between bouts of selling beloved DC comics on the stoops, three for a dime, simultaneously studiously work her way through the Webster English Dictionary one hot elementary school summer?

Cover to cover.

And when, American liberalism intruded into a conservative Spanish American home, via lovely handwritten invitations, didn't Rita mid-way politely leave, at those raging hormonal pubescent post-office birthday parties.

Dignidad.

Begging an early exit, so *yuchnat,* Mrs. Liebowitz, couldn't yell from the third floor window, across the street while Tanya sat on window sills, washing windows, "Ruth saw your daughter kissing Ira, in the clothing closet yesterday."

Didn't Rita have to be quieter than those four *meshugaas,* Polish American kids on the first floor? You know, that apartment mom warned not to visit on the way home from school. "*No andas con esos ninos.* The man is *shikker* all the time.*"* "But mom we're in tha same classes." "*Er toig nit.* He's no good." "We have the same teachers, mom and, I like them."

No sneaking up the fire escape to the fifth floor, to find *where the boys really are,* practicing their early manhood, on the budding overly mascaraed, hair teased, *libertinas.*

A shande.

You know, that apartment with the three very attractive brothers, Paul, Mitchell and Stephen, whose parents were neva home, because they were building a business in Long Island City. That was fine for the bad gurls. But not for this *hija honrada.*

Dignidad.

Sure she'd sitting beside mom, chins comfortably on hands, leaning out the window sill to capture a cool summer breeze, watch the stick ball games, double dutch and captain below. Sure she'd skip the staircase, preferring skeletal fire escapes, running nimbly up to enter a best friend's apartment, (the only Jewish *goy* family in the neighborhood) unannounced, hoisting into the kitchen, through an unlocked opened window, lifting a slice of warm freshly made *babka* on the way to the friend's bedroom. *La familia* could not be confused with those *spics* living in Spanish Harlem. One could hope.

Or.

Wouldn't they be asked to move, if they weren't better conducted, cleaner, neater, quieter than everyone else?

Invisible.

Didn't Tanya have to put a towel at the door's base so the "*oy vey*, their using garlic, *ipish*" comments wouldn't be shouted in protest at their door next to the *mezuzah*?

Defensive, "Sew *gefilte* fish, doesn't stink?"
"*Seas respectosa*, be respectful."
"Our foods betta!" Rita retorted.

Opening the refrigerator, "Whaddayagot to *nosh,* mom."

Rita carried proverbial *hija honrada kultur* plates like an expert waitress.

Plates full of *Dignidad*,
Of Daughter.
Of American.
Of Dignidad.
Of Bronx gurl.
Of Goy.
Of Spanish gurl,
Of Dignidad.
Of *Americana.*
Of Sister.
Of Good student.
Of *Hija.*
Of Dignidad.
Of *Hermana.*
Of Good girl
Of *Hija querida.*
Of *Honrada.*
Of Dignidad

And Rita, never dared drop the plates.

Exceptionalism,
    was *la familias* expectation.

Nothing, *nunca* less.

Chapter 5

Idol-A-Try, No!

Turning to Kat, "So let's dew it!"

Weeks before the scheduled nation-wide talent search, on a hot summer's day, in a hipster styled crowded, eclectic living-dining room, lined with shelves, filled with music sheets, books, cd's, cellos, violins, toys, opera and Broadway playbills sits Rita. Still petite, now middle aged, looking ten years younger than anyone guessed. Reddish brown straight shoulder length hair, she enjoys wearing down, usually topped by a favorite purple summertime straw hat.

Rita intently watches the pop reality television program, *Idol-a-try*. Sitting nearby, is Kat. Rita's daughter, has luminous raven shoulder length hair. Kat's long lashed dark eyes are large, doeful. Nose, small, delicate, lips smoldering. Face sharply oval. Curvy, more reminiscent of a 50's girl, than the pencil thin cheerleading type, she went to conservatory with. Nor does her body represent the uber-thin high maintenance women Kat sells clothing to in a high end Washington, DC couture shop.

Rita, unemployed, is now living with Kat somewhere in northern Virginia. Things are tense, but there's much love and obsessive talk on the mothers' part about their futures. "Kat, let's dew it!"

This is one of the few days home the exhausted daughter has. "Do what?" Kat bracing. Rita is distressed; Kat left a conservatory to work, helping Rita through the collapse during the Bush economic crash, taking half of the middle class, never mind what it did to the poor, whose ranks Rita was tap dancing hard to avoid.

"Idol-A-Try."

Kat is pained by Rita's obsession regarding her musical career. Eyes rolling, "No, no way. Not interested. Don't like the program." Kat turns away from the fashion magazine, looks towards child-like graphic urban paintings, hanging on alternately painted mahogany brown and orange walls.

Ignoring Kat's attitude, "Yeah, but sew what!" Rita adjusting layers of loosely fitted warm clothes. The room and conversation are about to turn more frigid.

"No! I'm not auditioning for THAT! Can't stand *Idol-A-Try.*"
"Yew cud dew it. It'll be fun."
"No," exasperated, "mom." looking downwards. "Not interested."
"Yeah, audition for it."
"No, can't, don't like it."
"Why not?"
"Don't know." Insecurely, "Don't know my chest voice." Emphatically, "Know my classical voice. I'm a soprano. Can't sing in my chest voice." Voice rising, "I'm training now."

While the uncertainty of their future divides, music is a passion both share. Neither knows how to escape or bridge their great divide. They talk delicately of it.

"I like it."

Kat leans towards Rita, "Got it, mom? I sing classical, I need to focus on my technique for conservatory auditions." Rita ever sure of Kat's beautiful melodic soprano voice, responds reassuringly, "Know yew say yew don't, not yur style." Joyfully, "But it cud happen."

"Can't do *other* stuff. No! No, no more auditions." Immovable force Rita keeps on, "Yeah." Ignoring the response, turning away, "Sew it's not yur style. Give it, give it a try. Cum on," leaning a shoulder against Kat's as if to cuddle, on the sofa. "Yew ova think singin' jis,"

Annoyed Kat replies, "Not doing it!"
Continuing without an ounce of trepidation,
"Think of it this way. Make it tew tha top ten."
Thumbs pointing upwards.
"A possibility."
"Talent, check!"
"Voice, check!"
"Looks, check!"

Smiling, "Try, why not? Try, fer heaven's sake! Nuthin' tew loose? We go," eagerly pointing to herself and Kat. Waiting a moment to continue, "Yew, audition. Yew hang in dere." Excitedly continues, "Think, think of tha connections, yew *shmooz* wit' David Foster. He cud hear yew sing. That's tha prize." Pleading, nasal northern Bronx accent increasing. "Ta-hav a record pra-ducer like 'im hear yew. Then yew'll work on a song he'll pra-duce."

Grieved by this conversation, Kat looks down,

turning glossy magazine pages, "Can't hear you."

Listening to the pause, Rita realizes she's got to reassure Kat this isn't a lark. Not another audition where rejection is flat, hard, exhausting. Softly, "Yeah, I kno' ya wanna classical career. That's a long road. This isn't about tha winning. Luk, yur' beaw-tiful, luk at yur face. Yur looks! An' whatta voice, what's not-ta love. Give it a try. Cum on!"

"No, mom."
"Sure, try, try."
"No. No, Mom! ... Oh, I don't know. You're pressuring me."

Facing Kat, stands, holding arms outstretched on Kat's shoulders, lovingly, "Ya kno' yew cud dew it. This isn't the Borsht circuit." Softly, Rita, "Remember, the West Side Story audition?" Painfully, "Sure I remember. Don't want to do this tho'. My chest voice is different from my head voice."

"Yew sed it was a waste of time, but yew came in second ... You've got tha voice." Annoyed by Rita's insistence, angst filled voice replies, "No, I didn't want to audition for that either! Had to take a few days off. It cost ME, DO you understand. I sung from the soul for that audition."

Rita changing the tone, cheerfully, "They loved yew an' THAT wuz a Broadway musical." Exasperated, "YOU! as usual mom, you, arranged that without my knowing. *Idol-A-Try* is pop, not classical. I'm not doing it." Emphatically, "They needed a classically trained soprano for Maria." Rita insisting, "Love that song, Can I hear some of that?"

Kat sings a bar, wistfully relives emotions, "Wish that happened. Meant so much." choking up. "Can't get my hopes up for wishes anymore. Mentally, emotionally." Shaking, "No." Annoyed, determined, "Mom, I … I … won't do it. I'm an opera singer. Not a pop star!"

Rita knowing Kat intimately stopped for a moment. Braced. Old memories, emerged; remembering all the "no's" heard from this beautiful gifted talented child. Moments of 'no' could turn into hours of insecurity, hesitation. Performances, auditions, required every ounce of stamina, energy, commitment. Kat found talents, honed them to perfection. Kat was a quiet, shy child.

Losing momentum, after leaving conservatory, insecurities returned. The 'no' child never disappointed with a steadfast ability to resist.

Rita cajoled, offering images of happiness, success, inclusion. Sitting in their car an hour, watching others wave, entering a birthday party or small informal gatherings was the norm. Mental hijinks emanated from Rita, "So, just imagine there's a wall in ya mind," continuing, "an' ya wanna be on tha other side, but ya havta climb it, cuz being on tha outside, on this side that you don't wanna be … well, if yew don't climb it, well, yew'll be in more pain later on if yew don't, so …"

High jinks worked no longer, Kat wasn't a little girl. Rita tried bravado, "Oh, ged over yerself, just SING! They need ta hear yew! Yew need ta give a try! Whatdaya think? Iz it a go? Can yew dew it? Do we get bus tickets? Hotel tickets, no, not that! Can't afford that ... we'll have ta find another way ta stay ova-night. Or, is it becuz of Dweeb? Yew know, the Prince of Darkness."

Disgusted, exasperated that Rita reduced the boyfriend to a democrat anti-Dick Cheney slur, Kat responds, "His name's not Dweeb!"

"It's not PRINCE, either!" Rita yells.
"Mom, its' Mohammed. And, leave him out of this."
Snit-fully "Whatever!" Rita responds.

"Anyways ... mom, I'd have to find a song, take time off of classical music. You don't know how hard it is! Finally got my technique back. Don't want to ruin it for a fluke, that's not going to happen." Softly, lovingly, "Cum on Kat ... *Chutzpah*, that's all ya need!

Hesitantly, Kat opens up to the idea, "Maybe, maybe a David Foster song? I love his music. But, (*insecurely*), pops not me. Guess I could do Ave Maria, by Beyoncé." Brightly, Rita embraces hope, possibilities, "Alright now! Let me hear some of that." Kat sings. "Yes, gud, dat's gud, that song. *Bubala*, yew got tha talent ta dew either. This cud be a short cut ta gettin' noticed. That's all yew need is tew be noticed. Winning's, not important."

Springing, mental panic. Stepping back emotionally, physically, an avalanche of insecurity escapes, "Noooo, nope, no. See I'm an alto in chest voice, No, can't belt high notes. ... Soprano ... That's me. No." Mentally, reliving, trauma, rejection, "Why bother?"

Pleading, momentum lost, "Yes, please, cum on." Grabbing Kat's hand, "There's an encyclopedia of song in that hed. Did it all in school, wha' didn't yew sing? Or dance?" Standing, sways hips, pretends tap, trying to make it an upbeat moment, always having to tap dance for this child.

"No."

"Yeah, see yew want it. I, please. It's not so inconvenient. It's outside the City. Cud, sleep at yur cousins in Manhattan." Kat loved the Manhattan cousins. Rita continued, "There's a cupla weeks ta prepare."

Kats face brightens, "Yes? Ohhh ... Maybe? Ok, mom. I'll go. But you make the arrangements. I don't have time. Can't sleep in Manhattan, need to stay in Jersey. Maybe we could see our cousins after the audition. Too much pressure, going back and forth." Walks to Rita looks into her eyes. "Do it, set it up."

"Yes?" Rita hoping they'd climb over the wall.
"Yes." Kat walks out of the room.
From a distance, "Night, mom. Luv you." Trailing off, "Going to bed." Softly, warmly calling Kat by a childhood nickname, "Luv ya more, Petunia, night!"

On the web that night, not taking chances, Rita immediately books round trip tickets on one of those DC to New York City double-decker buses college students discovered. Prints tickets, places them on Kat's desk. Tickets bought, it's a reality.

Weeks pass, its departure day. Feeling its weight, Rita wakes hours before the work shift begins, starts the coffee maker, to bring calm and reassurance. Kat awakens, prepares for work. Quietly, routine movements go on. Finally, approaching a nervous Rita, "Are, you, excited, mom?"

"Yes, yew?" Cupping Kats' face, "Here, lunch," handing Kat a sandwich in a small brown bag. Minutes pass, "Yes," shyly.
Thankful, Kat was game for this venture, hugging, "Should be awesome!"
Tepidly, "Sure."
Reassuring, "A good time!"
"Bye, see ya mom."

Rita waits, moves quietly opening the door. Holding a warm coffee cup, lets go a soft breadth, prays a short prayer, distantly, Rita, softly, "Luv ya more, Petunia."

Listening for Kat's soft muffled footsteps against the plush carpeted corridor to the lobby stop. Finally stilettoes meet marble steps. Hearing lobby doors close, Rita pulls back. The clock is ticking.

There's a lot to do.

Chapter 6

Redline. Bus Stop.
DC

Hurriedly running across several busy NW, DC streets Rita makes way to an outdoor parking lot, scheduled to meet, Kat. The planned boarding, a 6:30 evening bus to New York City. Looking about, walks to a Hispanic attendant, "Over there. By the sign."

Reaching the sign, settles a wheeled suitcase, makes herself comfortable. First in line. Conservatively but smartly attired, Rita thought laboriously about the upcoming four days. The filled suitcase accommodated two distinct personalities. An itinerary of clothing had to fit into one travel easy suitcase. Kat, invoked fashion house names with the same rhapsody of spirit, as lay persons and clergymen invoked the name of God during Sunday choir practice. Realizing this was DC, where one is either smartly attired, Neimenly attired, or just plain poorly attired, Rita took great care in packing.

Wearing an upswept 'do,' purple bowler straw hat, black crocs, a loosely fitted dress, gold open toed Cuban pump sandals Rita prepared for a bus, train, taxi, rain, heat, running, or standing. Sparkling golden sandals reflected a free spirit. Contemplating their single parent road map, Rita felt good. Rita was proud of Kat. This was another quest towards the wannabe opera-pop-superstar goal. Looking forward to the post wannabe like Woodstock, four day musical voyage.

Shouting to a man sitting on a bench, "Dew yew

know tha time?"

"Its 5:15 pm."
"Thanks!" Perspiring, wiping a brow.

Speaking to anyone. "Gawd, cudn't ged more uncomfortable. Christ DC's humidity can kill. And, oh, tha Red Line is impossible. Those ice hockey tourists goin' ta Gallery Place, torture. And, tha single track thing, shit, whadda we payin' for?" Making the forty-five minute ride from northern Virginia to the DC, Chinatown inter-state make-shift bus station with record efficiency, "Damn, tuk foreva ta get 'ere. Livin' in Arlington, don't need ta drive. Not always sure of tha metro-bus schedule."

Bench person, looks up, smiles, nods in agreement, gets back to reading. Kicking suitcase wheels, "Shud be here. I know tha bus isn't leaving till 6:30, but its, its ... Gawd, hope they let'er get out of work." Rita, shifts. Steps out of Cuban heeled golden sandals. Gazes down at bare feet. Stretches aching toes. Leaving suitcase, shoes, at bus stop sign, joins fellow bus voyager.

"You goin' ta New Yawk?"
"No. No, I'm waitin' for the Philly bus. Should be leaving at six."
"Waitin' for my dawter. Tha bus gits crowded. We like sittin' t'gether. That's why I got 'ere early. Like ta sit in tha front, up high. If she gets 'ere on time we cud dew that. Gonna dew tha *Idol-A-Try* thing."

"Hey that's great. She nervous? My kids watch. She excited?"
"No, it wuz my idea. I'm not one of those stage

moms. She's classically trained. Doesn't think they'll like 'er soprano voice. It's a beautiful voice, needs tha exposure."

Checking the line, bench person adds, "Big career for those kids, after they get on the program."

"She's *exceptional*."

Bench person nods.

"They told her so at art school. She'd rather not go, working on conservatory applications, thinks it's impossible ta win. But I think Kat can sing anything." Proudly, "Got a gift!"

"Gotta go, my bus is filling up. Good luck to your daughter! Break a leg!"

Bus attendant announces, "Line up, over here. Where's your ticket, *Senora*?" Rita presses a ticket into the agents' hand. Looking around, agent asks, "*La otra persona*? Where's the other person?" Anguished, "Not 'ere yet, on her way."

"*Senora* I can't let you board. Move to the side, *por favor*." "Oh, please we like ta sit ta-gether, she'll be 'ere any minute," hoping a quick change to Spanish will help, "*lo prometo!*"

Agent not beguiled, "*No puedo*. Can't, let you on. *Mira*, look, *tanta gente*, look at how many people behind you. *Al lado, por favor*. Move aside, *déjà que la gente te pasan, por favor.*"

Moves away from bus line, "Christ, Kat hurry."

"Mom! Hey, mom," shouting, waving. "Sorry, I got off the wrong metro stop, that Redline is impossible ... and," speaking rapidly, "been walking ... in circles." Face perspiring, make-up running, and out of breadth, "I'm sooo ... hot."

Kat adjusts the navy blue YSL jacket, pulls at the hem of an Italian diagonal biased draped, multi-colored silk, tightly fitted dress.

Pointing to Kat's dress, "Gawd, think yew'll be comf'table in that? On, tha bus?"

"I'll change when everybody sits down." Rita pushes through to the bus attendant, "*Llego* ... arrived. *Senorita*? OK?" Irritated, "Ok, ladies, step up, move quickly."

Kat and Rita board. It's 6:25 pm. As is their routine, they sit on the second floor of the double-decker bus. Kat changes in the bathroom, returns, plugs in an Ipod, nestles into a seat. Rita, pulls a lavender Indian inspired shawl over her body. Needing no inducement, quickly falls asleep. Hour's lapse. Passengers safely unaware of surroundings, slumber, passing DC, Maryland, Delaware and New Jersey.

Chapter 7

Taxi! Please

Like a hand into a glove, the bus slips into the Lincoln Tunnel. Abruptly darkness, ends as flashing lights shine through the glass ceiling. Slowly everyone awakens. Its late night. Rita lowers the shawl, looks over to Kat gently tugs a sleeve. Kat removes the IPod from its connection, starts pulling items together. Adjusting the seat, gazing out the window as the bus passes sooty, elegant old buildings arriving into a bustling thoroughfare. Riveted by sudden activity, both stare at pedestrians challenging street traffic. The Washington, DC double decker bus stops on a lower west side street of Manhattan.

Rita and Kat, stepping onto a makeshift sidewalk stops, feeling comfortable, at home, moves toward the rear of the bus to retrieve luggage. The air is languidly warm, but not as humid as Washington. Holding a smartphone in hand, checking for information, Kat asks, "Where's the Port Authority? It's 11:05. We have to catch the 11:40 commuter bus 164 to the Meadowlands. It's the last bus. Mom, how far is it? This is 28th & 8th."

"Taxi, we havta catch a taxi. Its twelve blocks uptown. Times Square! Hurry, ged tha baggage, I'll ged tha taxi."

Leaving Kat to handle the suitcase, Rita walks past the bus's rear, past the sidewalk curb, finally bridging the corner of two streets, moving aggressively into traffics' militia of yellow cabs whizzing past, raising a hand, shouts, "TAXI!"

Rita's demeanor challenges the cue hailing crowd. To the right a taxi stops before a well-dressed man. Confidently, briskly, Rita walks towards the cab reaching the door handle, simultaneously, they grab it. Uncomfortable with the sudden movement, he obligingly steps aside.

"Uh, hey, you can have it." Uncompromisingly, beckons Kat. Looking at the taxi stranger, "Yew, sure?"
"Uh, *si*, sure, *seguro*."
"Thanks!" Seconds transpiring during the cordial exchange, are too long for the cabbie; pressing foot to metal, it speeds away.

Rita lifts a hand, "TAXI!"
"TAXI!" yells taxi stranger.
Taxi stops.
An exact scene plays out. Taxi stranger moves aside, relinquishes, "Take it." Opening cab door, Rita waving to Kat, "Thanks, let's go!" Getting into the cab, "Christ, can't believe you took two taxi's from that guy." Rita worried about the time, "What time is it?"

"11:15." Leaning forward Rita abruptly barks, "Driver, Port Authority, please. Hav' only fifteen minutes tew git tha bus, its tha last one. Kat, when we ged outta tha taxi, run!"

Arriving, Kat pays, pushing luggage out onto the crowded street. Rita exits on the other side. Pushing past hordes of tourist, they run, towards the Information Booth. Kat reaching it first asks, "Where do we buy tickets for the Meadowlands?"

"All the way down to the end of the building and up the stairs to your left." Rita suggests, "Your younger, run, I'll catch up."

"Hurry!" Kat, pushing ahead, runs past late night commuters, homeless people, tourist, police and reaches the ticket line. Rita running, hauling luggage catches up. Ticket buyers slow the ticket master with questions.

"Holy d*reck*, these people tawk too much"
"Shhsh, mom!"
"Well, dey dew."
"Mommmmm, please, quiet!"
An exasperated impatient Rita nudges Kat, "Hurry, aesk, aesk."
"Hey! Mom, move (nudging back) away!"
"Aesk, aesk, (nudging) aesk."
"Stop it! Mom."
Redirecting her attention Kat speaks, "Tickets to the Meadowlands."
Elbow nudging Rita's ribcage.
"Bus 164, please. Does it go to the Meadowlands? What time does it leave?"
"11:40, yew only gotts ten minutes ta make it. Whereyugoing? Yew, one of doze singers, whads it called? Contestants?"
"Hurry, hurry up. Tell 'im ta stop tawking!"
"Shhhhhhh, mom! Do you mean, Idol-A-Try?"
"Well, yes. I mean, uh, anybody else looking for a ticket to that?"
"I've 'ad a City full of people fer tickets! Bubi, 'ere ta-day! Giv'ya ticket if yew sing," holding tickets over his cap, "me a song ."
"Oh, but there isn't any time to,"

Re-thinking "Oh, okay, … I'll sing a few high notes of Ave."

Ticket Master smiles, hands the ticket to Kat. "Gud luck! See ya on TV!

Thanking "Gawd" that the ordeal was over, Rita yells, "Run! Run ahead an' ged on line. Bus 164 tew tha Meadowlands."

"I know … mom."

"Hurry up, down towards the front of the Port Authority."

Exasperated, "God mom! I know, we just passed it on the way in!"

Making a mad dash towards the elevator, down the escalator, dozens of bus stands, they push thru crowds.

"Excuse me, excuse me. Christ, ged,"

"Sorry,"

"Where tha hell dew all dese people cum from?"

"… Excuse me, sorry."

Running past lines of commuters, "Sorry, mom, shhh."

"Please, *schmuck* muv."

"Stop! ... Stop, saying, that."

Pointing, "Run down that corridor, its jammed pack. It's frickin' crowded"

"They can hear you."

"Maybe there's information. Don't know where the heck we're supposed ta go."

Stopping, Rita asks a handsomely dressed businessman, "Sir, dew ya know where ta catch tha 164 bus?" Distracted, walks away. "*Shit dreck*! I'm tired, let's stop for a moment. Gotta stretch my neck, it's hurting. Hey, luk, up there, there's information fer tha 164, 163."

"Damn, mom, it's here already!"
"Let's run."
"That way. Hurry!"

Sprinting, their run abruptly ends in a *mishmash* of humanity. Quickly, aggressively stepping into the line formation, Rita is dismayed, a couple moved behind. Looking for Kat who had fallen behind in the crowd Rita finds Kat anxiously, waits for Kat to move into the line formation. Kat walks hesitantly towards the line.

"*Schleping* the Gawd damn frick'n luggage," through crowds, unintentionally trampling more toes than ever imagined possible. Feeling stressed from moving through crowds of hundreds of commuters, wondering how many she'd physically offended, then how many Rita verbally offended, Kat hesitated. Walking towards Rita. Stops, hesitates. So how many toes, accidental pushes, elbows in mid-section, verbal assaults had been executed to get to this spot?

Panic.
Her focus narrowed.
Brain hic-cup.
Paralysis.

Kat wanted to run. Run in the opposite direction. Away. Away from Rita. Kat didn't want to be here. Where, ever, here, was. Kat wanted to drop the luggage and run. Run up the stairs, past the crowds of commuters, homeless people, frankfurter stands, tourists, news booth vendors, police officers, *tchotchke* shops, run to those Manhattan cousins. Kat wanted to run towards, relief.

Relief.
Comfort.
Un abrazo.

A warm welcome. Laughter, a meal with rational *familia*, with normal expectations of Kat, in the rational upper East Side. Nothing exceptional expected, maybe a glass of wine. To kick off heels, to rest. Rationally. Feeling impulses run hot in veins. In bones. In feet. That insane fleeting feeling 'What am I doing?' entered her psyche. Kat wanted to cut and run.

Panic.

Kat stood still for what seemed to be an eternity to Rita. Rita understood. Kat looked like a deer in headlights. Kat stared down the crowded, aged, exhausted corridor. Pennsylvania Station spelled it out. Everything about it was spent. The dingy white walls. The half lit florescent lights. The missing ceiling tiles and grey '80s plastic tile flooring, chipped. The electronic neon signs, mostly dead. Floor signs, hand written, replacing electronic signs, in disrepair. Then, finally its people.

Exhausted.
Spent, tired, worn.
Like Kat.

Worker bees, all of them. Rumpled suits and dresses said it all. This was not energetic Fifth Avenue, not frenetic Madison Avenue, not potent Pennsylvania Avenue. This was a line, in truth, she didn't want to join. Between full time work, studying, practicing and courses, Kat was over-extended. Commiserating. Eighteen hours into this day, feeling their pain. Over extended worker bees.

And here Kat was, with a woman, who never understood the word, *'no.'* Not on this level. Understood it if you were asking for peas, while passing the butter. But in the big scheme of things, 'No,' didn't exist. Coming from parents who neva accepts 'no,' either.

'No, you can't live here.' 'No, you're child can't swim here.' 'No, you can't join our club.' 'No you can't go to school here.' 'No you're children aren't as smart as ours.' 'No your hair isn't as straight as ours.' 'No your features aren't as fine as ours.' 'No your people aren't as good as ours.' 'No your kids won't go to college." "No your children won't become professionals.' 'No you're not attractive.' And finally, 'No you're not as good as us.' That Bronx *shtetl* made her Teflon proof resistant to the word 'no.'

> *Maybe the question wasn't*
> *how did they get into*
> *the red-lined segregated northern Bronx,*
> *it was more really,*
> *how did they survive*
> *that shtetl with ego,*
> *spirit, and psyche intact?*

Exhausted, tired of the long day, and in truth tired of that ambiguous meandering road called 'success' in the artist lane, she wanted to run. Kat looked at Rita, and thought of her people's *exceptionalism.* They had not been defeated, in the face of so many discriminating bigoted odds assuring defeat. Pushing them down, but promising *'this land is your land, this land is my land.'* Saying 'no' to her mother, was something she couldn't do, in the end. So Kat joined the line.

But kept the distance.

Tired from the running, Rita waited for Kat to join her. But Kat refused. Rita was confused, worried. Making, futile hand signal attempts, still no acknowledgement. Rita continued to engage Kat. Kat looked away, several times. Rita intensely worried about seating decided it was best to force the situation. Fully aware she was about to annoy, Rita spoke.

"Kat, cum-up, 'ere. Don't be a *putz."* Kat looks away.
"Kat." More forcefully.
"Noooo." Turning away.
Talking past the couple, "We need ta be ta-gether. Muv up."
Motioning to a spot.
"No."
Annoyed, insisting, "Ok, if tha bus cums an' tha line ends wit' me, AND, I'm tha last person on tha bus … Yew'll be on tamorrow's bus! Damn Kat! Muv!"
Angrily, "Fine, ok, that's fine. I'm not cutting in. I'm not moving!"
Rita giving up, asks the next person in line, "Iz this Bus 164, tew tha Meadowlands?"
No response.
Continuing, "Hey, dew ya know what bus stop this iz?"
"*Senora* who knows. Maybe the 164, maybe not. We're waiting for the 163."

"Honey, we all wanna ged home," added the woman standing next to him.

Beyond the windowed doors separating everyone from the large parking garage buses arrived constantly. Each bus landed before a door marked by painted white lines on the asphalt. Rita can see an unnumbered bus approaching. It finally pulls into the area where Rita is waiting.

"Kat, there's a bus arrivin' now in tha parking area. Muv up."

Kat resists. The line starts to move. Rita inches past the terminal exit, steps outside. Looking behind to make sure Kat isn't too far away. Rita decides to stand beside the bus door, waits for Kat, letting others pass. Kat stands beside Rita, finally boarding the bus.

"Hi! Is this tha 164 tew tha Meadowland?"

"No, led me call my dispatcher to see what's goin' on. It shudave arrived."

"Yew can wait out there."

"Out there?" Rita, slowly steps down, "Damn."

Kat follows. "Out there?"

Abruptly, harshly, the door slams shut, the bus pulls away.

"What? Where iz, … iz that bus going? He said he wud check on tha 164 fer us." Looking at the person on line behind them, "What bus wuz that?"

"That was the 163 … tha 164 is late."

Accidently Rita and Kat are first in line. While relieved by a sudden win, day long exhaustion creeps, again into already worn bones. Stepping back into the line, Rita leans against the door. Kat, leaves the open area. Standing against the heavy white painted wooden door, leaning into one another, they wait. Needing the door to hold them up, shoulders meshed, leaning into one another for emotional strength.

Motherhood, daughterhood.
Intertwined intimate fabric,
holding them up.

Invisible
threads.

Familia.

Chapter 8

The Highway Trek, Meadowland Adventura

*Looking towards the young
man, softens becoming calmer, "Uh,
huh, sure, uh, well dat wus jist yew and
that sista in the back . A fava for you
and the sista, yew kno." "But, but
mam, you're going too far. We needed
to get off back there, mam. Mam,
you're making it really hard on us now,
please mam, let us off." "We're with
him." Looking across the aisle, "We'll
get off with him." "But I wus gonna
leave 'im off arounds near tha last
area to the highway exit, I don't know
if your mother, is, dat your mother?"
"Yeah." "Don't know if she cud dew
dat. We're past it all now. I mean the
Meadowland and it's dangerous on tha
highway. OK, I'm stoppin' now."
Decelerating. Loudly, on the overhead
speaker announces, "Ok, anybody
wanna go ta tha Izod Center dis is tha
closest I can git ya."*

Kat drops the luggage onto the floor, pushes it
between cramped chairs, through the narrow aisle,
down, steps. It lands on a bluish grey pebbled, grassy
road. Rita follows, squeezing tired, 'I can't believe this
shtup is dropping me off in the middle of no where,'
body past her new worst enemy. Harshly, accidently
poking, pulling the seat, Bus 164 mega sister lets out a

defensive scowl. Tinkering with explosive thoughts, Rita knows it's better to move on and uncharacteristically decides to stay quiet. A line waiting to exit, forms behind.

Cautiously holding door handles, Rita's golden sandals tepidly manage the last step and footings are found. Clumsily between sleeping passengers, six exit and step onto a highway shoulder. Angry gurlfriend bus 164 driver waits, for the last wannabe *Idol-A-Try* contestant to move away from the bus. The heavy silver metal door harshly slams shut. The bus wheels accelerate. Bus 164, swings wide, away, and turns left onto the empty, automobile-less, highway.

Six. Strangers. Dumped. Walk past, the black gaseous bus vapors and huddle.

Its marshland quiet, dark, warm and the middle of the night. They are the only persons in sight. Standing alone, yet together, as strangers, their worry for their safety emerges and becomes imminent, communal. A shared awareness, fear and concern awakened in their being, the moment they individually took that first step onto the pebbled shoulder.

This was no city street. No suburban road. Treeless. Cattails. Sedges. Rushes. Round man made waterholes hugging the highway. Standing on the bare naked inter-state highway at this point, off in the distance, four miles away hotel hospitality awaits, comfort could be found by registering at the hotel for the night, seventy-five minutes away from the City.

So there it was. Two distinct paths; one, offering hotel comfort, the other, offering the open road. But none seem to have comfort on their mind. Comfort wasn't part of the plan. All knew that. Even if they hadn't planned on this. Who would? Who could imagine this? A mega multi-million dollar talent reality TV show neva mentioned this. Or the snarly bigoted, profiling, bus driver. Looking about it sunk into their psyche that Bus 164 *was* the last bus for the night, out of the City. No cars or taxis' in sight.

Tiredly ambivalent, a giddiness, restlessness, gladness over comes them. The last fifteen minutes on Meadowlands Bus 164 had been fraught with insecurity, fear, confusion, tension. Bus tickets promised them a destination. Hadn't they checked, re-checked and re-checked the *Idol-a-Try* website?

Bus 164.
Izod Center.
Bus 164.
Meadowlands.
Bus 164.
New Jersey.
Bus 164.
The last bus.

They had checked, re-checked and re-checked the *Idol-a-Try* website. *Los chabos,* money, was short. For all of them. Again and again they had checked the website. Returning to the City was not an option. Not for anyone.

Disembarked, was a cross section of America, at a reality TV crossroads freak moment. Two Blacks, two Hispanics, and two Anglos. Each looked the other over. So this was the competition. Out on the open road, this was somehow a more intimate way of meeting. And this was beginning to feel surreal. Here, in the middle of nowhere they discovered one another, a chance meeting of like aspirations. *Dreamers*. Perhaps they had like talents, perhaps not. Heeding a musical call, testing waters, pushing the envelope of opportunity, timing and circumstance, finding themselves here.

Eyes roamed gently, inhaling cool fresh meadowland air. Stark incredulity made them laugh quietly, openly, then loudly. Out stretched before them was a concrete and asphalt medusa's labyrinth of highway. A cosmic joke of some kind, landing there, in the middle of nowhere each thought. Definitely, four miles from their destination, looking towards a highway exit, further down the road. Here they stood, together. This was destiny each thought. Somehow they were meant to be, together.

Looking towards the lamplight halo of the moon, relief entered their bones. It loomed large, clear, round, lucid, and spacious, elucidating the highway. Outstretched before them, was nothing but highway, bulkheads, road, wired fences, bridges, more road, several overpasses and off in the distance, glowing, the Izod Center, a massive rectangular expanse of neon metal colors. It would become the Center of their universe for four days, and the aim of their imminent trek. Huddling, paths discussed, fingers pointed to the other side of the highway. A consensus reached to climb over the highway medium and bulwark and walk on alongside the cattail highway winding towards their musical Mecca destination.

A distance away, Kat's finger outlines the arching bridge across the highway, then to a bridge to the other side of the road, with many more road barriers. So they started, it is all they could do, they wouldn't continue to stand there so they start to walk, briskly with determination. Realizing there are others like them, leaving their comfortable beds in the middle of the night to be here, to line up, with an open desire and need to be first in line, on the road to Hollywood, to a vinyl deal. That motivation, to be first in line, makes them walk faster.

The trek to somewhere over the vinyl rainbow begins.

Without hesitating, Timothy, suggests "Ok, so I guess we have to go, go towards that bridge, avoid the tract of low wet land, we don't know what's in that water, but we need to cross the highway to get there. Everybody, game or does anybody want to go it alone, their own way. Where you guys coming from?"

"DC, I'm Rita. Tho' from New Yawk, originally."
"DC, northern Virginia, I'm, Kat, this is my mom."
"Manhattan by way of South Carolina, my name is Jay."
"Baltimore. Timothy."
"Connecticut. Dustin."
"Maryland, I'm Chloe. Can we call you Miss? I'm from the South, Miss is how we do it."
"Sure, it's usually Miss in DC or northern Virginia."

"So, so anybody want to go their own, own way?"

"No, I'm for staying together. It's dark and nobodies out here," Chloe responds without hesitation. "Right," Rita concurs. "I'll take the luggage mom, you just keep up."

Jay can't resist expressing anger "God! Could you believe that fuckin' bitch, bus driver. Drove right past the Izod Center, thru the fucking Izod Center. Thru it! Damn wench! I waved at it, as we drove past the fuckin' building."

"Hey honey calm down. Maybe we should call a cab?" Laughter erupts. "And where exactly are we?" "Oh mister cab driver," chimes in Jay, "yeah just drive through the Izod Center. No, no, don't stop there, keep going. Then leave the fuckin Izod Center and when you can't see it in your rear-view mirror, THAT's where you'll find us."

"God damn fuckin' bitch."
"Like they say in tha old hood, that bitch wuz *meshugenah*, dewing her sistahood *shtik* ."

"Let's keep moving."

Reaching the medium, Kat hoists the luggage and wonders, out loud. "WHAT did you bring?" Heatedly, "What do you have in here? Why do you always pack too much? Christ mom!" Rita's eyes roll. Dustin grabs luggage from Kat, tosses it easily over the bulwark. "Okay, sew how does my *klutzy* body get ova that?" Dustin and Kat, steady Rita's body leaning atop the concrete divider, gently moves backward, lifting legs carefully.

"Could have stopped, could have stopped right in front of the damn building. What was her problem?

Damn fuckin' bitch!" Calmly, Timothy replies, "I don't know Jay, but, but thank God we got left here. It's closer than," Pointing Kat interrupts, "Ok, so we just have to get to that bridge. That way."

Observing the hike ahead, Dustin mentally maps the route, offers, "We'll have to walk on the other side, along the highway." Determined that nothing will stop her, Chloe adds, "I'm game! Yeah, I can do this. As long as I can throw my bag over the fence or push it through, I'm ok. Forget the f'n bitch, I can do this."

Feeling limitations Rita offers, "I'll keep up. Yew all *schlep*, walk ahead. Kat its best yew stay wit' them. I'll be comf'bly behind. Seeing yew up a'hed." "Ok, but, Mom, can you walk in those shoes?" "Yeah, jist keep *schlepin'* stay wit' 'em." "Ok, mom, but don't fall too far behind. You needed better shoes. I could have gotten you better shoes at Neimen's. Why didn't you ask? Those will hurt your feet. Why didn't you wear better shoes?"

Throat tightening, trying to thoughtfully measure words, failing, "Damn, Kat, who tha frikin' knew we'd meet tha anointed Saint, guardian angel of tha Meadowlands, full of malarkey, protecting hotel lobbies."

"Guess the driver thought the worse of us, mom"

"Sista Souljah not wanting tha likes of yew an' I hangin' tew night in tha fuckin' Izod Center, wannabee central. Or a frickin' hotel. Wha tha hell did the bitch think we were gonna dew in tha fuckin' hotel lobby?"

"No hotel reservations. I guess we couldn't make that up convincingly."

"Saw two *chicas* and thought, Jezus they're gonna steal the planters. The silverware. Mmmm no! Can't let 'em in no hotel lobby! Open tha servants entrance, for dese two."

"Yeah Miss Rita, you're gonna put that planter in your suitcase. What the fuck was that hotel shit all about? I don't remember the website saying we needed a reservation. I'm staying with family in the Bronx."

"Think we're gonna pick pocket our way back tew tha Port Authority? Tha bitch wus supposed tew stop at tha Meadowlands. Sista drove through tha frickin' place."

Reaching a twelve foot tall chain link fence, stopping to evaluate their dexterity, ability to get past it. Twisting the lock, Dustin announces, "It's locked. I can't get it opened. Jay can you help here?" "Sure, hey, I'll pull this side. You take the other side." "Can you make it through mom? I'll help you." "Yeah, help squeeze tha luggage thru. Jist push it hard." Timothy approaches, "I'll hold the bottom. Got it." Understanding calamity Chloe extorts, "Christ this mother is only the beginning."

Squeezing between steel metal poles, taking turns. Patiently, carefully hands grab mesh wire. Pushing through, noses get pinched. One at a time, carefully shifting a pelvis. Then a foot, followed by a leg. Tucked stomachs. Arms twisted. A knapsack wedged here, a bag jammed there. Somehow each makes it.

Knowing friends are forged through such experiences, Rita doesn't want Kat to miss out on conversation with these travelers. Whenever Kat looks behind to check on Rita, Rita shouts "Don't slow down, Kat, keep *schlepin'* with 'em, they're muvin' along." Rita was tired of people, Kat was entering life, not leaving it. This was a possibility, perhaps a connection to a musical future. Pop wannabe moments.

"Damn! Wish Kat wud dump tha Dweeb. Look at 'er, laughin'. Neva dew that if the Prince wuz around."

The neon monolithic metallic Izod Center looms in the distance. Finally reaching the high point of a bridge, stopping, catching his breath, Timothy breaks out into song, "over the yellow ...." There's laughter at the end of the song.

Jay taking Timothy's cue sings. Calling up from memory Broadway show tunes he's sung from audition to audition, he entertains. Having escaped the sardine like enclosure of Bus 164, his energy level is high. Jay is best standing at the pinnacle of the highway bridge, star gazing, singing from the soul. Grabbing his audience's attention, he taps. Movements lithe, practiced, comfortable. Audition, after audition has fine-tuned Jay's body. Tap, jazz, ballet, influenced movement.

Timothy and Jay share their songs atop the bridge. Feeling free, triumphant, they are ready to conquer. The climb down the bridge went quickly, as they continue walking along the highway.

Timothy opens up, "I knew that bus driver

wasn't gonna stop for you. Didn't think she would let us off once you started talking. Had me worried. I thought oh Lord, don't do it. Promised me when I got on. We had a moment there."

"Oh, yeah, that bitch wasn't stopping for us. Wud not stop *kvetshing* about how we didn't hava a hotel reservation. Thank Gawd yew spoke up. People are like that in DC, sucks if you're Hispanic, white an' tryin' tew deal with someone from tha hood."

"Yeah, I heard it all. Kept hoping she'd stop when we were at the Izod Center. Only wanted to help a black brother," Timothy adds.

"Dang, she told me she would stop. I'm a sista, you know. Or, can't you tell? Thought, oh no, I don't know where the fuck I am and this sista bus lady won't stop, to give you a bigoted hard time." Chuckling, "I'm thinking if this bus doesn't stop where the fuck is the 164 going?" Chloe wasn't offering excuses. "Cud see right through 'er black ass bigoted bitchin."

Chloe continues, "Well, I got worried when I heard her shaking you down. Wondered, where would it, I mean the 164, be taking me? I already spent one hundred dollars on some dumb ass Black Jamaican cabbie who didn't know what the fuck he was doing in the Bronx. Yeah well I guess it's not only tha police who profiled. It wasn't no police car. I was a paying customer."

"Driving up and down, pretending he knew how to get to Jersey. Shit. I was worried, you know. I'm not from the Bronx, I'm staying with family. Came in from Maryland, what the fuck do I know of the

Bronx?" Sniggering, "That fool, took, me for a ride. Yes he did! A grand tour of the Bronx, that's what I got! I gave him one hundred, he didn't have change."

"Oh, no, please tell me he gave you change. DC gypsie cabbies pull that nonsense."

"Right, how could a cabbie not have change? Tourist, that's what he saw on my face, outta town suburban African American tourist. My people are from the islands too. Guess I don't speak Jamaican. All I saw was tenement this, and tenement that. And Co-op City, what the fuck is a Co-op City, isn't it all New York City. Where the fuck and what the fuck, it took forever. Dang, I was in the fuckin' cab forever, with that dumb ass Black Jamaican."

Jay laughs, "Look, I see the Izod Center! Neon, show time lights! Hell yes, here we come!" The laughter is contagious, their pace quickens towards the highway bridge. "Two miles, maybe two and a half fuckin' miles. I can see that from up here. God, this is as messed up as dealin' with that fuckin' Jamaican cabbie."

"Shit, oh fuck, really? Couldn't stop? No, more than two and half miles. What the fuck did we pay for?" Dustin wonders.

"Awww, well at least we're not alone. Cud yew imagine walkin' in tha dark alone through all this?" Dustin looks around, "At least another fifty minutes of walking, what do you think?" Jay pushes on with momentum, "Keep going, let's speed up. I don't want too many people getting in front of us." "You ok mom? You alright?" "Yeah, yew walk ahead with 'em."

"Do you think there are lots of people there? It's only 1:50. We're the only ones on the 164. I worried about getting here on time from Long Island City."

Finally reaching the end of the highway, making haste through the coarse ankle deep thicket squeezing itself between the asphalt, gravel and concrete. Neither car, truck, or, police crossed their path. Not only had they taken the last bus into the Meadowlands, but they had ridden the very last vehicle to their vinyl Mecca. Period. There were no other travelers in sight. After a time, they reached the parking lot in front of the Izod Center.

Before them stood what all hoped would be the last of the twelve foot tall fences. Circumventing the parking lot directly in front of the Izod Center, like the highway, this was another barrier to their Mecca. Stopping to assess gaps between poles, tired, but not deterred, and realizing it to be too small for the luggage piece, Kat and Rita, consulted one another. Estimating, mentally measuring, looking past fences, the distance to the Izod Center appeared to be half a mile away.

Divine serendipity reigns.

Impatiently Jay offers, "Cutting through the parking lot, we'll be on the other side quicker than if we walk around. Squeezing through, we can toss the sacks over the top."

"Ok, don't ruin my bag, let me push it through. Hold the gate open. It'll squeeze through." "Can you do this? Mom?"

"Can't get tha luggage through. Think we can dew better if we *schlep* along tha perimeter of tha fence. It'll take us ..." "Longer mom, it'll take us more time."

"I can squeeze this bro's Black body, cut through the parkin' lot with them." Dustin conferring, "Yeah, I'm going this way. It'll be faster." Jay waves, walking away quickly, "We'll meet up on the other side."

"Think I can dew it more easily on tha perimeter." "Well, I'm not going to leave you alone." They both turn and wave, "Bye guys, see you later." Walking quickly, Rita and Kat continue along the perimeter of the fence. Chloe blows a kiss from a distance, "Ok, see you on the other side. We'll meet up. See you folks there. I'll hold a spot for you!"

"If you hurry up, we can make it down the hill quickly. How's your shoes for that?" "Gawd, this sucks. But I'm game, let's go." "Can you run in them? And we won't be climbing over anything." "Yew muv ahead."

"At least it's asphalt, mom." "Yeah, aren't we lucky, endless asphat in Gawd damn middle of fuckin' nowhere. I'll keep up behind yew."

Kat, walks aggressively, towing luggage. Rita runs a few steps behind. After fifteen minutes, stopping. "Hey, look back, see them. They're having trouble climbing over that inner fence." "Uh, oh. Let's keep goin'." "They've stopped, mom. Wait. But I'm sure they'll still get there before us."

Rita at Kat's side looks toward the interior of the chain link perimeter road. "Look, Chloe, seems tew be havin' problems! Luk, Timothy's at 'er side. But tha others, oh, tha others are muvin' ahead." "You ok? mom. We can't do anything about it. Chloe's not alone, she'll be fine. Let's get a move on."

Rita and Kat re-start and quicken their pace. Clickity-clack, clack, clack. Clickity-clack, clickity, clack, clack. Clickity-clack, clack, clack golden Cuban heels are heard encircling the expansive perimeter of the chain link fenced parking lot.

Chapter 9

Hay mas?

The land of dreams, that was these *United States of America.* Nothing less. Tanya, arrived as an immigrant, 'above board,' in 1929. One of the most onerous American years to land in these United States of America. Tanya arrived with *suenos.* Dreams. But then, who didn't? Who didn't come seeking their fortune? To change their identify? To forget old Gods. Create new idolatries? Who didn't leave something so familiar, so intrinsically, singularly themselves to recreate a new persona? Tanya was part of the latest horde of immigrants, working, buying, stealing, begging into that dream. Would anyone notice her arrival?

Once upon a time, Tanya, *una senorita elegante y hermosa*, strong willed, independent was wanting a way out of her parent's vast third world Latin American empire. A way out of *machismo.* A way out of stupefying Catholicism, mahogany, sugarcane, cattle homesteads, corrupt *politicos*, and the more corrupt, *assesinos*, whose families Tanya might have to marry into or be relegated to *la familias' rancho* because she was her high strung, aristocratic mother's independent daughter.

Anos de las cosas politico, the family survived, that wrenching, delicate dance done between *los partidos* in *el Capital* in *periodicos*, speeches, pen and bully pulpits. But, executed with assassinations, *machetes,* rapes, *pistolas,* torture, kidnapping, house burnings, and flat out land seizure wars. Tanya's father,

Don Rafael ruled vast *hacienda rancho* holdings with a benevolent hand. *Dona Dela*, his wife an unparalleled beauty, towering over most *mestizo* ranch hands, European elegant with crisp blue green eyes, alabaster white skin covered by layers of cotton, protection, never shied of working lands beside *campesinos*. *Dona Dela* led men. *Dona Dela* did not walk to their side or behind them.

Known to visit their capital city house ignoring the comings and goings of her *politico* husband and its hornary, gossiping, sociopathic, *sociedad*. Running a large agricultural empire, with responsibilities of workers, animals, crops across the country, there was never a slumbering moment. *Dona Dela* considered *las cosa politicas* a waste of time. Capital city visits were busy with coffee cartels, *maize* distributors, American mahogany and silver conglomerates. Theirs was a matriarchal family. Never questioning, *Don Rafael*, comfortably left *la Dona* in charge of *el rancho, "Seguro que todo esta bien."* during weeks or months long absences, touring vast holdings.

Dona Dela bought, bartered, sold, traded, discarded, all things theirs. Raised, or grown on owned properties. *Caballos*, *maize*, pine, *oro*, cattle, *pavos*, silver, sugar cane, *frijoles, arroz,* ocelot skins*, pollos*, eggs, *café*, flowers, *mansanas*, mangoes, *platanos*. Trading with the best of *los rancheros* in the mercantile market, unlike her, benevolent husband, *la Dona* was a force to be reckoned with. Possessing a linguistic artistry and deft tongue, equal to her beauty, merchants, *campesinos*, wives, cautiously transacted business. While, *El Don* raged eloquent wars of words on capital state house stages through *periodicos*, hers' was a war of *lempiras*. Together controlling the largest tracts of mahogany rainforest, north and west of *el Capital*, reaching out to the Atlantic, their lives always on line, never cowering. Working from a sense of *exceptionalism*, endurance hardened arteries.

Eran poderoso. They were powerful. Properties, livelihood, gave them wealth, but endangered *la familia*. Violence, a norm, boundless, constant. Especially at mahogany outposts which *el Don*, surveilled with an entourage of pistol holding, *machete* militia. Leaving *la Dona* and Tanya alone, travelling with sons.

This for Tanya was a parlor game binding her solidly to an unwanted future. One filled with crude men, *hombres duro, bruto, pistoleros*, and disappearances. Tanya, spirited, unshackled freely roamed parrot, monkey, ocelot filled humid rain forests, crossed rivers high on majestic willful horses. Travelling through thousands of acres alongside *el Don*, brothers, uncles.

Los ceritos, whose gnarled ancient *sapodilla* pine valley's, deep clear watered pebbled *rios* Tanya knew for hundreds miles around, were a back drop to each dawns' darkly illuminated adobe *fogon lena* fires, daunting, exhausting hard work, endless battles with tree swallowing violent earth moving hurricanes, searing crop consuming heat waves, skin encroaching battles with mud, crocodiles, venomous snakes, spider monkeys, thickened vines, mosquitos, tapirs, worms and things unseen but crawling, sneaking, slithering, snaking about.

Mother Earth, no dainty lady here, *en la Mosquitia* rain forest. Predator spotted jaguars, pumas, cougars with stocky limbs powerful jaws, roamed, capturing small children, stealing them for a meal. Graceful, hostile eagles hunting, picking monkeys and sloths from trees. Jabiru's with thick black neck ringed red and white feathers flew above tree lines.

Mother Earth expected *exceptional* senses. Visual prowess. Subdued stillness. Instinctual ability to stay alive. Ginger movement. Foraging. To find water. To hear. To hear, silence in a cacophony of noise. *Mother Earth* never retreated. Always testing a man's worth.

La Mosquitia, wasn't for the faint. Smart men, like *Don Rafael*, knew to fear *Mother Earth* in these environs. Always respectful. Always cautious. Always disciplined. Sweltering humidity, torrential down pours, ground pits appearing from nowhere, grabbed whole men. Animals unseen. Watching. Hunting. Slinking beneath grasses and vegetation. The hunted, being hunted. Its interiors, darkened by mahogany stories tall. Irresistible, was this *caoba* rainforest. Trees thirty men, extending their arms around. Bountiful because of *la Mosquitia's* harshness. Three weeks by donkey, horse, and foot from civilization. Impenetrable to the common man. It held its wealth quietly for thousands of years. One had to be a hard man or woman to entertain survival en *la Mosquitia*.

But no longer. American conglomerates noticed. Vast their land holdings, power and responsibilities. But Tanya, wanted more than Third World stifling centuries old Spanish Catholic traditions. Those assigning boundaries, duties to women. "There must be more," Tanya thought, no longer wanting to be here. Unlike the young women of her day, Tanya wandered about *Tegoose calles* unchaperoned. A liberty *Dona Dela* heard whispers about, but never a confrontation. Hushed conversations fed gossip, at *sociedad* tea parties she had little time for. Stopping into interior court yards, to pay respect to bored rich Senora's, *las mujeres de sociedad*, held tongues and opinions. *Chisme*, silenced with a glance.

Tanya continued roaming, questioning *todo*. Searching through fields, sitting at rivers edge, in brush, looking out at *la familias'* lands stretching out beyond the seeing eye. Most, sat in awe of their vast holds. Yet for Tanya, a gut feeling of dissatisfaction, in tranquility with this *rancho* way of *vida* was real. Desire. Wanting something different, Tanya waited for the right *momento*. Tanya prayed to *las estrellas* showering the rain forest for answers. *Con humilidad*, waiting, knowing *el momento* would come.

Finally, after the last *maize, caoba* and other harvests were sent to Tegucigalpa, and her parents were back to rest, after weeks in *el Capitol* selling or trading their bounty, they returned to regroup. During one of those end of day quiet moments when *la familia* gathered on the large shaded, cooled front veranda, after paying, feeding *peones, compesinos, lavanderas*, maids, cooks and putting the last *lena* embers of the *adobe fogon* out, Tanya quietly approached *el Don*, lumbering through a book, Tanya pulled a chair towards him. Sat beside *el Don*.

Hesitating.

Raising eyes for one last moment, towards an elegant, aging exhausted mother, rhythmically moving to and fro in a *hamaca*. Having changed from work day clothes, to a simple embroidered clean frock, covering *Dona Dela's* long thin exhausted body, down to ankles. The six foot frame stretched casually. One arm raised languorously above over head, covering her eyes, exposing white thin muscular ballerina-like arms. Hair released from the tight work day braid, *Dona Della* took great pains to wrap at the top of her head, clasped at the nape of her neck, with a mantilla broach, made of delicately carved mother of pearl. Comb tooth, long, wired thin, gathering, locking in hair which was past her waist. "*Mama's pelo*," blonde, gray, white, straight. "White, too soon?" Tanya wondered.

Slumbering, *Mama's* eyes closed. Tanya never tired of looking into her mother's bright blue green eyes. Envying their color since childhood. Changing *el color* depending on *Dona Dela's* mood. Becoming most multi-colored vibrant when wronged. Coolest *azul* when calmed, her mind resting. Tanya knew how to tease, just enough to see the colors change. Most times Tanya elicited the sparkling blue green. *La Dona* so pleased with Tanya. But then, Tanya was the last child. The child who sneaked into the womb, when everyone thought *Dona Dela* was done birthing. And, this was the child everyone wanted. Tanya was *la nina esperada*. The one they hoped would be second after *el hombresito*. But it didn't happen that way. Seven boys. Then the time when a women's womb becomes empty, dried. Unforgiving womanhood, still-birthing too many, hope of a *nina* cautiously abandoned. After passing years, heartbreak, consultation with doctors' *la familia* moved on. There was an empire to run. Continued with *la vida que tenian*. A hardworking good life. *Mother Earth's* abundance blessed *la familia. Dona Dela and el Don* could not complain.

Miraculously God's will blew a subtle whisper. Out riding, watching grazing cattle across *terrenos*, with sons, a sutble movement. Quietly, alone, *Dona Dela* consulted *el doctor*. And there it was, *vida*. Heatbeat. Fear entered. Anguished questions arose; Would she lose this child? Could she carry it to term? Would it impact her health? Would she lose her life? Many died leaving children behind, half orphaned, anguished thoughts entered. Loving *la familia nuestra*, so totally. Was she too old to bear? Would she carry it dead in womb, like the others? *Dona Dela*, advised by *el doctor* did something never done before; Taking to bed for six months praying to God. Eventually birth in the guise of *una nina querida*. *Muy querida*. Prayers, *bendiciones*, answered.

Tanya waited, finally finding the moment. This was a conversation not to be had with "*Mama*."

"*Las lagrimas*," tears would come too soon, Tanya would lose courage. Leaning in, *el Don's* luminescent large green eyes, looked squarely at dark amber eyes, searching. A wisp of curl moved down, covering a brow. Gently, a thick, coarse calloused finger moved it. For a second, *el Don's* heart quivered with fear, trepidation. A fear never felt *con assesinos, hombres borachos, hombres crudos.* Somehow, knowing a tidal wave of loss foreseen. But then, having taken every care to watch over Tanya's well being, riding together side by side through mountainous pine ranges, over years, always anticipating, Tanya's fears, joys, grievances. Such was their relationship. "*La misma mama*." Not a restful spirit.

"*Si mija? Que te precupa?*" "*Di me?*" (Yes, my daughter. What bothers you? Tell me.)

"Hay mas?" (Is there more?)

A worldly *politico*, university educated engineer, rancher, newspaper publisher, loving his daughter totally, *el Don* told a truth knowing, it would tear heart and soul. A truth *la Dona*, didn't want the independent fearless daughter to learn.

"Si mija, hay mas."

That said, in the coming few months, *Don Rafael* and *Dona Dela* prepared to let the caged *pajarito* fly. Letters of introduction, transit papers, planned itineraries were prepared meticulously for *la hija querida*.

Then finally with parent's blessings, Tanya booked passage on the banana boat, *Platanos*. Tegucigalpa to Puerto Cortes, to Nuevo Orleans, to the Port of New York. Passing the Statue of Liberty.

Dignidad. Familia. Suenos. Si hay mas.
Siempre. Hay mas. Adventura. Dreamers.

Chapter 10

Izod Center, Meadowlands

Parking lot circumference conquered … *"Oi gevalt!* Ova, finally. I can't *schlep* this any further."
Four miles, walked. Climbed. "What a *schlemiel*, that woman wuz. a *shlimazel. Schlemiel, shimazel."*

Uncomfortably tugging a medium sized black four wheel suitcase, Rita and Kat nervously reached the bottom of the hill, their hurried pace slackened. Approaching gingerly, adjusting city street wise wits, stopping, intrinsically together, simultaneously. Startled, mother and daughter, emerged, from dimness under twinkling navy blue Milky Way blanketed skies. Gymnastic obstacle course parking lot circumference conquered, no longer a challenge, now, before them stood their asphalt marshland mecca, the Izod Center, Meadowlands.

Their destination.

Kaleidoscopic lights emblazed against a nine-hundred foot towering white concrete backdrop, hovered before them. Brand logo embellished by neon greens, florescent reds, zigged blues, zagged yellows, iridescent purples, broke tone dusky darkness.

Continuing, "What wuz tha TV show that sed that? How did that go?" Rita's exhaustion turning to silliness.

"It was Laverne & Shirley, mom."
"Whad were tha words?"
"I don't know something like, *schlemiel,*

schlimazel, hasenpfeffer incorporated, don't know after that."

"That's it! Yew got it!"

Rita repeats, *"Schlemiel, schlimazel, hasenpfeffer incorporated*!"

Kat stared at exhausted Rita, wondered who the adult was? She'd seen this before. You know on those nights, after, the last note sung, the last late night of National Opera House performance, the concert, the play, the private performance, the show choir competition, the drive back home, in the middle of a major f'n snow blizzard, over the 14th street bridge, visibility zero, at 1, or 2, or 3 am. Always, becoming silliest during those hours. The most sleep deprived moments.

Kat's friends who Rita drove home in the opposite direction, because their parents couldn't, or wouldn't, always enjoyed this time. Rita was the mom who turned up unannounced to discuss what the 'hey that school' wasn't doing right, who on her way to the Principals' office, made *shure* Kat's classmates were where they were supposed to be. Calling out first names, shuddering cell phones flipped open, announcing Rita's arrival. Diminutive, like Moses, parting seas.

Kat took it all in stride. This was the mom, who turned up, no *matta* what. Single parenting *bravado*, more demanding. *Chutzpah* and *cojones*. After all, wasn't everyone more demanding, critical, of a single parent? Just ask a single parent.

Fearless.

Their physical pain forgotten for a few moments, returned. The bright lights met harshly on unsuspecting irises. Blinking eyes slowly, then rapidly, after hearing rasping eyelids, grate against contacts, Kat tried adjusting, dried out contact lenses, pushing an index finger against an iris. Sorely, "Did you pack the stuff for my contacts? Please tell me you did." Rita rubbed her eyes. "Of course."

"Whadda ordeal."
"Well thank God for *Tin Man* mom."

"Yeah, thank Gawd they're not all bigots," Rita shot back in anger. Emotionally taxed from the longer than need be journey, wondering if asking Kat to do this was the right thing. After all Kat wasn't totally convinced this was worth it. Kat, had doubts, but Rita was unusually convincing this time. No, no to be fair, in truth nothing changed. Rita was always unusually convincing.

Exceptionally, convincing.

But this, this journey was just too much. "Who knew of such t'ings?" This would go down in family annals as *exceptional*. Exceptionally, hard. Knowing the drill, this would become family folklore, in a nanosecond. Envisioning family gatherings 'round the dining room table,' someone telling, at every Thanksgiving. Every frickin' fuckin' Thanksgiving, fur eva. 'Pass, the salt.' Then a pause, 'And oh did you hear 'bout how she dragged Kat.' It starts, continuing to, 'Yeah, they were dumped.' 'No, kidding, for real?' 'On the side of what?' Eyes laser focused on Rita. Laughter ensued. Yeah, family folklore fodder. Heard it all before.

And still, auditions hadn't even started. "Auditions, auditions, auditions. Damn weren't they always, always hard." Rita hated auditions, neva mind Kat's impressions of them.

"He stepped up. It's generational mom."

"Don't I kno' that? An' exactly what generation wuz that over-sized ridic'lous sista from? Felt like yur high school. Gurlfriend had color issues an' I kno' gotta be light years outta high school. What a *schmo*. We didn't pay for color issues. I. No, yew and I paid for a frickin' bus ticket tew tha Izod Center. Nuthin' less, nuthin' more."

Working through exhaustion, anger, neither really recognized where they were. Well, not exactly. Remembering they'd seen this spot. Passed it, hours ago. Returning to this very same spot. Finally coming to the end of a daunting four mile journey, but not being from Jersey or ever visiting the Meadowlands before, they were disoriented. And why wouldn't they be? Disoriented, that is. They had seen bulwarks. Wired fences. Highway. Bridges. Not what they imagined. What they imagined was a smooth late night ride to a bus stop at the Izod Center.

Unawares while standing in their testy anger, abruptly an envelopment, cacophony of movement, sound exploded. Twirling about them, deftly, playing itself out, like one light piano stroke at a time, the scene danced itself into a vortex of TV show reality; one human, two humans, five, fifteen, then a crescendo of hundreds of shouting human throng. Cars honk imperviously. Crossing guards blow hard silver shrilly whistles. Muscular, ominous, bristly State Police officers holler threats, marching orders to someone, to no one, to everyone.

Hands flaying, a New Jersey State Trooper barks, "Muv along." Pointing his finger harshly at no one in particular, "Cum on. YEW, DERE, MUV! Don't stop in da middle of tha cross walk!"

Streams of contestant millennials walk past them chatting animatedly, stridently. Dizzying, encircling, encroaching movement brings them back to the four day main event. Further along another State Trooper stands amidst a confused traffic mixture of crowds, vendors, event crews, cameras, cabs, vans, moving food pavilions, he admonishingly taunts a group of bike riders, "Hey! Youse! Youse wit da Bike Cyc-cules, muv on, muv along."

"Whadya dew, bring da whole calvacade? Didn't know Dey were doin' a bike race 'ere! Cum on now, can't bring dose t'ings in 'ere. Yuse can't ride dem 'ere. Can't park 'em on tha sidewalk."

A perturbed bike rider, dismounting, launches into the first stanza of the Queen song, "Bicycle! Bicycle! I want to ride my Bicycle! Bicycle! Bicyle! I want to ride my bicycle. I want to ride my bike, I want to ride my bicyle, I want to ride it where I like." Laughing, he bows to the State Trooper, who chides "Muv on, cum on yew. Muv on, cum on youse holding everybody up. Leave dose in da parking lot."

Flood lights brighten the sidewalk with a third rate, movie set, like quality, lacking a Director. Walking past the well-armed State Trooper, moving onto the side walk, an event person in an *Idol-A-Try* t-shirt and hat, points the crowd to a cordoned area which Rita and Kat join. The event person commandeers a baton, loud speaker, channeling spigots of bodies past, around, over thousands of feet of red, black, yellow electrical cords, generators, and generations of lamps.

Yellow, black plastic crime scene tape carves out space wraping groups of bodies inside a marked area designating, *you've made it.* You, your fate are tied to the circumference of the light emblazed Izod Center.

Mecca.

TV

reality show,

Mecca.

Blowing a whistle the State Trooper carries on with country boy swagger, "Yeah, like I sed, keep gawing. Get 'em parked ova dere in tha parking lot fellas!"

An impromptu dusk to dawn outdoor four day music festival forms at the foot of the neon wannabes castle. The air is full of song, rhythm, harmonies, melody. Random orchestral tuning sounds of banjos, flutes, guitars, ukuleles, accordions, mandolins, being tuned, guttural notes, pitched squeals, laughter, greetings, shouts surround them.

Remembering that all six, *Bus 164* passengers promised to meet, somewhere in this ambush, Kat and Rita looked about hoping to see Timothy, Dustin, Chloe or Jay. Separating, taking the longer but, easier pathway around the circumference of the circular parking lot they knew they might not meet too soon. Optimists, fervently looking for the other *Bus 164* passengers, as they walked to a final resting spot.

Head spinning, Rita whispers, "Holy *dreck*, dey cud be anywhere."

The Meadowlands.

The Izod Center.

Mecca.

Chapter 11

First Night, Izod Center

Exhausted Rita and Kat, walked within the plastic yellow and black ribbon leading to and outlining the second opened area. Four day journey only beginning, Rita felt long in tooth. Walking behind songful purveyors; traffickers of illusion, joy, delusion, hope, sorrow, energy, synergy, grand gestures of theatrical idolatry in one form or another, reliving flashes of Kat's youthful life time of auditions. Arriving in this grand PT Barnum outdoor festival, "Might, just might, pay off."

Finally, relaxin', eyeballing the scene, grasping there's at least a thousand in the section ahead, Kat and Rita, drop their handbags, seizing an area on the concrete floor. Like marbles in a glass jar, the area fills immediately with gyrating ill-fitting bodies, chairs, bags, pillows, coolers, umbrellas, blankets, mats, food, instruments. Waves of tiredness come over their bodies. Traveling eight hours to reach this point, wasn't anti-climatic, the air thick with excited anticipation, breadth renewed energy into their being. Their bodies hug the concrete floor with abandoned relief.

Rita pulls a blanket from the luggage, spreading it on the concrete. Laughingly announces, "There, now we can sit." Feeling every step of the journey slowly lowers herself, "Houston, ... tha eagle has landed. Jist a little somethin' between our *tokhis*, an' tha concrete, tu-night."

Looking hard, "A blanket! Really mom, a

blanket?" "Love it or sit elsewhere." Incredulously, "A blanket? Okay ... Luv it, won't argue," waiting a moment before continuing. "But really, is THAT what we've been hauling? Struggled with that suitcase for this? Mom, really." Pivoting, "Oh, hey, look over there, there's more room, let's move over there."

"Why not stay 'ere? I'm tired, don't wanna muv 'round any longer. Why muv? Let's stay 'ere." Moving the blanket, "Over, here. Come on! Mom." "Oh Lord, why? Ova there? Why?" Moving the bag, "There's more room over here."

Changing subjects, "Wonder if we'll eva see dose guys again? I lost sight of 'em."

On all fours, Kat continues to move the blanket and bags, "No, don't think we'll see them again, they're probably up in front of us. We're at the beginning of this line though. Dustin and Jay are ahead of Timothy and Chloe. Chloe, must have slowed them down with her bag." Laughing, "Great bag. I wouldn't give it up either. Retail mark down, it's still expensive. Thought we'd stay together, but the crowds' real large maybe we're too hard to find, and they're really far ahead of us." Exhausted by the ordeal of getting to this spot Rita admonishes, "But I'm ok ova 'ere."

Looking around, "Hey! Over there, look mom! It's Jay! No one else though." "Really Kat, I'm too tired ta muv anoth'r inch!" "Let's move closer to him, mom. There's room." Moving about on all fours, deciding to not respond, waits before moving anything. "Jay!" Walking towards him, *schleping* her bag. "Where's everybody? Mom and I just got here."

"Hey! Hey! Got separated up at the fence. Dustin's walking around saying hi to some of his friends. Seems he knows everybody from Connecticut. Chole got stuck, we decided to meet up here. Timothy, the Tin Man, stayed with her. Don't know where they are." Moving luggage, bag closer to Jay without Kat's help. "Kid! How ya dewing?" "Hey!" They'd journey far, harshly, getting up Jay envelopes petite Rita. "Hello!"

Kat imitating Rita, "Well who wuddathought we'd be 'ere first! Where are they?" Unsure, "Don't know what happened, I kept moving along. We had a ways to go." Rita and Kat sit comfortably on the blanket, putting their bags on its edges, securing space. Every inch on the concrete was coveted and mattered.

Timothy and Chloe arrive. Chloe drops the large leather designer bag on the blanket's edge. Timothy lowers his knapsack slowly towards them. Shouting "Hey guys! You got here first?" Laughing, "Mother freakin' fuck! How'd that happen?" Rita and Kat's heads turn. "Rita, Hey, how did you guys get here … first?" Timothy, speaking to Chloe, "Gurl, knew you slowed us down. Didn't think we were so behind. You guys had to walk all the way around. Did you cut through anywhere?" Chloe bends, lowers her body, arms outstretched. Hugs, kisses fly about. Laughter bubbles up from within their exhausted, wrought bodies.

"Ha! We thought, you were up there." Chloe, squeezing herself onto the blanket. "Can I join you? I mean I already sat, but IS it OK, that I stay?" Relieved and excited that most of the original journey group, had re-grouped, Kat stretches the blanket, "Sit, sit!"

Rita chuckling, accommodates, "Sit ova 'ere. We've got more than enuf blanket. *Kvetch,* here. " Making space from thin air, where there is none.

"Am I getting too comfortable for you? Miss Rita?" Moving along on her knees. Rita, pleased to have them back in her circle, offers, "Oh, hey, grab a corner." Seeing Chloe and Timothy felt good. "Am I too forward?" Chloe asks Kat. "Naw, we wondered about you."

"Shit, what an ordeal! I mean we're like family now, aren't we? All colors of the rainbow type family?" Nods, exhausted, an inner warmth rises, kindred spirits these Bus 164 outcasts, Rita answers, "Sure, sure, you're *mishpocheh.* Family, shares. I'll move ova a little. Not much space off tha blanket, sew many people, but we can squeeze on it."

"Hey!" Timothy walks over to Jay. Fist bumping, "You guys made it." Acknowledging Chloe. "Where's Dustin? Jay, what are you doing all the way over there? Keeping your distance? Why? I see you left us back there. Couldn't wait for this gurl to get her booty through?" "He's around, finding friends. Hey, you know how it is, the line and all. We were gonna save you a place once we got here. It mattered, getting here."

Chloe sits on the blanket near Kat. Timothy returns to where Rita and Kat are. *"Bubbeleh,* sit ova here," he finally, plants his thin, angular, long body on the ground. Squeezing onto a crevice of space, knees crossed pulled up to his chest, between the edges of the blanket, a pile of knapsacks, almost behind Rita. Rita, pulls the baggage towards her and starts rifling through the luggage.

"Christ, would you believe I got stuck on one of those mother fuckin' fences."

"Looked a little tough to climb over. That's why we went around the fence, we thought it would take longer than going through. How'd you get stuck?" Kat asks.

"Oh Chloe got more than stuck. It was, more like you got blasted by the fence. Couldn't move you. It was tough going for a while. Sure wish," Chloe looking at Timothy, chimes in, "Tough, shit yeah, it was an ordeal. Cripe, we made it past that fence you left us at, then we climbed over bulwarks, (excitedly) then there was this other tall fence that we came to and I grabbed hold (stretching out her right hand), and I felt a tingle, but then,"

Simultaneously, Kat and Rita, gasp "What? A Tingle????" Kat asks, "Timothy, what kind of tingle?" Chuckling nervously, "Yeah, a tingle I felt it too. Hey Jay, did you feel that at the fence?"

Accusatorially, Chloe spits, "Like in electricity! Jay?" Staring at Chloe, "Awww shit, you didn't grab," "Like, uh, you know, well, I felt it run through my body, kind of like something funny. You know?" Concurring Timothy adds, "Yeah I felt some sort of electricity go through me too."

"Then, the tingle got worse when I grabbed the chain, hoping to get my balance. Psssst, bzzzzz! Dang, Shit, I thought I was gonna die! I couldn't let go … I tried!"   Timothy, aggrieved, "Yeah, a tingle, when I touched the fence but, I didn't hold on hard like you did with your,"

"Shit, well, I, while I was touching the mother fucking fence, squeezing my body thru, I put," Standing, stretches out an arm, holding the fence. "My foot on this other thing," tretching, standing, raises hands high above, and extends the left foot way behind, her body spread across and over the blanket. "You know, I stretched out to get my balance on that other fence or bulwark or whatever the fuck it was, and I felt, well electricity, then …"

Rita horrified, "Electricity? *Oye*, No, way!" "My body parts shook, like my boobs were jiggling!" Shakes her body to demonstrate the electricity going through it. "My booty was, was shaking, like that." Chloe demonstrates wriggling, "Thought my hair was gonna get on fire. I was all stretched out. My hands up here! My feet way back, over there. Shit!"

"Electricity? Those fences were electrified? Chloe they shudda had signs saying that."   Timothy laughing nervously, "Yeah, well I felt the tingle on the last fence, but I didn't touch the other thing."

"Couldn't let go, I tried. Don't know whether it was minutes or seconds, but shit I was holding on and couldn't let go." "Chloe was, stuck. Well, if, if you got a booty and all, and you gotta squeeze through that was, was sure as heck tough to get through." "Don't think I didn't want to. Let go of the mother fuckin' fence, that is."   "Well, it's not like a guy. A guy can suck it in. And, I got this skinny black body! Bones, Tin Man thin bones are what I have." Chloe looked pained, "I didn't know whether to grab 'er or not, cause,"

"I was electrocuted, I mean it!"
Shaking his head, "I couldn't do anything."

"Electrified! By those mother fucking fences in the parking lot. Why the hell would they put electric fences in the parking lot? You tell me."

"Miss Rita, I should've gone with you guys." Cautiously Rita leans forward, "Yew ok? I mean really. Chloe? Are yew okay?" Snickering, "It looked longer, but shit that was harder feeling electricity run through my body. Thought of my baby and everything," Concerned Rita suggests, "Why don't yew lay down, or maybe not. Don't know if lying down is wise."

"Thought, dear God you must be really loving me to put me through this much shit for this audition."

Rita, hesitating, "Not sure."

"I thought, yeah well, electricity or no electricity, this ain't gonna stop me. No, not at all. This dear Lord is not how it's going to end! I'm not leaving this earth before the audition! No way, no fuckin' way, at least not here in the parking lot."

Laughing, worried, each traveler collectively, searching Chloe's face to find signs of something. What they're looking for is up for grabs. What exactly does someone look for when they've been electrocuted, they wondered? After minutes of silence and anxiety about Chloe's well-being, Rita brings up a childhood memory.

"My mom wuz zapped while takin' clothes off a wire line. We were on vacation in tha Caribbean, stayin' wit friends. Mom wuz on 'er back for a week. Cud've killed 'er. Had a doctor check in every day."

Kat asks, "Do you wanna go see a Doctor? That happened to me when I was in Italy."
"What?" Stunned, Rita turns.
"Know how you feel. How's your head?"
"What happened tew yew?"
"Told you about it, mom."
"While yew were in Italy?"
"About the laundry wire, remember-r-r-r."

Delighted Chloe asks, "You went to Italy?"
"Yeah, when I was sixteen."
"NOOOOO, yew didn't, tell me."

Chloe wanting to forget about the recent electrocution, "Hey what were you doing there? I've always wanted to go." "Mom sent me to a Comedia D'ell Arte camp through Italy and France."

Maddened, "YEW DID NOT, tell me."
"How long were you there?"
"Six weeks."
"Kat! Noooo, yew didn't. What laundry wire?"
"Yes! I did. Wrote you about it."
"Electrocuted. In, Italy? No, yew,"
"Sent you a post card."
"Neva got post cards from yew."
"Told you on the phone."
"No, no yew didn't. Cudn't reach yew on the phone!"

Interrupting, Chloe asks, "So, what happened?"

"Mom! Shhhhh! Never mind!"

"Well I went out to collect my laundry. We were staying at a large rustic stone castle. Nobody told me that in Italy they use metal wire for their clothes lines. What do I know? I'm a DC northern Virginia City kid. We don't use clothes lines. Well, it was raining really hard. I didn't want my clothing to get wet. I ran out and all of a sudden ... it gets dark, ... and ... the wind comes up ... and outta nowhere there's a flash of lightning. I lost my balance, the lightening scared me, I grabbed the wire, hard."

"Christ! Yew didn't tell me, that!"
"Yesssss, I did!"
"No ... Way!"
"Whatever!"
"I'd like ta beat those *meshuggeh* camp counselors."
Annoyed, "It's not important now MOM! I'm here aren't I?"
"No, shit! And, it ain't because of those counselors."
"Hey ... CHLOE,"
"I hated those assholes, what else didn't they ... yew, tell me?"
"Told you, mom."
"Yew neva wrote about that. Hardly got letters from yew! Definitely didn't get post cards, I think yew brought them back with yew."
"Anyways, when I, grabbed the metal wire, I felt a tingle run through my entire body.
"Yeah, that's how I feel, weak. My head hurts."
"I couldn't let go or move, I felt weak. My head was spinning. I saw the castle moving 'round."

113

"I'm feeling lethargic, my body hurts in an odd way."

"I felt like I was going to pass out. I think I did while I was standing there. But my hand wouldn't let go of the wire clothing line."

"And my coordination is off."

"My nose started to bleed."

"Nose bleed!"

"Yew didn't tell me, Holy shit, mudder of Christ, did they call a doctor? Electrocuted! In Italy … damn. So what tha heck happened ta yew in France? What else don't I know?"

"Mommm … Chloe needs,"

"Chloe, uh, hey, yew sure we don't need ta take yew ta a doctor?" Grabs Chloe's wrist, feels its pulse.

"No, I'm not going anywhere. Shit, I got fuckin' electrocuted to be here. God has a plan for me. I'm not leaving. I prayed to God to make this happen. Make this audition my ticket out. My family needs this. I said, 'God make this happen.' Had a dream about being here, so it must be right. But shit I didn't expect to get fuckin' electrocuted."

Dustin shows up. Sits, joins the group to the right of the blanket, where Kat and Chloe are sitting. "How you doing?" Fist bumping Timothy, "Hey." Chloe still annoyed by Dustin's abandonment, "I don't know. Find your friends? You got ahead of us. I could have used your help at that fence."

"Did you get caught at that last fence? It was hard getting through, but I squeezed through." "Thought we were staying together to protect one another." Dustin answers, "We looked behind, you seem to hang."

"Yeah, well, the operative word is hang, yeah. I hung there, like a mutha freakin fool." "Did you have problems getting through?" "I was being electrocuted, by the mother ..." Jay speaking to Dustin, "Chloe was hands on." "Oh did you grab the fence too hard? I think it had a sign."

"Uh well, you don't ... Man, you cud have told us. You were ahead. I didn't read all the fuckin' signs." "I felt the tingle too! Chloe."

"Why the fuck would they have electricity running through a damn parking lot in the middle of grasslands, fucking nowhere? My body felt toasted. Tell me." Timothy looking to Jay, "I felt it too, but, Chloe grabbed both fences at the same time. It must have doubled zapped." Jay responding, "Yeah well I didn't hold onto it. I touched it, I squeezed through and I didn't touch that other thing. It had a sign posted saying, caution, electric."

"How are you feeling Chloe? I didn't feel right for days after that. I was weak."
"No, damn way, yew didn't,"
Eyeing Kat hard, "There's no way yew told me about that. Christ, yew were electrocuted in Italy at that God damn music camp? And yew had a nose bleed? What tha fuck were those counselors being paid fer?"
"Ok, Yes, mom, alright already! Chloe, are you okay?"
Everyone takes a hard look towards Chloe.

"Hey I'm gonna join my friends over there, see you guys later." Dustin steps away carefully over bodies, guitars, food bags, luggage and lawn chairs.

Rita pulls two large black garbage bags out of the luggage, handing them to Timothy and Jay.

"What else do you have in THERE mom? Garbage bags, really ... MOM? Chloe, you okay?"

"I'm not going anywhere. Shit, I handed out most of my money to that damn Jamaican Bronx cabdriver. Let me look through my money. See how much I have left." Shifting through her large designer handbag. "I'm staying, headache or no headache." Counting money. "Ten dollars, twenty dollars. Forty dollars. Ok, I think I have enough to get back. Shit, I don't know where I am. Where am I gonna go? I'm staying with relatives in the Bronx. I have twinkies, packed them. Anybody want one?"

"I cud always nosh, yes please," Rita's, everyone's hands extend. "What a freakin' long day. Met the strangest people today. Company excluded."

These bus 164 voyagers finally settled down to their black garbage bag spots on the concrete sidewalk in front of the illuminating Izod Center. Timothy, Jay stretched out on the plastic garbage bags. It's about 2:30 am. Looking up, Timothy shares, "Hey Rita, thanks for the bag. I didn't bring anything. Didn't have time to, to shop, get supplies up at the bus station either. Had problems getting outta work early. Might be fired, don't know. But I had to, to be here. Take a shot at this. This is my turn. I know it. I really want it."

"Yeah, I left from work too. Taking the, next three days off. Had to take vacation days. Should have been able to pull two regular off days, they wouldn't buy it. It's not how retail works in DC or probably anywhere. Won't have any vacation for the end of the year, so it sucks."

Timothy leans up from the black plastic bag mattress, "I just moved to, to the New York City area and it's a new retail job. I'm working in a plumbing store. Have a little know how from my mom's place in Maryland. We renovated. I worked with our cars. My dad taught me what he could, he's an electrician. I talk pipes this, pipes that, nuts, bolts, you know. But, I'm missing home, the people are hard in the store, they're hard in the hood. Mr. Pacinni, the store owner is suspicious. His sons never take their eyes off me. You'd think they never saw a Black man before."

"Where you living?" Kat asks.

"Long Island City. Went into the store early so I could commute into the City on the LIRR. They're pissed, 'cause I told'em I wouldn't be in tomorrow. You know today was just about getting here. The commute is long. Waited to the last minute to tell them. Knew they wouldn't give it to me. So, as I was walking out the door, I said, 'I won't be in tomorrow, gotta catch the train."

"But Tim, this is what it's all about. That recording deal contract. It could happen. This could be the break." Jay responds.

Timothy, moves his thin angular body on the square crevice that is his. "Audition is tomorrow and the way these guns run the show, we could be in and out early, or we could be here all day. Depends on their filming schedule. Couldn't chance it. So yeah, they were pissed. Don't know if I'll have a job when I get back."

Jay moves closer as more wannabees inch their way in squeezing him to contortions, "Glad we got here when we did. It's filling up fast." Timothy responds, "Yeah, had to be here on time. It's important."

Angrily recalling the trek, Jay adds, "We could be back at the bus depot the way that bitch bus driver was talking. Who the fuck knew they didn't stop at the Meadowlands? They took my fucking money and the sign said Bus 164 Meadowlands! In fuckin' lights, with large letters. The website didn't offer a fuckin' highway tour."

Mockingly, "Here it is folks the 164 special. We'll drop you off somewhere, why anywhere, or, the middle of nowhere, so you can deal with asphalt, marshland elements, bulwarks, electric fences for added excitement, with a dash of homespun gurlfriend city bigotry."

Chloe, "You got that right, her and the frickin' cabbie figuring we were all from somewhere else. What an experience."

"I just moved into another place. Long Island City has cheaper rentals. Manhattan's too expensive. I'll commute in for auditions, but damn, who knows if that's gonna pan out. I do this, I could get an in to the recording industry and get my music out. And, I really want a recording deal. Broadway or theater is not for me. I just want to sing."

Ever the curious mother, "Where'd yew go to school?"

"Baltimore School of the Arts."

"Hey, Kat went to the DC art high school. Kat, hear that? You both went to art high schools."

"Oh, yeah? Really?"

"Did you like it?"

Kat gives Timothy a nod, "It was an exhausting experience."

Rita complained, "I spent more time in the Principal's office protecting Kat from the bullying of one Black prima donna soprano and an oversized show choir talent than at my business."

"I was resented. I survived, got a great arts education. It was a 60's holdout for some of the parent's, some of the teachers. I wasn't there to worry about their anger. We didn't know DC was segregated. What a shock. We moved in from the suburbs. Never occurred to us that being Hispanic would be a problem. My mom stepped in, when the shit hit the fan."

"I got in like everybody else, I tested into two majors. Voice and Strings. Only person had done that in 25 years. So, what the hey, I was there for an education. But yeah, it was like dealing with the bus driver. Hostile, did I say exhausting? But, I met really talented fabulous people, made some good friends, who worked as hard as I did for my art. Got a couple of friends at Morgan, one at Peabody. They love Baltimore. That's a really good art high school. Music is colorless. It's about the art, the sound. I worked around the bullshit."

"That's tough, man. My school wasn't about that. We got along. You had the talent, you got in, you worked hard, you stayed. We had people from all over Baltimore City and the county. So, it was mixed. It was a great experience. Lots of real talent. But, this here, not sure they'll pick me." insists Timothy, "I'm not like most of, of the singers here."

"Wize that?" Rita wonders.

"Studied classically. Most of these people, just sing or they're into musical theater stuff. My training is different. My school doesn't do just the gospel stuff. Or the Broadway show stuff. They get into the classical. My voice reflects that. It reflects that training. I just want to record now."

"Well you're in New Yawk, now. Go afta tha producers. There must be a way to meet 'em. Parties, work. Yew know David Foster watches, likes gud voices. Make it to tha top ten. Maybe he'll be a judge."

"Yeah well I had a chance with Sony but, blew it. Interned. When they signed me up, they pressed that, that I wasn't supposed to approach anybody. But after I left I heard about interns, making connections." Feeling his pain Rita adds, "Well, independent producers are making it anyone's game."

"I'm classically trained too. Kno' what you mean. I'm listening to people and thinking, Christ you don't know what the heck you're doing. But they're singing and they're here and I don't know what they're looking for. It was mom's idea to come. So I thought, ok, why not? Give it a try, give it my best shot. But yeah, they don't do classically trained voices from what

I've seen. I'm not R&B, not rock, not country, so, a recording deal would be nice. But, I don't think it's going to happen, but if it did, it'd have to be me, my music, my idea of me."

Timothy leaning in towards Kat, "Thinking of today, do you know, '*If I Got My Ticket, Can I Ride*.'" Smiling Kat replies, "Yeah, we did that. My freshman year, in show choir went all over the country performing it. I know it and all the spirituals forwards and backwards."

"But let's change the words. Instead of, 'Ride away to heaven on the morning train,' let's change the words to bus and 164!" I'll start acapella, and we do the chorus."

"I'm game, bus and 164, it is!"
"Let's do it gurl!!!"

Timothy stands on the small black garbage bag crevice that is his, looks out to the sky, begins the spiritual, acapella, "Oh, if I had my ticket Lord, can I ride
I said, if I had my ticket Lord, can I ride
Ride away to heaven on the one-sixty-four."

The surrounding crowd takes notice, becoming quiet.

Kat sings from the floor the chorus, Timothy joins in: "Oooh, this bus, is a Holy bus, can I ride
Oooh, this bus, is a Holy bus, can I ride
I said, this bus, is a Holy bus, can I ride
Ride away to heaven on the one-sixty-four."

Clapping, rhythmic clapping surrounds them, they continue.

"Oooh, if I had my ticket Lord, can I ride
Oooh, if I had my ticket Lord, can I ride
I said, if I had my ticket Lord, can I ride
Ride away to heaven on the one-sixty-four."

Others, knowing the spiritual, join.

"Ooh, can I, can I, can I ride
Ooh, can I, can I, can I ride
I said, can I, can I, can I ride
Ride away to heaven on the, one-sixty-four."

Oooh, this bus, is a Holy bus, can I ride
Oooh, this bus, is a Holy bus, can I ride
I said, this bus is a Holy bus, can I ride
Ride away to heaven on the one-sixty-four."*

*Traditional Negro Spiritual

Timothy bends his long thin angular body mid-way giving a bow. Applause erupts around them. Gentlemanly points to Kat, who rises and bows. Their moment lasts a few seconds. A resounding success. Done with the song, Kat extends a hand to her mother, helping her land squarely. Tin Man, easily lowers his body on the small corner of the black plastic bag. Hugging them both Rita shares, "Hey! Cud hear ya both sing all night, happily! Magic."

Chloe votes her pleasure, "Got that right!"

Chapter 12

Jersey

A constant stream of humanity walks past, pointing, questioning, engaging, pleading to join them. The highly prized cordoned off area gets more crowded. Anxious, impatient auditioners ask friends to let them into the coveted area. Acquaintances, family squeeze under, past the yellow tape, joining others.

Waves of last minute pre-dawn crashers slink into their cordoned area. No one speaks of impropriety. Pre-dawn johnny-come-lately bodies, are accommodated without rancor, and usually with a loud raucous hug. Room is made for everyone. Humanity is in deep, tight for the night.

Dustin comes by again. "Hey! Folks, I see some people I know from home. I'm gonna stay with my friends. Jay, do you want to come?"

"No, don't know anybody. I'll stay here. Go ahead, I'll see you later. Got your cell number." "See you guys. I'm just going over there." "Stay in touch man, so that we can hook up later." Speaking to Jay, "You ok? You sure?"

"Maybe you can come over to my new flat in Jersey, if I don't see you again." Bends down, hugs Jay. Moves onto another group. The group becomes five. Although losing one, they become part of a larger membrane. Their small group listens in on surrounding conversations. Vocals absorb the air.

"Hey, I'm sorry. I'll stretch out the other way." Timothy brushing against a body behind his, further contorts long limbs better onto the garbage bag, moving closer to the blanket, folds a knapsack under his head and tries to sleep amidst the constant movement.

"Well I'm not sleepy, I never sleep during a sleepover. Ask my mom. Used to have sleepovers and never understood why they called them sleepovers! More like, stay-ups. Stay up for a movie! Stay up for popcorn, stay up don't let anybody fall asleep, mom, hey mom, didn't I love it! And, I'm especially not going to sleep here! I'm wired." Answering, "I know, but I'm tired."

"Well you know I'm still not feeling right. My head's fuzzy."

"Then let's stay up, it's not the most comfortable situation. Not my sleepovers. Hey Jay, how's Jersey?"

"Well, so far I love it. I've been in the City for the past two years. And yeah well that's cool, but I'm from the country, South Carolina."

Kat responds, "That's country alright."

"I so lucked out. Picture this if you'll let yourself imagine, a play. Off, off, off Broadway." Jay chuckles. "A small cozy theater house. Intimate. One balcony. They can hear me without a mike. The kind of playhouse I used to read about in *The Village Voice*. The stage isn't all that large. Lights up." Jay stands "Curtains up. I walk out onto the stage. Stage right, there's a spotlight on a white fence. Then the focus of the spotlight expands. The stage is lit. There's another light, it finds me. I'm in it. I walk. This particular spotlight follows me."

Standing, Jay's worn navy jeans, loose fitting tennis shirt shows off a tall athletic body.

"Stay with me, I walk towards a porch. It's a small 1940's white stucco two storied house. It's nestled tightly between a row of other white stucco two storied buildings. Really, non-descript. Two curtain covered windows on the porch. The curtains are checkered. You know like those checkered table clothes you see in Italian restaurants. A bank of windows, on the second floor. Nothing special, but then again, if you've been living like a stacked sardine can in cavernous Manhattan type buildings, and you come from where I come from, this little stucco house is magical. It's transformative."

Looking into the distance a warm resonant brilliance enters his voice, "For me, it's a small, tortuous rendition of southern small town life. Actually it's a faint snif, a sensory smell, of childhood memories. It's a place that doesn't exist, any longer. Certainly not here. Not for me. Not in Manhattan. Not with my meager earnings. Haven't headlined, anywhere. Not getting union contract work. Nobodies calling me up to the front chorus line, and I'm not getting callbacks. Well at least not yet."

"So, this little house, it's beckoning. It's pulling from the inner recess of my brain those small nuances of tranquility, space. Can you imagine space? A room, another room. A separate kitchen. Sweet Jesus, did I get lucky. A closet. Well maybe not a large one, but one that I'm not living in. Expansive sky, I took for granted and couldn't move away from fast enough. Then, stay, with me, I approach the steps. Steps on a porch! Can you imagine a porch? As I approach I realized, hallelujah, it's not a stoop."

Gleefully, "It's two steps to the porch. I take them, the wood creaks, from the weight of my body. I'm on the porch. Then I lean against the wooden railing. Imagine, my body leaning, my hands feeling the wood. There are chairs. Old ones. You know those metal 1950s style chairs you see on the beach. I'm not hearing the constant buzz of buses or cars whizzing by. Across the street there's a small playing field."

Jay continues, "It's a warm humid Jersey night. But it's not like the breezeless nights of my bedroom in the back of the building. I'm lightly dressed. There's a small front yard. I've got my dog with me. I'm throwing a Frisbee. My dog fetches."

Breaking from his trance admitting, "That's me. It's the quintessential me. I look up to the sky. I find solace in the sky. Its stellar visage, its limitless space, it offers tranquility" Quietly, thoughtfully, "And, you know, I need open sky," looks up towards the sky, "open space." Wistfully, "I like to see the stars. My old place didn't have open sky. Who does in New York? My old place, it was a walk up, on the Upper West Side. Looking out over an alley, a bunch of garbage cans."

"It was your typical new comer's apartment. Convenient." Looks towards the sky, open space. "Had, subways, all over the place. But tight, you know what I mean. No air. I could stretch my arm out the window, touch the next building. So after two years, I thought it was time to look. I went to Craigslist, called around. Most o' the places were in the city, then this ad turns up for a place in Jersey."

"It's like easy access to downtown. Hard to have a dog in the City, but I didn't want to give him up. The walking part with him is good. Get to walk in the park, it makes it less enclosed. I get to meet other people. Dog people. But, could you imagine, a yard?" Sees the future, glances stage right. Watches his dog, run unleashed. Walks along the porches narrow length. Shoes meeting the creaking aged wooden planks, throws again, to his dog.

"I think in the City I'm mostly outdoors. Going from audition to audition. I'm always walking. It's what you do in the City. But still, it'd be a dream to be able to see the open blue sky stretched overhead from Jersey to the city. But see it, you know, from your own place."

"So," Kat asks, "the place in Jersey has a blue sky?"

"Yeah, and a back yard. I mean it's not huge. It's not like my parent's large place where I grew up in South Carolina, but it's a yard, there's another small porch, the minute I saw that, I thought, YES! This is it. I gotta live here. It's not any further than any of the other boroughs, probably closer than your place, Timothy, in Long Island City. I get in and out of the City easily. My dog has a yard where he can run a little without being on a leash, I can sit on the porch or look out my window and yeah, can you imagine? See, the blue sky."

"So," Kat continues, "life's simple pleasure, you found in Jersey City?

"Yeah, and I'm not giving up anything. You know, I can't wait to get back there. I just moved in. I feel so lucky. Just imagine, me, a small town South Carolina boy, working it up by day in some recording studio and by night, staring at that great big blue New Jersey sky."

"I couldn't wish for anything more. What more could I possible want?"

Chapter 13

There's a First Time For Everybody

American standards ruminate through the air; 60s, 70s, 80s, 90s. Uniform of the night includes shorts, hoodies, jeans, t-shirts, sweats, flip-flops, sneakers, boots, hats, sandals, barefoot. It's past 3 am, bodies huddle, throwing on whatever's available to generate heat, like embers in a campfire, energy comes and goes.

One performance ends, another alights. Teenagers from nowhere stand, own the moment, singing, gyrating, dancing, trying out standards. A captive audience's attention moves onto the next wannabe. Others hide under hoodies, vocalizing. Voices screech, hoarseness starts to creep into what had earlier been clear strong full throttle voices.

Rita wants nothing more than to sleep. But Kat and Chloe have other things on mind. Not wanting to miss out on anything transpiring, Chloe engages Kat in ceaseless chatter, rustles through her bag for more food. "Wait, let me see if, where are they? Ok, still looking, somewhere, there are creme pies in here. Kat, do you want one? Brought lots. Rita, you awake over there?" Hesitantly, "Yeah, yeah, I'm awake." Barely audible, "But don't want yew ta know it. Pay me no mind, like in, pretend I'm not 'ere an' don't tawk tew me anymore! *Comprende!*"

Rita, prostrate on the blanketed concrete floor, squeezed onto a space at the base of a lawn chair belonging to a teenage girl and family. The girls' fortyish mother stands. Points, rising from a lawn chair. "It's a long line. Can see that from here. I'm walking over to those Johns over there. Be back in a little while. Babe, don't go anywhere."

Chair hovering overhead, at the girls' bare feet, resting six inches away from Rita's nose, Rita finally comfortable, stares at the cloudless blue sky. A familiar voice breaks the silence. Rita ponders its identity. Finally, recognizes the voice. Looming, casting a shadow, the tall slender young man greets the teenage girl.

"Hey! Saw your mom. Said hi."

"Hi! Dustin. Yeah going to the John." Politely asking, "Can I sit here?" "Yeah, on the blanket got plenty of space." "Thanks, this is awesome. You ready, you got a song?" "Yeah, doing, Carrie Underwood's," interrupting, "Oh that's nice. You practice?" "Yeah."

Adjusts into the lawn chair. Looking up from the blanket knees criss crossed, "I'm going to sing, 'Every breath you take' by Police." Dustin sings a few bars. "That's a good song. You ready, I'm really nervous. I still sing in church, but this is different. Could you believe the crowd already here? Thought we'd be up there somewhere. The website said no overnight camping."

"This is my second try out, people camped out at that one too, so I was sure we could tonight. I came with my friend Jay. Over there." "The website" Tiffany, cuts in, "yeah, well we didn't believe the site either, they always show people camping out on the show. So we planned on hanging out here."

"Hey, I'm really tired, I'm gonna lie down by your side. Okay with you?" Pullling her hoodie, "Yeah, go ahead, everybody's walking around. I'm happy to be sitting. Thank God we brought these lawn chairs. The floor is hard and cold. I'm more comfortable up here, its cold tonight. Glad it didn't rain. Wanna blanket?" "Still going to the same church choir?" "Yeah, still the same. You're missed, Dustin." "You know its nice being out here. But, I'm outta my element, tho'."

Tiffany, not understanding, "How do you mean?"

"Well there are all sorts of people here. Normally I'm playing it low. People, girls, guys are hooking up, all over the place. It rocks. Can meet someone here, maybe never see them again. The largest crowd I ever come across singing, was at church. Can meet some really nice girls at church." "Yeah, haven't seen you in church, in a while. Guess college keeps you away."

"Miss that."
"What?"
"Being away at school now. Not getting home, seeing the same people. My school, classes are small."

"People at church sometimes ask about you. What school you going to? Do you still sing in a church choir?"

Lifts himself, "State U. Uh, yeah, at school, it's a good way to meet other people my age. Hey, do you think your mom's on 'er way back?" "That John line is gonna take forever." "You got another blanket? I'd like to get warm." Looking for a blanket, "Sure, yeah, you can use,"

"You know I really want this."

Leaning forward, reaching out, tugging the arm chair. "What's that? This? Oh, me too. I can really feel," Moving closer, "Yeah, I can feel it too." "You know the energy, the opportunity. I know I might be too young." "You don't seem too young for me."

Tiffany re-adjusts the hoodie. The cool night air just got cooler. "I've been wanting this forever."

Dustin seizes an opening, "Wanting it? Really? How old are you?"
"I'm sixteen, but they changed the rules this year. We can try out."
"Sixteen, huh, you're young. I'm twenty now. You seemed older."

"Really? Wow."

"You're kinda like the girls I used to meet. At church. Its nice knowing there's girls like you. Still out there. Mom's done a good job." "Uh, yeah, thanks, sure she'll appreciate hearing that (pause) she likes you."

"Really? That's nice to know. Yes, mom has done a good job. You know I'm saving myself. What the church preaches is," Uncomfortably, "Uh, okay. Saving yourself?"

Grabbing the moment, "Yeah, it's important."

"Like saving yourself for God?"

"Well, when I'm dating a girl, I like to put that out front. That I'm saving myself for that first girl. That,"

"Um, sure (pause) you still want a blanket?" Dustin carefully, slowly delivers, "First experience," Nervously Tiffany asks, "Do you think my mom coming?" Pointing, "Getting cold, up there? Might be warmer down here."

Pulling feet away from Dustin, bringing them closer towards the inside of the chair, brushing up against Rita's nose, "Uh, no. I'm okay up here." "Yeah, like I was saying, I think it's important to know up front what your standards are. You know, like what kind of experience Do you have? Is there a first?" Tiffany wonders out loud, "Standards?"

"Yeah, like, what," he continues.

Tiffany, squeezes hoodie tightly. "Like in, how much experience a girl has with a guy? Or," Dustin holds arm chair tightly, slithering python like forward, springs, "I want a girl to know I'm (hesitating) I'm still a virgin. I'm twenty, almost twenty-one. It's important to let a girl know. I don't wanna have sex before marriage." Sixteen year old Tiffany inhales deeply, exhales, "You ask a girl if she's a virgin?" Practiced, coolly, "Well, I put it out there. That, I'm a virgin, that's important to me. You know." Naively, "You really believe that? That it's important to be a virgin."

Speaking.
Tentatively.

Softly, "When I meet a girl, I like to have a conversation about that." Curiously, "You talk about it with her?" Greek letter practiced, "I want her to understand that being, having that first experience is the most, that sharing with me, that I'm the first is the most important thing."

Incredulously, "Like, you bring it up?" "Yeah. When I go out with a girl I tell her that. That being the first, being a virgin is important to me. Are you cold?" Extending the blanket, "We could, uh, you like to share." "Hmm, ah, well, it is getting a bit nippy now. Here you keep the," tossing the blanket back.

"Thanks, I let her know that I'm a virgin. That we have to stay committed. That, I'm willing to wait. That, we could be together, you know without hooking up. You warm? We could," Nervously, shuffles her slippers, bumping into Rita, "Oh. No, I'm okay up here. Got my hoodie, thanks."

Pulling closer, "But. I, I've learned, sadly, girls my age usually can't commit to that, they've already experienced, too much. You seem like a nice girl. It would be nice to be around a girl like you. You know, commit, have, first experiences together. You, I could, I mean we wouldn't hook up, just be,"

"Hey, here comes my mom." Unsuspecting mom returns, sits on the vacant lawn chair.

Dustin, changes the conversation. "You've got a really nice girl here Mrs."

Chapter 14

Life, It Ain't the Movies

Back at Kat's blanket Chloe, turns to Kat, "Well isn't it a night to be telling everything. Guess that's where it is. I prayed to God for this. Prayed, told him, God lead me to where I should be. Well here I am. So if it's going to be, it's meant to be."

Leaning towards Chloe, also having heard Dustin's attempts, Kat replies, "I guess. Sounds like another frat boy. Isn't worth, *Bubkes*."

Not wanting to sleep Chloe offers, "You know, I was in a hospital, had a dream about this."

"Hospital?" Rita's proximity to Tiffany's chair and feet, kept Rita partially awake, over hearing the entire the conversation.

Chloe answers, "Well you know it's interesting how people don't read people right. How people can be really mean to one another."

Rita risks, "What were yew in tha hospital for?"

Not caring who listens, Chloe, addressing no one in particular knowing everyone would be an audience, their proximity, made powerful moments. Speak, cry, sing, shout, or seduce, the hard concrete sidewalk was anyone's stage for the next four days. And Chloe wanted attention.

"You know I noticed how people don't read

people right. Noticed this guy. I was really depressed. Got the best care. Yeah, well, my mom thought University Hospital was the best place, so that's where I was. But this guy, a patient on the same floor, was all twisted up, talking to himself. Nobody paid attention. He was like scared at our meetings. I was having my own issues."

"Hate to be a *yenta*, but how long were yew there?"

"Was there for a month, so you know I got to know this guy. I wasn't locked in or anything. I was in there to get help with depression."

"For a full month? At University Hospital?"

"Yeah, needed help. I couldn't handle things anymore. Got so I couldn't move out of bed. Can't handle mean people, things had gotten mean. Just couldn't deal with it any more. But let me tell you about this guy. No one seemed to notice he was really frightened. I did. I wondered why they could be so mean, so uncaring. But they were."

Sleepover queen Kat is engaged, "What was wrong with him?"

"Thought they'd help, but they didn't seem to care. You know you're in there with medical professionals, like doctors and all, and nurses."

"Why was he there?"

"He'd come to group sessions. We're supposed to talk about what's bothering. He never talked, but I could see there was something going on. Like, he was really troubled, frightened."

Wondering after all the turmoil, the electrocution, the Black Jamaican cab driver, wondering if this indeed was where Chloe should be, Rita doesn't hesitate, "Depression? When, were, yew in?"

"Well, a couple of months ago. Guess we both had that. Depression. Ever been depressed? So depressed you can't do nothing? Like everything is wrong? Like it's not going on for you? That's how I felt. Like nobody cares, or can fix it and you can't fix it for yourself? That's how I felt about my baby's daddy."

"Baby? Yur tew young ... ta,"

Sleep over queen, brightens, "You have a baby? That's so sweet."

"Yeah, a big boy, like his football dad, eighteen months old. Handsome, that's my family. Wanna see a picture? I've got a picture, let me find it." Chloe rummages through the large designer bag. "Have it here somewhere. Always carry it. His daddy was mean. Don't know if you've ever had a guy be mean towards you." Searching. "Thought I could handle it, but I couldn't. My mom had to take care of us."

Looking quietly, motherly, for a few moments. Finding the personal treasure, hands a small rim torn color photo lovingly to Kat. Kat leans in, sharing the picture in their cusped hands, "Oh, adorable. What's his name? Mom looka, a little guy. I like the football outfit going on. Here."

"Trevor, we named him after my dad. Well Miss Rita, I thought he'd be there for us. You know like a family. Thought he'd want to have a family. That's all I want, is to have a family. Be married, be happy, but it didn't play out like that. Like you see in the pictures, you know. Crazy, huh? Thinking that stuff, in the movies is real. Guys don't care just because you have their baby. He walked away."

Wistfully, chuckling, "Oh, how I wish Kat had one of those. Yew kno', one that walked away, but no gettin' rid of Dweeb. She's dating a Mohammed."

"Mom! It's Mohammed, not *A Mohammed*."

Mohammed, sporting superficial 'elite' connections was an easy going college student, who smoothly stole the confidences of Kat, and family. Multi-talented, over achieving. Kat's life became a classic vinyl 33 rpm notched up to 78 rpm's. Managing a full double major, national show choir performances, personal appearances; while looking for light hearted diversions, Kat somehow sandwiched in a friendship with the eccentric beguiling intern, Mohammed.

Acidly, "Looks good on paper, he does! Mentor-delish credentials! Yew know those Asians …. Always looking good in tha curriculum vitae department! Hispanics can't compete wit tha Pollyanna deceit." Burnt out by racially inflicted, unexpected strife at the elite predominantly Black high school, Rita welcomed the friendship.

"Mom!! Hush! Don't go any further, won't talk

about him, he's not here to defend himself. So, NOT hearing it! Chloe, go on. She's fit to be tied, about Mohammed. You'd think she'd appreciate."

"Beguilingly subdued. He wuz. As, accommodating as a new pair of Italian designer shoes." Rita continues.

Secretly, cell phonically, nightly, as Rita slept, tribal doors shuttered. Smilingly, culturally oppressive towards women, twenty year old Mohammed lulled sixteen year old, Kat, away from music, fourth generation Spanish-American culture, and family.

"Imagine having to listen to this. Mom's coy. Plays it slyly, … this, … this, lands on my ear. Sometimes, in a verbally cautious nuanced pitch, only I can hear. As if, because I'm her daughter it's okay to wail disapproval, privately. Treats me as tho' I've no common sense. But I need somebody, he's my choice. Yet she lingers, in some remote mental fantasy of what … a 'Mr. Right,' is for me. I work hard all day. Work 'til I drop. It's my whim, my fancy. Get over it, mom, Chloe, I'm listening, go on,"

Chloe, grasping disconsonant discord, tries to bring calm "Well, no matter what you do. If a guy doesn't want to be there, they're not. I tried hard to please, you know to be the sex kitten, the smart gurlfriend, but no matter how I re-invented myself, it didn't matter. Anyways, this guy in the hospital looked like he needed help. I thought, what about him? What's going on with him?"

Stressed but engaged Rita asks, "So, what does this father dew for yew? He support you emotionally?

Does he show up? Tha father, Chloe, iz he payin'? I mean dew yew get some sorta check? Yew girls let guys schlep all ova yew. Kat, can't visit too long. He fusses an' she leaves! Make excuses." Bristling from life long experiences with narcissistic men, Rita's mind pivots from the past to Chloe's dilemma.

Checkmating, Chloe's comments, against Kat's over indulgent acceptance of all things, Mohammed, Rita, knew she was complicit. Rita, remained silent when Mohammed pushed aside eating utensils, refused beloved *perniel*, wore flip-flops and shorts to Kat's elegant occasions, overlooking differences, believing Kat deserved personal space. Knarled thoughts emerged. "Why? Do women do this? What was in our DNA?" Rita worked benevolently to incorporate all things Mohammed, but remained distantly insecure.

"Kat, you tolerate that?" Rita accommodated Kat's friends uniqueness, believing it all to be a youthful lark, a rite of passage, road of self-discovery. "I mean do you let him separate you from yours? I wouldn't accept that. I get we have differences, but, nobody can come between me and mine."

"He's not as bad as all that. Not exactly an '*all*' American boy. I'm not into the shot glass frat boy, if you know what I mean. Mom, doesn't get that the average white college boy is all about lap dances, getting skunk drunk, and scoring. Mohammed, well, he's got standards, maybe old fashioned ones, which you'd think she'd appreciate. I understand he's got cultural kinks, yeah I guess so, but I understand him. And, that's what matters. I matter. My comfort zone matters."

"Not as bad as all that? Only family Kat sees, is his, an' that's tew clean their frickin' business office. His mother offers, 'oh help at tha office ...' Bullshit! She saw a Hispanic girl an' thought, 'oh housemaid!' No sir Muslims' not here ta bomb tha shit outta of us! They're here ta steal away our dawters! make 'em servants!" Tangling verbally, admonishing, "I didn't pay fur voice, cello, violin, ballet, piano, art, tap, modern dance lessons fur yew tew be a fuckin' Latina housemaid in a God damn third world Muslim household," sparing with Kat.

"Mom, don't go there! Not here! Not now. Can't believe you said that! So not having that conversation. Save it."

Snapping, Rita chimes, "Tell'er 'bout Christmas, an' those fuckin' evil Christmas movies. No, Christmas classics! Imagine! No 'White Christmas.' Sacre Bleu! No 'Mr. Scrooge (indignantly)!' But he found God damn Santa vampires. Evil priests! Controlled (putting her hand out, as if holding a remote) the damn remote! And oh, no (incredulous) gifts! Pshhaawww!"

"Mom! Stop! Chloe, pay no mind. Mohammed's different, alright. Odd at times. But what a relief. High school boys, testosterone city! Freshmen college guys, yeah ... give me armor! They're winners, alright! They win beer guzzling, shot glass toting, inebriated banging contests at the beach! Noch, noch, notch, panty collection! Mom!"

Complaints continuing, "Yeah, well, 'we,' cudn't hear tha Messiah!' (Indignantly.) 'Or listen tew Christmas music. Imagine raising a classically trained musician, an' not listening tew Christmas music. An' I had tew hide that Italian renaissance bible."

For a time, Mohammed's omnificent male domineering narcissistic ways supplanted Kat's disciplined musical traditions, accommodating his foreignness, became her new practiced vocation. "Lord mom, give it up! It's his place. He has a right to," "Right tew what? Diminish, denigrade your upbringing?" Both endured anguished bitter moments, hours of heart battering diatribes. "So I thought screw dis. When his Ramadan comes 'round, he expects us tew genufleck, suck up tew his food schedule. Fuck that. He eats wit his fuckin' hands! Hardly knows how tew use utensils!"

"Jesus, Mom! Stop … He's got his customs. Respect that. Why does he have to assimilate? Who's that important to? Certainly, not me. It didn't used to matter to you. He's doing as he pleases in his home. Can't believe you sometimes, you're the one who taught me to be open minded, to not judge."

Each knew; mother, daughter alike, they were one another's life boat, but how to mend splintered emotional wars, was something both roughly navigated. Kat, was after all a woman. The very type of woman, Rita strove to raise. Independent, self-sufficient, cultured, city-smart savvy, artistic. Rita was staring at her very own creation, and smarting by it.

"Who knew people cud replicate Third World livin' conditions in a damn northern condo. So, I put tha damn renaissance bible square in my room. Fuck'im! I wuz waitin'. It's Christmas, for Christs' sake. But she's tongue tied."

Rita felt fear, dread, powerless. Insecure. Rita held tightly onto the identity this outsider, was chipping away. "There are cultural markers under these *United States of America bandera*." A tug of war, sometimes between soul, identity, and spirit surfaced.

"Ditto! Mom! ... Wish you'd be tongue tied. Give it a rest! Change the subject, Chloe. Chloe tell me more about,"

"Phonies! That's what those people are. Cum 'ere tew change our people. Screw assimilation. They want tew take us ova, one freakin' virgin atta time."

To Rita, to *visabuelos* along the way coming 'from here,' meant one gave up *cosas intima,* mother country traditions, rituals, languages, and for some memories of things too cruel, even God was dropped. Such was the price of being from these United States of America. No, *American-o schtick*. It was God Bless America all the way.

"Shit Kat, gotta listen to your mom, doesn't sound good. I don't care what religion, Muslim, whatever. Control freak takes you away from family, your own people, shit girl, when things get tough, family is all you have. Remember that!"

And there it was. Chloe was right.

Comprende?
Fershtay?
Understand.
La familia.

It was the further scattering of tribal heritage Rita found subliminally most alarming. An invader arrived in guise of amity. Vanquishing protective, *familia*, with its melded *American-o* traditions, nuances, limitations Rita rhythmically conducted, like conservatory musician *Papi,* beloved Tanya, and their landowning *visabuelos.*

Alarmingly, *déjà vu*, this was the *shtetl* experience of her childhood, once again, her tribe being circled, silenced. Kat was becoming *invisible.* To family. Being abducted to another *shtetl*, a Muslim *shtetl.*

"He cares for people alright. His people. Hind sight is twenty, twenty."

Losing to this interloper, "What nerve! *Gavalt!*" Asking Kat to give up her fire and brimstone, Methodist, cross hanging, *Jesu Cristo,* made Rita indignant.. "Wasn't it the idea of these *United States of America,* to give up a lit bit to live and let live? To evolve into that American fabric?" Rita balanced old plates, new ones. Why couldn't he? Let Kat keep some old plates, that is, adding new ones. Rita, cherished those plates of *exceptionalism*, her parents balanced. *Exceptionalism* allowed her psyche, her people to survive. Providing for, expecting much of Kat, so she evolved, more easily than Rita, and *familia* had in those old Brooklyn and Bronx *shtetl*s.

"I'm giving up the house." Rita remained independent, scraping up mortgages, repairs on an aging house. So, after a time, while waiting for Kat to return, she quietly packed, discarding remnants of *familia* to move on.

"Shudda, wuddof, cuddof! I muved in with 'em. Shudda stayed on my own."

"Oh, that's being stuck. Dang. Guess you could say I was stuck too. Yeah, Miss Rita I have to fight him for the support and he's mean, and I don't like mean. That meanness made me sick."

"Then, walk away. Don't wait on 'im. You got your life an' tha baby. Don't like men not meeting obligations. Go after a check, support. Take 'im ta court. Yew dewing that?"

"Uh, well, no, not exactly." Emphatically, "Then fu-ged 'im." Turning, finding space on the blanket, Rita decides to calm inner insecurities, becoming silent.

"Hey, Kat, uh, I think your mom's pissed. She turned away. Miss Rita, it isn't like that, it's not easy. I had to put up with a lot. He's got a harmful meanness about 'im. I've been through a lot. We've known one another for five years. He's into football. We were tight. He can make money when they sign him. Good money. He's not signed right now. So no, he can't help."

Warmly, "Miss Rita, I wanted to be happy, just thought, what about a baby? A baby would make a family. You know, I think that's the nicest, kindest thing. Having ... a family, my people are from the Caribbean. Caribbean people have a passion for family. So, I had a baby."

Breaking silence, "Well, if he's not givin' yew a

check, ged past 'im.''

Turning to Kat, "God your mom's pissed. I don't like meanness now. You know. That's why I was in the hospital. I couldn't handle it. Living with him, got slam punching mean, my people aren't mean. My Caribbean people are a loving kind." Rita sensed something in Chloe provoking profound stirrings of things knowingly buried.

Connection. "Ah, yes, bandaged." Damaged. Injured.

Rita's vulnerabilities were carefully wrapped away beneath layers upon layers of sublime curative psyche gauze. Intrepidly, every emotional wound, individually, carefully bandaged. Uncharacteristically, theirs was a soft interior, not hiding in plain sight, their individual public persona was facetious, bold, brazen, thorny, prickly hard. Rita never wilted. Molted, sometimes. Off came emotional bandages. Never met a challenge she couldn't take on. Challenges cost. Wounds inflicted.

Chloe was packaged like a Black Monroe. A cornucopia of smoldering sexuality, a rich brown chocolate scrumptious, morsel. Smooth, chinaware mahogany colored facial skin patina. Iridescent. Lustrous, perfectly cut, beyond shoulders, straight black hair. Gurlfriends' men hoped to be invited towards and couldn't take their eyes off. But with all that going on in an almost childlike innocence, she exposed deep insecurities through constant chatter. Easily sharing inner most privately fragile thoughts, as though in sharing she might capture from them something missing, repairing a damaged psyche. An open wound looking soulfully for bandages.

Rita understood. "Meanness," Chloe said.

Bingo.

Nineteen-fifties racist *meanness* Rita experienced left her wounded, bleeding that neva stopped. No matter where.

This land is your land, this land is my land, from California to the New York Island.

They sung in those Bronx *shtetl* schools. She believed it. Year after year, bought into it. But they had lied. Teachers, neighbors, ministers, rabbis. Authority figures demanding she sing that song righteously. Loudly, with hand on heart. The meanness surfaced *in this land of you and me,* time and again, no matter how far and hard she ran from the bigotry. No matter how many band aides used to mend. No matter how often or hard she sung that *damn* beloved song.

It was as if the *shtetl* followed, everywhere. Every practice of assimilation wounded.

This land,

Perfectamundo English,
band aide,

is your

College education,
band aide,

land

middle management,
band aide,

This land

rising executive,
band aide,

is my land

English centric,
band aide

From California

expensive homes,
band aide,

To the New York Island

more education,
band aide,

From the Redwood Forests

foreign languages,
band aide,

To the Gulf Stream waters

international experience,
band aide,

This land was made for you

national recognition,
band aide.

And me.*

*Woody Guthrie

Still the *meanness,* after all these years, met her.
Didn't *Papi* and *Tanya* assure, by working harder than
everyone else, life would be easier? Play by the rules.
Assimilate. Immersion. Yet, growing older, Rita got
tripped up by holes, in that great American fabric.
Found falsehoods, mythology, promises ringing <u>hollow</u>.
The great American fabric was covering up its self-
inflicted wounds. And, hers.

Wondering, "What life was supposed to be
better" Materialistic life, or spiritual life? Everyday
life? From the very earliest of time experiencing,
meanness tugging. Festering, like molten lava,
everywhere. These United States of America was one
heck of a *meanness* melting pot.

Myth melting pot was boiling over with bigoted
meanness. Didn't homeboy, Donald Trump, that orange
haired demigod playboy rustle it up too easily. Like his
KKK, John Birch, worshipping white supremacist,
practicing father. You know that other landlord bigot
from Queens who red-lined those buildings in Queens
and da Bronx. To keep her people out. How about
Robert Moses, the grand puba of concrete highways,
byways, walls. Robert Moses, trumped Trumps' wall
erection desires, keeping those Spics out, back in the
1930s, 40s, 50s. Same as the Donald was wanting to do
with those "Mexican rapists" on the southern border.

You know, where *Tejanos* have lived forever. Before the Orange haired pervert's family ever landed. Ever ... in any part of these United States.

Remembering the earliest wounds. The racism exercised, terrorizing a child. Impinging on innocence. Holding her Methodist *Jesu Cristo*, accountable. Her supposed Inquisition ancestor's responsible. At the candy store. Over banana splits, with a cherry on top.

Guilt. *Shmilt.*

The daily re-accounting by gentle *bubbe*'s of Brother's Grimm like stories of dark forests, beatings, starvation, numbers tattooed on body parts, skin made into lamp shades, unruly mobs, ethnic cleansing, demigods, skeletons, rapes, beatings, starvation, gas chambers, soldiers and wars, left her frightened, damaged.

Her parents lathe, then bandaged those early childhood wounds with stories of heroism, *dignidad* by *Papi* who landed in France as a Medic saving the wounded. Unarmed.

Dignidad.

Bandaging wounds during the D-Day Normandy beach landing, later in the fields, farmlands of France. Bandaging mortal wounds of his own fellow American soldiers, *brothers, hermanos,* in trenches, roadsides, hospitals. Bandaging wounds of French soldiers, French civilians. Later still, of other Europeans fighting.

But yet after so much sacrifice, the *meanness*

greeted *Spics*, when they got back to the States.

Shunted.
Marginalized.
Made Invisible.

"Dad served in World War II, my older brother in Korea, my younger in Vietnam. They were still *Spics*, when they returned from those wars."

Kat trying to soften memories, "It's a different time now. Lyndon Johnson thought about us, remember mom. You told me, because of his teaching experience in Texas, with the *Tejano* elementary school children, it was 'us' he actually thought about in the civil rights law."

"That's a foul word, *Spic*, an' I heard it plenty comin' up in *da Bronx*. My mother believed a gud education wuz the key tew a better life. Yeah, well we got educated alright, it was thirteen years of institutionalized bigotry."

Softly, "Oh Lord, mom, give it up, she's not you."

"Seriously, Miss Rita?"

"Yeah, tha Spanish kids were punished wit' a visit tew tha Principals' office an' met a ruler, if yew were learnin' Spanish at home. Every now an' then, one of tha Spanish kids who heard it at home and brought it to school, came outta tha principals office red faced wit tears streamin' down their cheeks. Didn't happen to kids who spoke *Yiddish*."

Sitting up, taking a look at Chloe, "Institutional bigotry. That's whad I call goin' tew tha' New Yawk City public school. I always wondered how my neighbors cud be sew bigoted afta experiencing sew much hate. After all my *Papi*, tha *Spic*, served for them, as well as us. He served to keep all of America safe. He served to keep the world safe from tribalism and bigotry. European encroaching hate."

Chapter 15

Ghosts That Go Thump In The Night

Laying on the floor, talking to Chloe brought a ground swell of tearful memories. Voice trembling, remembering the hurt, "Like their families weren't one generation off Ellis Island, their names weren't even their own. Anglicized."

"Mom, rest up."

"In my generation, if I had Kat wit my college sweetheart, tha *WASP*, and she wuz as beautiful and intelligent, it couldn't be becuz of 'my' side."

"Don't you wanna take a nap? Mom."

"No, sir! His mother wuz fricken' terrified. Her whole *WASP* middle American family, wuz terrified I'd conceive." Softly, "Come on now. These are post Obama times!"

Rita's voice warms, blows her nose, "We had more art, more warmth, than my ex's stuffy, smug, mid-west word-smitin' Mayflower people. He loved my mother, she returned tha favor."

"Sorry Chloe, should've told you to not get her started on men. Especially (laughing) dead beat dads!" "Before I left that marriage, I aesked, 'did yur people not approve, did they neva give me a chance because I'm Spanish?"

Laughing and trying to lighten the moment Kat

offers, "*Viva la Raza!*"

Rita, "Shamefully, crying he sed, 'yes.' So, after all tha trying tew please him, tha covering up, his four years of infidelity with that insipid pixie haired blonde talentless reporter bitch he sat next to in Florida, sew that he cud remain that 'perfect son,' by leaving I bore the brunt of his lies. I was so devoted. So, I found a way tew hava baby alone. Cudn't, dew it on tha "WASP, *oh my God this land is not your land,* dime."

Kat cuts in, "A 60's feminist. Gotta give 'er credit. Don't let those hippie beads fool ya. Offers a peace sign in one hand, and hit ya with a placard with the other, if you get the Bronx out."

"Chloe. I understand yur wantin' family, man at home or not. Holy *dreck*, there's nuthin' I'm not more proud of, than mine." "Luv mom, women, children, injustices. Grandma was the same. Card carrying Eleanor Roosevelt democrat! Democrat, with a big D."

Rita tries to impart wisdom. "This 'perfect son' bit, I guess it comes in every culture. Males hav' all tha privileges. It's in my culture, my-ex's, Kat's Dweeb."

Laughing, "Mom, comes from a long line of tough broads."

"Women propagate it, men demand it. Glad I neva had a boy. Wudn't kno' whatta dew wit' 'im. I'd feminist tha shit outta him! Make him responsible, and kind. Yeah, men can bring meanness to yur life."

Kat laughs, "Christ, she cried when Hilary lost to Obama. Says women are still second class citizens."

"Correction! Third class!"

"Right,"

"Chloe, damn hard work, single parent stuff. Yew need ta discover Chloe. Yur journey's important. I know I can't impart wisdom. Like I said ... this one, is under tha influence of Dweeb!"

"Mohammed, Mom!"

"Prince of ..."

"His name is Mohammed!"

"Third World Manipulator!"

"Mohammed, Mom!"

"And King of Deception."

"Mom, stop."

"Whatever! Like I sed before, I'm tired. I'm going ta sleep."

Rita lowering, crossed arms across her chest, pulled the beloved purple bowler over exhausted eyes, pretended to fall asleep. "Well how do you like that! I'm telling a bed time story. Your mom's going to sleep. I heard you Miss Rita."

"Night, Chloe."

"Guess I tell stories that put people to sleep. Even here, with all this noise, all these (laughs) people, hollering, singing. But I wanna tell Kat, about this guy. About, how I helped him." "Let her fall asleep, mom's tired. I'm listening."

"Late at night when visiting hours were over I'd walk around. I wasn't locked up. I had freedom to roam. Not much for sleeping I guess, Miss Rita. Well this guy was up too. We were all on meds, but his

155

seemed to be really strong. So I walked over to his room. The guy didn't talk much at first, but I kept visiting."

"I got him comfortable with me, and, one night I saw him cowering under a table in his room. I thought, shit, what's going on here? I pressed his room button. No one answered. Could you imagine? It could have been an emergency and those uncaring lazy nurses stayed at their station. So I walked over and said, 'hey, you gonna help him? I've been pressing that button.' You know what the nurse said to me?"

"No. What?"

"Said he's doing his thing." I asked, "What exactly is his thing? He's sitting under the damn table like some boogey man is gonna get him."

Told me "That's his thing. We have it under control."

"What control? He's not in his bed, he's bawling his eyes out. Can't you do something?' That's what I said. Looked at me like I was some space cadet who didn't matter."

"She told me to go back to my room, mind my own business. That's mean. I thought shit tomorrow morning I'm going to bring it up with the doctors. Christ you think, this is the fuckin' numero uno, big deal University Hospital Psychiatric Unit."

"Hey look at my mom, she looks like Michael Jackson. I'm gonna take a picture!"

"Oh my God! Hey, Miss Rita, you've got a Michael Jackson thing going on. You know the hat, and your arms all the way up in the air, like when he's dancing! Ha! Ha! Go on shoot!"

"Got it! Look. Oh my God, mom look, look!"

Uses her foot to nudge but Rita doesn't answer. Rita moves, changing position, kicking up against Kat, "Thanks, guys. Go tawk ta somebody else."

"So listen, the next morning the doctors come in I said, 'hey that guys in trouble.' They brushed me aside. Finally after two weeks, I approached and said, 'hey I don't know if you wanna talk to me, but I'm concerned. You hide under a table at night. What's going on? I mean, can you tell me, let me in a little bit?'"

"Did he tell you anything? Did he open up?"

"Yeah, well he told me he heard voices. They were telling him to do things. Scared the shit outta him. Could you imagine? Now I'm in there cause of the meanness about me, the stuff that got outta hand. I couldn't handle. Could you imagine, hearing voices? Imagine, people are inside your head and there's nothing that will make them go away. Shit, I wasn't in that bad of condition after all."

"His, shit was serious. I asked the guy if he told anyone about the voices, he said he hadn't. I said 'well you should.' I told one of the doctors, but he looked at me like it's none of your business. I thought that was mean too, mean of the doctors, mean of the nurses, mean of the institution. Hey! You awake Miss Rita?"

"Hey Chloe, I'm tired and cold. Thank God it's not raining. I think I'm finally sleepy. Can we end the sleepover?"

"Yeah well I'm cold too." Looks around. Starts talking to a Black couple to her left, "Hey, you, using the furry blanket? I mean like its cold, you don't have it wrapped on. So, can I use it?" "Uh, no, I mean, no we're not using it. I guess so."

Looking to the woman with him, "That ok with you honey?"

"I'm real cold, do you mind if I get under it? I don't have to bring it over here, I could go over there. You got a little more space for stretching out there, than here. Is that Okay?" Still looking at his female companion, "Sure, sure, I guess we're not using it. Make yourself comfortable."

Chloe rolls over to their area, grabs the blanket, stretches out, covers her body. "So, where are you guys from? Thanks for letting me use this. I didn't bring anything. You guys okay over there? I'm getting warm over here. These guys were real nice to share, don't ya think? We could use more people like this, sharing, with a neighbor. Nite Kat."

Before you know Kat's stretching out. "Yeah, uh, ok, sure, what time is it?" Rita looking at a cell responds, "3:30 am."

Chapter 16

Spicy

Izod Center awakens,
like a whiff of smoke,
the smell of a meal of possibilities
arouses bodies trying to slumber.

Fame's kinetic aura in the guise of a video producer moves slowly towards the once resting wannabees. Spit fire energy, movement resumes to the right of them, towards harshly illuminated street area.

"Over here! Over here!" Snoring whispers become loud gleeful pleas. Kids rise from the floor, run into the edge of the yellow and black tape. Shouting, "I'm 'IT' the next winner!"

The producer brings a camera closer, walks towards them. From within the crowd, a 5'8" rotund twenty-something, Anglo, t-shirted male rises from a lawn chair, walks under the yellow and black crime scene tape, onto the street. Strutting, gyrating, strumming a guitar, leans forward and sings into the camera. Twang, goes the guitar, bluesy resonating croons emanate from his throat. Holding the guitar tightly, swinging it left, then right. The camera dances along, body left, body right.

Capturing the act in its entirety, the video producer pans further into the crowd. Crouches under the yellow tape, walks tentatively over bags, blankets, bodies towards Kat, pans her face for fifteen seconds, then moves to the others. Jay, Timothy awakens at this point. Their bodies looking disheveled, crooked, uncomfortable, they adjust their clothing as the producer moves slightly left. Wearily, mechanically both wave. Peeved Jay comments, "That was irritating. Those floodlights woke me up."

The video producer moves on, further back through the crowd, towards the other ten thousand wannabes waiting for their celluloid Instagram.

Rita, "Wow, that guy ova there has a whole routine goin' on."

Timothy responds, "Yeah, bet he'll appear. Producers do clips of fans waiting in line. Sure shot at that. They did that back in the Baltimore try-outs. *Idol-A-Try* likes that."

Jay's voice gruff from the outdoor air adds, "He'll get thru further. That was smart."

Kat inquires, "What do you mean?"

Rita tries to ignore them, "I'm lying down. I can't sit up any longer. Must be my age. I don't go for brunch at 4 am any longer."

Timothy offers, "Producers look through the crowd for talent, then move them further along in the process. It's filling air time. Staff cruises all night long, if you got it going on, you're on. That's why people bring signs and dress up in those silly costumes. It'll get 'em on the show."

Ears perking up, "Really, hav' yew done this before? I mean how many times hav' yew auditioned?"

Timothy, "This is my third time. Learn something new each time. Producers got an agenda. It's a produced show. You'll see later on, he's got an in to the first round. That was smart. You know those street clips in the show, or the info on people. That's how it's done. I saw the connection in Baltimore."

Jay, "Yeah, I've done this six times. Every time something's on the north east I make it. Get a little further along each time. Maybe this is it this time. Got a better song, I watch the show to see where they're going. It's scripted."

Chloe standing, shouting, "Hey! Hey you, guitar man." Finger pointing, "Come over here!"

"Who me?" Twenty-something pointing to himself, laughing. "Sexy me?" Flirtatiously Chloe responds, "Yeah! You! Gaw on. Sexy," "Foxy lady! I'm gonna have to climb over a lot of half dead bodies to git to you."

"Mmmmm, I like what I'm hearing. Keep gawing, I wanna hear more. I like those lustful words."

Teasing back, "You gonna make it, worth it?" The 5'8" rotund Twenty-something starts walking towards Chloe.

"Makes me feel good to hear ya talkin' that way. You can do that closer!" Laughing, "You, you know that hip movement stuff?" Swaying her hips, "Some more of that please. That, was pretty good." Strumming his guitar, holding it right up close to his heart. Hips swaying back and forth, "A guy has to know. If a little foxy lady like you is gonna make it worth it?"

Carefully climbing over blankets, sleeping bodies Twenty-something continues walking towards Chloe.

Cooing, "You're pretty sexy, too. I mean you were making love (caressing her shoulders) to that guitar for the camera man. You've got a nice voice. Closer. Climb over everybody. Nobody'll notice. Do a little something for me, over here. This body's a little too tired to get over there."

"Sure thing, lovely lady! Anything for you. Bringing my gurl with me, see what we can do together as a threesome!"

"Ha! You're too funny. I don't know who you're coming on to more me, the camera … or your sexy guitar! Yeah, I like the songs you've been singing. You did a good turn for the producer. He caught everything. I like what you sang. Any songs you don't know? Heard you singing, over there … on your chair with that group."

Twenty-something, finally reaches Chloe. Leans up towards his face, into his guitar, flirting, "You're you know SPICY. Hey! That's what I'll call you." Standing, swaying her hips, he follows, stepping closer into her space. "You need a nick name. SPICY that's, the way you moved your hips, got it going!"

"I like that, SPICY. Never, been called that before."

"Awww, cum on, sing for me. I like your

sound. You got a good voice. I like Barry White, 'we could make it through the night.' Know any of his stuff? It's been rough here on this body you know."

"Sure sassy lady. Anything for you." Strumming the guitar, rubbing up close to a willing partner in Chloe. "You really worked it for the producers. Saving anything for the audition?" "Sure, but I knew they'd be roaming through the crowds."

Coyly, "You did? You knew that?" "My uncle over there and I came last year. Realized you have to come prepared to show them something. Do an act. Treat the street like a stage. I have songs ready when they come back. I wanna be heard. Want people to hear my music. I'm serious about this. It's my chance to get stuff out. Gotta come here, be ready. The producer gave me lots of time. That'll make the final cut, learned that the last time I was here."

"Really? It'll get to the show? So, you're already ahead of the game. So what do people like me do who come here with just a voice?"

"You gotta do something different. Something that will make them notice you. Sing your song differently. Make it yours, make it different. Be different, make them want to get your performance in the show. Make them want to use that clip."

A ukulele strutting, singing wannabee walks towards Spicy, "Hey, come over here. Bring your guitar, we can use it over there. We need some back up."

Walking away from Chloe, Spicy leaves her

warm side and joins the other group.

Chapter 17

Pla-ta-nos

One week into voyage, Tanya's mind raced, having already seen an expanse of *Mother Earth* not imagined. Beautiful her Honduras land, she had not realized how diverse, knowing only its ancient parochial Spanish colonial *Tegucigalpa*, cobble stone *pueblitos*, between *el Capital,* and verdant pine abounding cool *montanas*, ancient tropical rainforests, overflowing with pebbled streams, waterfalls, dark sand lined engorged rivers, profound gentle valleys. *La naturalez. El mundo Hondureno no era tan pequeno.* But her land was indeed small. There was more.

Si.
Mas.
Si hay mas.

La Mosquitia. Travelling, two, three, five days from the last of *la frontera* villages, singular white adobe churches, abutting small empty clean blue painted plazas, one entered *la Mosquitia,* trepidly. Respectfully. After all, rainforests hid, honorably, ancient limestone square steeped cathedrals to ancient Gods no longer prayed to. Forgotten, once all knowing, powerful angry, ruthless demanding Gods.

This *patria's meztijos* moved on. *El Maya* vanquished, conquered. Vanished, invisible Gods of Quetzalcoatl plumage, serpent slithering, transfigurational figurines, ocelot clothed, painted Gods whose people no longer recalled the numbered days, blood sacrifices and festivities, on two thousand year old calendars now covered in dark, emerald, blueish green jade colored vines, leaves, and vegetation so thick, thirty undulating strikes of swift forceful, swung machetes made little permanent punitive damage through it. *Mother Earth* did not cry at their strikes. No rain forest tear shed. *Mother Earth* watched these invasions, molested, humored, swallowed humans leaving nary a trace. Human mulch. Offering to ancient Gods, perhaps?

At first indistinguishable to the common ear, rainforests, like vinyl recordings, had layered track over layered track, of rhythms, harmonies, melodies, percussive lines of birds, ocelots, snakes, lizards, monkeys, speaking to one another. Their languages becoming blurred as humanity passed through. Dusk calling everyone home. Macaws, parrots reaching up high for safety. Ocelots leaning on low lying branches, laser vision focused on movements, crawling cautiously beneath them. Nights never restful. Children swiped from their *hamaca* cribs. Snakes creeping about for their next meal.

Calling up from memory, her noise filled *Mosquitia* rainforest, marveling at its opaque beauty. *Mother Earth* composing. Orchestral, symphonic, operatic. Competing voices, sounds, movements. Flying overhead the sky turned suddenly dark, crowded with macaws, parakeets, parrots, nightjars, toucans, hummingbirds, birds of every size, and color, swaying the tip top canopy of trees. "*Que me dicen, mis amigos?*" Never totally learning their language, didn't inhibit Tanya's ventures into their realm. In the depth of rainforest darkness bathing in pure clear water *cenotes*, comfortable knowing they knew her, her movements. They knew her voice. Left alone to bathe beyond *peones, hermanos y el Don,* sure no on would hear her pleas to *Mother Earth* she spoke with abandon. Tanya pleaded for the freedom her rainforest friends had. An ancient gift coveted.

Quickly, memories, freighted, pangs in her heart made her long for rainforest friends. *Su amor*, was drifting away. *Que mas,* what else would Tanya love with such fierceness? The new land she wondered, would it reveal, anything like this? Where would, she find those resonances? Swooshes of tall thick *cana,* never bending to her passage. Taking beatings, hacking of rhythmic *machetes* by *peones* clearing the way for *burros* and cargo. Unforgiving blade thin cuts of tall grasses landed on her youthful, soft skin, through layered material, covering svelte wounds. Rivers breathing, churling, foaming, spitting up, entangled, unsuspecting bathers accidently slipping on rocks into dangerous undercurrents. Rivers gamely, pulling, suffocating, unwatched children, a mother chasing behind, finally reaching *el nino*, falling, slipping away. Taking their last gasp of air. Their bodies to the underworld. Recoiling, she grieved *para la mama y el nino*. Tragedies, at every step with *Mother Earth*. "But what was to come," repeatedly asked.

The lowlands of her Honduras along the coast dotted with its new cash crop, bananas, pineapples, and chiles spoke of moneyed harvests. Here along, the ocean, was a world unknown, showering bounties of fish, gathered by coastal fishermen. Shimmering bountiful mounds, captured in fishing net. Her people were not a starving people. Poor yes. Barefoot, perhaps. *Campesinos, trabajando, duro, siempre.*

Small fishing vessels cloistered themselves comfortably along the deep waters of Hon-du-ras. San

Pedro Sula, Tela, Puerto Cortes, La Ceiba. Further up coast, tropical green tufted islands, crystalline white sands brush against orange, purple, yellow, striped, coral reefs. Filled with fish of every other color. *Pescado* swimming in waters so clear, Tanya stood on deck in languished awe. So this was *su pais, su amor*. A country only half known, a protected, unchaperoned woman *de su consequencia*, had no reason to know. Hers an interior life.

"*Hay mas?*" she asked *el Don*. Yes there was. Apprehension entered every fiber. Realizing more time, was needed in *las montanas*, savannahs, rainforests. An aching heart promised to return.

Moving slowly along the coast, grasping its differences, one state from another. Arthritic mountains, gnarled knuckles rising from a rugged hand, stretching out onto undulating waters. Waves heaving back, then gently crawling towards majestic, lowlands spreading out like a hemmed skirt, flat, crumpled, delineating its different peoples. In the distance, square pristine white adobe homes, palm thatched villages, fisherman casting nets catching the days meals. Naked children splashing, swimming, in reflective rippling sunray beams of aquamarine white, clear waters, skin tanned colors of mangoes, orange, vibrant brown. Lithe athletic bodies, "*con pelo de indios*," Maya, straight, as jet-black as '*lena*' after fires distinguished in the *adobe horno*. Like their Asian Bering Strait wandering forbearers.

Honduras, especially *el Capital* was *mestizo* with a rigid class structure. Its' *campesino* class, increasingly hobbled by multi-national *empresas*. Hours, days, weeks increasingly controlled by forces from beyond. American and European companies tortured sweat, every ounce of gold, silver, *caoba*, and natural resources, out of her country. *"Las cosas politicas y monedas lempiras,"* more and more under the influence of large foreign multi-national *empresas*. These, *United States of America,* buying *politicos*. Turning their Presidents' and *politicos* into puppets. Diminishing the *peones y compesinos lempira*.

Along its coast line Tanya could see the United Fruit Company's, hired hands, *peones*. *Platanos*, stopped before journeying further into the waters of the Atlantic, to load cargo, there she met their broad, strong, muscled, tall, English speaking Black men. Awed by their bilingual ease. Wishing she studied English, but she loved her freedom to roam, more.

Platanos sailed farther away from the coast, its people, the villages, the palm trees. The mountains increasingly more distant. Her heart fluttered. Thump, thump, thump. Sometimes, quiet, passive rhythmic thumps. Then thump, thump, whoosh, thump, whoosh. Feeling the thump, thump, becoming startled by the skipped beats. She recognized the disconsonant life force notes. Strength, weakness, happiness, sorrow. She heard it all, before in the rainforest.

One Central American state after another passed. Leaning against the ship's cabin, Tanya hugged her chest, trying to control its pronounced pounding fear. Traumatized by this separation, heart harshly pouncing against its cavity, embracing the ship's pillars, looking out, realizing she was no longer a part of her beloved land, Tanya wept. Openly. With abandon. *Mother Earth* still beneath her, sensing a profound loss, of her identity. Her *bandera*, pledge of allegiance oath tortured her heart. No longer able to endure the separation, Tanya left the top deck for the private cabin.

Chapter 18

Morning Of

It's light once again. Midnight coolness gives way to an early morning moist chill. Bodies start moving about. There's quietness. Some have slept. Some haven't. Hastily the group in front of them rises and advances.

Lifting, tugging, "You up? Heard guitars and singing all through the night." Stirring up from the floor, "What's goin' on up there?" Event people with loud speakers are heard in the distance. Contestants start packing possessions, moving closer together. "Think people are starting to be moved. Don't know, I can't make it out. Let me have your glasses."

First group moves forward, carefully. Exact words couldn't be heard, so everyone in Kat and Rita's group remain seated or laying still. Standing, "Yeah, they're moving, mom. Oh Christ, its' finally happening. They just cleared the area in front of us. Cudda used a couple more hours of sleep. And, I'm feeling tense. Hey Timothy, you gotta start getting up. Boy he's dead. Guess, he can sleep deeply anywhere." Moving slowly, "Ok, I'm up." "Jay, Chloe, guys we gotta get our stuff ta-gether."

Jay rising from the concrete floor, "I'm ok, been listening to them for the past half hour. Trying to ignore, hoping for more time." "Chloe, hey! Ova there, yew joining us? Kno' you're tired, yew spent most of tha night tawking." "Mom, I see somebody coming. Way over there. Look."

Finally, a crew member stands in front of them. Four other staff members join. The area gets quiet, everyone looks towards the Crew Leader. Speaking, "Ok, we're gonna move along. Everybody stay calm. Don't want anybody getting over excited. We're going to move the groups one by one. Everybody pay attention. Anybody not following instructions we will remove you and you will have to go to the end of the line. Don't want anybody getting out of control. Everybody understand?"

Someone in the crowd shouts, "Let's go already!" And another, "Yeah! Let's do it! *Idol-A-Try, Idol-A-Try!*" Finally everyone, "WOO, WOOO, woo, whooooooo !" Event Crew members stand to the left, right and front of yellow taped cordoned crowds. Contestants, having slept on hard concrete, or in collapsible chairs which made for a tough night, groan, muffling crews' loud speakers, limbs move slowly.

"We want everybody standing. Get all your stuff together. But don't move. I mean that. Get your stuff, just stand and wait." After the first 10 minutes, gathering belongings, the pace quickens. Chairs, blankets are folded. Hands, helping one another stand, pull friends, family up from the floor.

"Everybody got their stuff?" Kat continues, "We should stay together. But how are we gonna do that in this crowd. Close ranks, we gotta be up there, near the front." Finally standing Jay speaking from experience, "I think if we lock arms, we'll be ok. We can walk forward, together, like in a chorus line. You know like a dance line. I can feel the tension, in the air. Whatever open space there is, we have to fill in, tight."

Jockeying for closer proximity to the front starts to get aggressive. Rita's group stands tightly together. As the event crew raise their loudspeakers, the entire group moves forward.

Voice blasting into the loudspeaker. "Now, let me warn you. We don't want anyone rushing. We will ask you to move forward in unison. Anyone not paying attention will be removed. When I say go forward, I mean to go forward very slowly without any pushing. We don't want anyone getting hurt. We mean that. You can't move until we say to move. When we say stop you must stop. Again, we don't want any running, pushing or aggressiveness. Is this clear?"

Resounding "YEAH!" from the crowd. "Ok, so everyone move ahead, S-L-O-W-L-Y. No pushing! We will remove you from the line." Crowd moves in unison. "SLOWLY, remember what I said. Slowly! No pushing ahead. Keep the pace even!" Jay, Chloe, Timothy, Kat, lock arms at the waist, walking straight ahead as in a chorus line. Kat looks behind checks her mother. "You, okay, mom? Do you wanna come up here between us?"

"No. But, Christ, this is tense. Yew guys tense? I'm tense." Rita signals to keep moving.

Timothy looking back, "Yeah, I feel it. But a least we're finally moving. God only knows how long this will take."

"Hey mom." Rita looks up, *"Schlemiel."*
Rita laughing, *"Schlimazel, hasenpfeffer incorporated."*

Looking back, "They film this too you sure you don't want to come up here?" "Don't worry, I'm holding tightly onto Kat's shirt. I'm jist a smidgeon behind yew. I'll use tha luggage tew keep people away!"

Rita grabbed Kat's shirt not letting anyone squeeze in front. At first heeding the crew's words, they move slowly, aggressively. No one outpaces anyone, as they walk further, their stride becomes more confident, the walk brisker, tenser. They walk one hundred feet.

"HALT! Everyone halt. Ok. We're gonna stay here for a little while. We've got some cue cards with chants on them. So listen to me, I will give you a signal with my hand. When I raise the cue card over my head, you chant as loud as you can." Looking towards Jay, Chloe asks, "Shit, what's going on now?" Jay responds, "We do a bit for the camera. This could go on for hours." "Where's the camera? Oh my God, there's a helicopter overhead. Look up! Mom."

Airtight, walking in unison. Every crevice of space filled with youthful bodies. Incredulously, the filming crew is above them. Timothy looks around towards Rita, "You okay down there, your kinda little?" "*Schlemiel*," she responds. "*Schlimazel*," Kat exchanges. "*Hasenpfeffer*," Chloe adds. "*Incorporated*," Jay ends. Giddiness visits. Tim, "*Schlemiel*," "*Schlimazel*," Kat responds. "*Hasenpfeffer*," Chloe. "*Incorporated*," Jay ends. They're personal chant interrupted with the business of show business.

Reading from cue cards, "We're in the

Meadowlands, we're here for *Idol-A-Try*! Every time I raise the cue card you repeat those words. Ok, let's practice." Event crew raises the card. Crowd, "We're in the Meadowlands. We're here for Idol-A-Try!"

"Again!"
"We're in the Meadowlands. We're here for *Idol-A-Try*!"
"Again!"
"We're in the Meadowlands. We're here for *Idol-A-Try*!"

"OK, now this is going to be for real. On the count of three I'm going to raise the card. You're going to scream this at the top of your lungs. This one's for the camera. One! Two! Three!" Raises the cue card. To the right, a video producer pans the entire area. Roars rise from the crowd.

"We're in the Meadowlands. We're here for *Idol-A-Try*!"

The crowd noise subdues, becomes still. Rita, standing alone, sings, *"This is it, make no mistake where you are,"* Rita's mind runs through the Kenny Logins song. Thinking, "Hey! A Facebook friend sed they wud neva go tew a wrist band event, 'cuz she's too old. Not me!" Excitedly, "This is THE wristband of all wristband events! Twenty million people are gonna watch. Ha! So here, we are finally, at tha Meadowlands. Lord this is wannabe central." Turning looks about. Looking up above, at the helicopters. Then, finally looks at her wannabe family.

"Lord, I'm standing behind two fine girls Gawd, but Lord, I've got this need in my gut for yew ta hear me now. I feel resolutely Lord, that it cud happen for Kat. It's a long shot, but I know an' yew know Kat's talent. Lord, I feel that if they hear that splendid voice, an' with your blessings, that good fortune cud step in. Gawd forgive my arrogance, but Lord could yew help her? Cud yew help her tew tha top ten? Wud that be tew much tew ask?"

Video producer continues in and about them. When, the filming stopped, the crowds were given more lines to shout. On signal,

"IDOL-A-TRY!"

Overhead a helicopter flies closer. Thousands of hands rise, fluttering upwards, wildly waving. Once these moments are shot, the event crew moved the group closer, steadfastly, arduously towards their final destination, up the stairs and finally into the Izod Center. Announcing, "Please line up inside!" Event staffers direct wannabes to various sign on table tops. "Move to empty tables."

Jay sprints, "Over there! Let's go all the way down to the right. Nobody's at that table. Look!" Once inside the arena, the five run, to an empty line. Each listens intently, grabbing papers, fussing over one another.

"Ok. I need your paperwork. Put your arm out. Are you an auditioner? I've got to put a red wristband on you." "Yes!" Kat stretches her arm out. "That your mom?" Nervously, "Yes? That ok? Can she come in with me? We're traveling all the way from DC." Pulling Rita closer, protectively, "I don't want to separate."

"I've got to give you a green wristband. That tells us you're not auditioning, but you can come in with her. Ok, folks, listen up. Do not, do not get these wet! Okay, you understand me. Do not get them wet. And, they can't be torn off. The wristbands have to come back the way you got them, in excellent shape."

Timothy raising an arm, "Not taking this off, sister for anything! Wooo, whoooo!" Dancing Chloe, "You got that right! Who would take this thing off? Sista! After, all that waiting and shit happening? That'd be crazy!" Pointing to the door Jay walks briskly away, "Let's go outside, its' getting crowded in here."

Tagging gave them a robust sense of exhilaration. Running, from tables past exit doors, shouting, jumping hugging one another. Once outside, regrouping, admiring wristbands, they couldn't help but brim with an exaggerated sense of accomplishment. They'd made it, past the harrowing 164 highway shoulder drop, asphalt endless ribbon, bulwarks, bridges, electric fences. They'd survive in truth more than any contestant should have to, to engage ... to get a first round producer video notice.

Fist bumping, hugging, Timothy yells, "We did it!"
Kat high fiving, "Finally! Yes!!!"

"Okay everybody! *Schlemiel*," Rita shouts. "*Schlimazel*," Kat, "*Hasenpfeffer*," Chloe adds. "*Incorporated*," Jay, Tim, "*Schlemiel*," "*Schlimazel*," Kat responds. "*Hasenpfeffer*," Chloe. "*Incorporated*," Jay adds, "Picture!" Gathering everyone.

"We havta get a group pic-chure. Kat, let me use yur cell. Yew got yur ticket in! Congratulations!" Long minutes of high-fiving, fist bumping, hugging went on for what seemed a justified eternity. Standing together for a cell phone picture, capturing the momentous moment, "Cheese!!!!"

Pictures taken logistics step in. Everyone hungering for a real nights' sleep on a bed. Jay, finally feeling light laughs, "Ok, so where do we catch the 164 back to the City? Never did get off at a bus stop. Oh my God, I think this is the first time we've seen the front of the building in the light of day!" "God do I wanna get this skinny black ass back to Long Island City. Over there somewhere, there's a sign for buses. The 164 should stop there."

Looking at Kat and Rita, "You guys, you guys staying?" "Yeah, we got a reservation at the Sheraton. Called last night, the hotel said they'ld hold a room. How to get there, who knows. We'll manage. Don't want to wait (laughs) for the 164."

"Taxi, I've seen taxi's. I can't, or don't wanna figure any of this out. My mind iz exhausted. What time iz it?" Timothy checks his phone, "Eight am. Registering just took twenty minutes." "Yeah, the whole fuckin' night, and we're done in twenty minutes. Well, I'm going. Home to Jersey. Guess we're sitting together in the arena. So we'll see one another again."

Everyone lifts a cell "Let's get phone numbers. Mom you ready?" "Yeah, ok, we're done. We're outta here. Guys cum ova to tha hotel tha night before. We'll leave from there. Keep us posted!"

More last minute hugs, goodbyes. A well-deserved two day layover before the audition was scheduled between ticket seat pick up and the audition. "Bye! Bye! See ya guys later. Don't forget, we're at the Sheraton. Stay in touch! You hear me! Stay in touch! Call if anything changes!" Waving, parting, walking towards the street, Rita and Kat hail a cab.

Chapter 19

Consolation Prize

An 8:40 am arrival proves to be too early. Walking to the front desk, "I reserved a room for two nights." Politely, "The room won't be ready until 11:30. You can try the hotel restaurant." Famished, tired Kat and Rita walk to the hotel restaurant, ordering breakfast.

Thumbing through the menu, "Ok, Kat, let's luk at what we can afford." "We can do the buffet. How about eggs benedict? Damn that's expensive. Order what you like, we deserve it." "I'll git tha full breakfast, that way we'll hava lot of food between us. Cud use coffee. I'll take tha jars of jelly back tew tha room with us." "No, no, don't do that! Everybody's watching." "No, they're not, an' damn, we're paying fur it. It's not like we're stealing. Fuck that bus driver."

Deciding to mentally exhale, an order is placed. While lingering for an hour in the half filled dining room conversations are initiated with a grandparent and teenage girl sitting at the next table. Looking to book more time in the restaurant an order for another round of coffee, is made. Eagerly sharing insiders' information about the audition registration process at the Izod Center, eavesdropping, overhearing another mother and daughter fraught with exhaustion after a day's drive, discuss their itinerary, Kat offers advice. Finished with their meal Rita, unconsciously meanders, in the great lobby. Kat walks to the front desk, to check in. Rita plants their luggage near a sofa.

Kat walks to the front desk, "Is the room available? Can we check in?" "No miss, you can't, the room isn't clean, it's only 10:30." Eyeing plump sofas, they hunker in for the wait. Dropping luggage about them, Rita places a bag under her head doubling as a pillow. Another half hour passes, stretched out uncomfortably in the hotel lobby surrounded by excited milling contestants.

After about an hour, Kat rises from the sofa, "Can't sleep, mom, can't sleep. I'm going to check again." Walking to the front desk, "Is the room ready yet?" "Yes, miss, it's all cleaned up and ready." Shouting across the lobby, "Mom, its ready." Kat settles the credit card account. Rising from the sofa, Rita collects possessions walks exhaustedly to the elevators.

Together, quietly, they ride up to the ninth floor. Using the hotel key card, Kat pushes the door wide open, walks in. The room is clean, spacious, air conditioned. Pulling luggage behind, Rita enters. The windows wall-to-wall, curtained, affording an expansive view of the highway and the meadowlands.

Rita walks to the bed near the exit door and bathroom, parks the luggage, places a bag, glasses on the nightstand. Immediately, removes clothing, drops it beside the bed onto the floor. Without thought, delicately folds down clean white bed blankets, crisp sheets, dropping rumpled, soiled clothing at her feet, then slips in. Loosening, unclipping a hair barrette, her head hits pillows. Exhaustion engulfs.

Smidgeons of compulsive energy emanate from Kat as she removes items from the suitcase which Rita has left next to an already sleeping body. Kat places items on the desk top. Quietly, opens, closes empty bureau draws. Walks to closets, pulls folding doors open, counts hangers, pulls a hair dryer out of its sleeve.

Meticulously Kat hangs skirts, pajamas, blouses, pants packed by Rita. Neatly, slowly removing toiletry and make up from a bag, Kat meanders into the bathroom. Noticing the light switch she puts the light on, scoping out the distance from the sink to the bathtub, finger tips move over thick towels. Taking a towel into hand, holds it up to her face, inhaling its perfumed sweet scents. Noticing her body in the mirror she realizes how disheveled the night out on the street has left her. Exhausted, but unlike her mother, Kat needs to be soothed by scents, steaming water and lathering soap.

Concentrating, eying the bathtub, Kat finds a consolation prize, piece of solace for this jaunt into fame. It is the large comfortable bathtub with its pulsating showerhead. Body aching for comfort, tired after the ten hour work day, the seven hour bus ride, the hours walked over barricades, bulwarks, through wired fences, and the sleepless eight hour street night to late dawn.

Decidedly, remaining there for hours, enveloped by hot, steaming lathered comfort. Meanwhile in the darkened, cold room, Rita has slipped into a deep, deep slumber. Neither speaks another word 'til the next day. Practically comatose, sleeping fourteen hours straight, an occasional head lifts from a pillow, to eyeball the others' wellbeing.

Familia.
The threads of our lives.

Chapter 20

Hmmm Comfy, Chatter

Awaking separately, Kat remotely flipped through television channels, finding movies, local news, weather channels, pausing for a few minutes and watched half-heartedly. Snug under rich clean aloe scented, cotton sheets, down-filled comforters, a luxuriant queen size mattress, all to herself, her body had no reason to rise to start the day.

Dozing, background television noises occasionally, pull from a deep slumber, Rita, intermittently looked on, not caring about the plot. Both did this for a day and a night. For seconds, one awakens, asking the other for the hour, the day. Day and night in the darkened room, confused their work-a-day alarm clocks. Exhaustion was mirrored in their lack of interest for food, or creature comforts provided in the room fee.

The hotel room was not inexpensive, their budget infinitely smaller than either wanted to admit. Rita unemployed, struggled without unemployment benefits. Kat pushing to sell more, earn more. Both struggling. These years were lean, while they would not afford themselves vacations, this to Rita seemed to be a have to, 'a have to do.' Rationalizing it as career investment, with a little money saved up and Rita's birthday around the corner, they called this a birthday present, even if it couldn't be afforded, with more than one shared meal a day between them.

This was a celebration of possibilities

unforeseen.

Finally, fully awake, aware of hours passing, rested, hunger stabbed. Rifling through hotel menus, Kat offers, "It's a bit expensive, even for a breakfast, which they serve round the clock. Well, I guess this will have to be your birthday present. We can't afford it. These four days, we'll call our vacation. That okay with you? This'll be our little holiday. We'll celebrate with a cake when we get home. Can't, afford it here. But yeah, we could go, have a sauna later on. I'd like that. Don't do that at home." "Cud order somethin' an' split it. The portions shud be large. Make it one order, ok, we'll dew that?"

"There's a Star Bucks. Let's do that. Get dressed, we can afford that. I know the prices there." Looking out the window towards toll booths, "Sounds gud, besides we shud walk around, see what's 'ere."

Dressed comfortably riding an elevator down, Kat a Starbucks addict didn't think through the wall menu, ordered quickly, "Venti, white mocha." Rita, stood at the cash register for what seemed an eternity, asked a few questions about what contained coffee what didn't. Deciding between a dessert coffee and a "cawfee, cawfee" was almost too much mental effort, but at last Rita opted for something which would jump start her body, "Pike Peak venti, please."

The day passed effortlessly, quietly, quickly, unpressured, walking through hotel grounds. Resting outside in an unpopulated sculptured garden for, cool breezes ran through tall thin sparsely layered evergreen trees. Sitting unobtrusively, in a shaded area, on granite benches, staring at a ten-story post '90s glass building across the courtyard, suddenly a rustling sound, brought their attention and eyes down to the well-manicured grassy knoll. A chipmunk ran across the grounds in front of them. Rita, pointing to the chipmunk, Kat hurried to the grate, crouched over it, but instantly, the chipmunk was gone.

Squeezing through a metal grate crevice seemingly too small for the tiny body, Rita, commiserated, feeling squeezed, but managing.

"Ay-Yay-Yay! Such a small space." Kat laughing, "Gone." Rita, rising from the bench, "Ok, let's hed back, before deese tired old bones stiffen."

Once in the room, Rita climbs under the splendid blankets and sheets. Changing, Kat decides to scout out the exercise room alone. A few more hours pass, Kat returns, orders dinner from room service. "Might as well splurge and eat something. Let's see, not a really fabulous menu. It'll have to do." "Unaffordable, but we hav'ta eat before we get back out there. Usually tha portions are large. Order a burger ta split. Whadda ya think?" "Good. Should be enough, I saw some food machines downstairs. Probably cheaper to do the sodas that way."

"I checked out tha gift store while yew were in tha exercise room. Everything was so expensive. Milk, was four bucks for a small two ounce container. So, I went to tha restaurant and gotta two dollar glass from tha bar for tha cawffee. At least I was able to get more cawffee and tea from tha maid dis morning. Pays tew habla Espanol in (both laugh) places like these."

Lifing the hotel phone, "Room service, yes, a

hamburger, medium rare. Uh, no, nothing to drink. Thank you. Twenty minutes, sure, sure that's fine. We'll be waiting." "What kinda soda do yew want from tha machines?" "Stay, I'll go and get Gatorade. Vitamins will give me an energy boost." Exiting the room, "Be right back. So what kind do you want?" "Got tha coffee, I'm happy."

Minutes later Kat returns with the Gatorade. There's a knock on the door. "Yes?" "Food service." Rita opens the door. A Hispanic young woman walks in with a tray of food. "Where? Adonde? Senorita, where would you like it? Senora." "Ova here, is fine." Clearing a table by the TV. Foodservice lady hands Kat the check. Kat reviews it, signs it and gives the woman a tip. The foodservice lady lingers. "Uh," Kat asks, "Is that alright?" "Uh, you sure? Segura? Senorita?" Sweetly, "Yes, thank you so much"

"Oh, okay, well then thank you (smiling she exits), gracias, muchisimo!"

Rita looking over the bill, "She seemed to wanna say somethin'. Wow, it's more than I thought. Sixty bucks for this? Enjoy!" "How could that be? I saw the prices, let me look at the bill?" Kat takes the bill from her mothers' hand, "Oh, oh." "What?" "Oh, that's why she looked at me. There's a twenty percent tip already in the bill!" Laughing, "Aw, yeah, that's what they dew. Shudda, told yew."

Rita divides the meal, making sure, there's a little extra for Kat. The cell phone rings, lifting the cell, "Hello?" "Hey girl how you been?" Excitedly, "Chloe? Is that you?" "Aesk 'er where she iz?" "Hey, I'm coming in, is it okay that I join you at the Sheraton?"

"Yeah, of course, where are you now?" "I'm on my way to that hotel we saw down the road from where we got off." Laughing, "The 164 does stop there during the day, not like, the highway."

"Yeah come on over. But how are you going to get here, Chloe?" "Well, maybe a cab. Not sure, I'll let you know when I get there. Ok, bye, have to go."

What seems only a few minutes later, Chloe, calls again. Kat answers her cell, "Chloe's at another hotel says there's a free private shuttle that'll bring her over." "Well, finish up yur food, we don't hav' enuf ta share, an' we don't hav' enuf ta buy another meal. Glad tha shuttle is free, things are tight for 'er too." Minutes later, there's a knock on the door. Kat swings the door open. Chloe, Kat hug. Rita, walks to the door, hugs Chloe.

Without saying a word laughter begins.

"Well, I made it. You guys going over tomorrow?" "We're goin' ova tonight." "Tonight? Why tonight?" "Yeah, we're goin' ta sleep in for a c'uple of hours then ged ovea there by midnight." "Mom, that's a little too early. Let's go in later, sleep in. It's paid for through tomorrow." Chloe hoping, wishing, "You gonna sleep out on the street again? Don't you want to rest up, here?" "Wish we cud, but tha line will start early again. Yeah, we'll have ta pull all our stuff out of tha room."

"Rooms good till check out. If we get there early again, we'll be out of the place quickly, we're paid up. Let's come back, sleep until the very last minute. Rest, after the audition." "How much did the room cost you?" "Three hundred a night, without tha *comida*." Laughing, "We just ate, split a meal, we can't afford." "Yeah, I just over tipped the waitress."

"How'd you do that?" "Didn't know a twenty percent tip is included in the bill, tipped twenty percent, she looked at me quizzically. So, I tipped forty percent, she doesn't (laughing) get that every day." "Damn things must be tight for you guys." "Tight enuf, but we're gud for now. We're ok. How wuz your trip tew tha Bronx?"

"Well you know I rode back with Timothy and Jay. They were alright. We talked some on the bus. Timothy was going back to Long Island. Jay, was hunkering to get back to his Jersey City flat. We said good bye at the Port Authority. I tried calling them today."

"Oh, I heard from Jay, while I was downstairs getting sodas. Said something, about sleeping on, or walking the street all night, at the park, after he had an altercation with his roommate."

"An altercation? He hit somebody? He doesn't look the type. He's got that Zac Efron, clean boy look."

"No, from what I understand, he got back to Jersey City. You know how happy he was about having that place, how he just moved in with a new roommate? There was all the room, the wonderful blue sky he could see? The yard for the dog?"

"Yeah, the Craigslist ashram, he was looking forward to, kicking back in." "Well turns out he's gonna have to find another place. He started practicing his song, you know vocalizing, like trained singers do, for a little while."

"Shur, of course. Yew dew that all tha time."

"Well, roomie has anger management issues." "Whadaya mean?" "Jay, really didn't know this guy. Hey, Craigslist is a crap shoot. Well turns out that when he was vocalizing, the guy didn't like him vocalizing, smashed the door down, started punching him. Started beating him up for vocalizing." "No way! Jay's got an awesome voice!"

"Good voice or not, that roomie guy didn't wanna hear it."

"So, what happened afta that?" "Well Jay says he hit the street, grabbed whatever, while this guy was still beating him, he's spent the whole night walking around." "Damn, who would do that to somebody? I hate harmful people."

"It was pretty late when this happened. So he spent the night out in Central Park. Jay, and his dog."

"Maybe he's catching up on his sleeping."

"I'm not sure. He was walking, sleeping on park benches all night. Thank God he has a dog, so he's safe. He was really stressed." "Unreachable. I tried on the way over to the Sheraton." "He's got a couple of friends in the City," Kat continues, "I imagine that's where he is now, he waited for them to get up before knocking on their doorstep."

Chloe asks, "He was walking? In the park? All

night? Damn that's sad. He, was so happy yesterday. You guys get back here ok?" "Yeah, hailed a cab. Took about eighteen minutes, cost twenty-five dollars. We're not that far but because of all the highway loops, you know, all the stuff we climbed over. Well the cabbie took a short cut, couldn't tell you if he saved us any money. We got here, that's all that matters. Didn't walk," laughing, "or take the 164, feeling too tired to care."

"Room's nice and comfy. Hmmm, nice view. Is that what we crossed over? Couldn't see where we walked the other night. Is that the Izod Center?"

"No, that's on tha other side." "Chloe, let's get sodas from the machines." "Okay, let's go." While the gals went to the soda and food machines, Rita starts gathering belongings. Opening bureau draws, closets, pulling items out, dropping them into luggage. Making a last stop at the bathroom, folds towels, cleans the sink, places the toiletries back into the suitcase. After checking garbage cans for fallen incidentals when all is put away Rita sits on her bed, awaiting their return.

Kat, suddenly opens the door, arms laden with soda and chips, walks to the bureau placing soda on the bureau top.   Chloe behind Kat eyes Rita's bed. Greeting them, "Hey! Yew gals got back quickly."

"Got you soda. Hope it's the right kind."

"Put it over there. Thanks, I'll be right back." Lifting herself from the bed, Rita walks to the bathroom, when she returns Chloe has effortlessly moved onto the bed.

Pressing her head against the headboard, "Mmm, this is comfy."

"Gosh, it was crazy down there. People walking all over the place. It's really filled up. Let's watch some movies. I'm not up for anything. I'm still tired. How about you Chloe?" "Oh, I'm okay for catching a movie, eating something, anything and sleeping. How about you Miss Rita?"

"My sentiments exactly. Eat chips, sleep some an' then let's getta muv on."

Rita, sits at the foot of the bed on a leather back desk chair. She doesn't ask Chloe to move, deciding it better, not to. Slowly Chloe is under covers becoming apparent she plans to stay, snuggly, for the duration. "Sure mom, yeah, best plan for the night."

Not protesting, Rita realizes she knew Kat's habits. No sudden surprises. Chloe, on the other hand she wasn't sure of, not so much because she didn't trust her, but more because Chloe was injured the first night. Getting 'electrically fried,' still had Rita worried. More than anything, Rita wanted to get some sleep. Rita hoped, if Chloe had the bed, she'd stop chattering, fall asleep. Quietness might have been Rita's wishes, but it didn't happen too soon.

Rita's host generosity only made Chloe chatter more abstractly.

"Chloe, have you heard from Tim? I tried calling him, but he didn't answer." Chloe doesn't respond. Nudging her foot, "Yew hear from 'im? Chloe? Any word from Tim?" Sipping a soda, "Yeah, well it took Tim all day to get back to Long Island City. I haven't heard from him today. He had to go to work, I think. That's what he told me when he was still up on the 164. He was exhausted. Once we got on the highway, I looked over at him, he was out. He slept through most of the ride."

"Anybody want some chips? Last I saw of him was at the Port Authority."

Chapter 21

Pizza Man, Me-he-co

Back at the hotel Chloe continued her story …

"Well, you know, it took me six hours to get back to my family's place in the Bronx. I didn't know where the fuck I was. Got lost someplace in mid-town Manhattan. Got lost just walking thru the mother frickin' subway tunnels. Got confused, about what number subway to take. The Port Authority, connections to the subway, the streets all interconnected, I was under avenue this, but I had to be on avenue that. I couldn't find the shuttles, so I walked. I don't know where the fuck I was."

"I walked underground fuckin' forever. I came up on one hundred something street. Thought well let me see if I can get some dumb ass Black Jamaican to take me all the way. I was too fuckin' tired to continue walking around. Thought, well if I get off the subway, somewhere in Manhattan a cabbie will take me the rest of the way."

Continuing, "Hey did you folks know that there's no sense in trying to get a cabbie to the Bronx? From around 110th? Miss Rita did you know that?" "Yes, hon, I did." "I tried. Put my pretty body out there, but like no cabbie would stop. So I continued walking. What the fuck, I was finally seeing something of Manhattan."

"I saw a brother around 125th, and asked him why the cabbies wouldn't stop." "I saw stars coming outta his eyes." He said, "Honey dew yew know where yew are? You're in Harlem, babe. No white man's cabbie is coming through here. Babe, even as good as yew look they're not gonna stop. Sista yew apparently aren't from around these parts. Where ya goin'?"

"The Bronx."

"Da Bronx." He laughed harder, "There's no cabbie who's gonna take yew past 89th street tew begin with. And they sure as hell ain't no yellow cabbie gonna take yew to that land on the other side of the bridge."

"What bridge," I asked. "Yew baby gurl, are on an island, and yew havta go over the bridge to get to Da Bronx. Da Bronx, sista, yew gotta get a Dominican cab, and it's gonna cost yew. Especially yew."

"Who knew the Bronx was on the other side of a bridge … Had my fill of bridges to get to the Izod Center. They sure do love bridges 'round here."

"Well there's no fuckin' way I was gonna spend another hundred on some fuckin' Dominican cabbie. I'd already seen Co-op City, and the likes of every burnt out tenement with that fuckin' Jamaican cabbie trying to reach Jersey. So I asked him for subway directions to the Bronx. The brother was kind, and directed me to my family in the Bronx. Did I say, I walked all over the fuckin' City? Took me six fuckin' hours to get home."

By closing the blinds to darken the room turning the TV off, Rita was finally able to relax. After a while Rita and Kat stopped participating in the on, going chatter which Chloe provided finally the two girls fall asleep. Looking at Chloe with blankets overhead, Rita coveted the expensive mattress comfort, covers and pillow, but this would do. She got over her desire for creature comforts knowing it was a short nap for everyone.

At some point in the darkened night Kat awoke, "Oh gosh, you're on the chair, mom, I'm sorry do you want me to move over." "Naw, I'm okay 'ere."

Rita remained upright, legs, feet stretched over the foot of Kat's bed until 12 am. An alarm went off. Noticing no movement on the beds, "Chloe! Kat! Time ta go ladies. Time ta ged up." Lowering the blankets, enshrouding her head, Chloe pleads, "Do we all have to? I don't need to get there that early, it's too early." "Yep, don't know when we'll get back here. Have ta move our stuff out. Let's go. Rise an' shine."

Kat was up, then Chloe. Gathering their things, they walked to the elevator. The hallway was quiet. As the elevator rode down, other contestants got on and off, arms filled with chips, sodas, candy. Giddy anticipation of late night parties made them rowdy, anxious. Riding down only a few more stops, the elevator door opened onto the lobby floor. Pulling luggage across the lobby, they walked slowly towards the unmanned Concierge's desk.

Rita leans the luggage against the desk, "Let's wait." Concierge appears from behind a closed door. "Hello, may I help you?" "Like, tew leave my luggage 'ere, get it around noon?" "Yes, that would be fine. I'll give you a receipt. Is there anything else you need?" "No. That'll be it for now. Thank yew." Rita leaves the lobby, joins the girls outside, under the canopied hotel driveway. While sitting, waiting on a bench for their cab, a small automobile drives towards them with an ad lit atop its roof. The lighted ad reads, Amalfi's Pizza.

In unison the gals shout, "Pizzzzzza!" "Oh my God, pizza, there's pizza. Look he's stopping, grab him! He's delivering to the hotel. Why didn't we think of that?" "You could have ordered pizza! Oh, I'm hungry." "Ged over an' aesk 'im how late he delivers." "Do you think he'll deliver to the Izod Center? We're not gonna be here." "Don't know, go aesk, hurry up, he's getting outta 'is car." Kat rushes over to the pizza man who is pulling pizzas out of the car.

"Helloooo, how late do you deliver?" "Up until three am." "Uh, do you deliver to the Izod Center?" "Hon, where at the Izod Center? Ain't that closed? Do ya mean tomorrow?" "No, tonight. Like later on. Have to get there first. Actually, don't know where. I have a cell. Somewhere, in the parking lot? I think, I mean we don't know, but once we get there we could call you, you'd get lots of orders once you get there." "Well, I dunno, hon. Neva, dun dat before."

Trying to sound convincing, "Lots of people, I mean, tons of people would see, YOU! you know, there's tons of people sitting out there for Idol-A-Try, waiting the night out on the street." "Okay, guess I cud hav' my man Joe keep cukin' Youse ask fur me, Tony. Got it, Tony. I'll rememba yew. Gotta, call it in an' tell me where tew meet, once yew get dere. Yeah, sure what the hey, I'll deliver. Up until three am. Rememba three am, then we close. Can't take any more orders 'cause tha oven closes, dis old man likes tew go home."

"It's a deal. Got, your number, Tony. Woo Hoooo!!"

"Oh my Gawd, pizza, pizza! I'm still hungry." "Me too, that hamburger wasn't enough." "Ask him for his menu. Gurl, I could use some food just about now. I'll chip in. Split it, three ways." Pizza man walks into the lobby. "Get it when he comes back down." Tony, the pizza man returns from delivering. As he opens the cars' door, Kat and Chloe, hover nearby with the finesse of rock star groupies. Leaning into the backseat, he rifles through pizza boxes, food, clothing and paper. Undeterred by the clutter, clumsily lifts a glossy menu, hands it to them.

Smiling, "Call. Fur yew, we deliver! Anywhere. Yeah even the Izod Center! Good luck, gurls." Delighted, they high-five! "Okay! We'll do that once we get there."

Returning to the bench, crouching, huddling tightly, fingers excitedly flick through the menu's colorful glossy pages. Hungrily eyes rove over pictures, words. This imaginary encounter with food was almost too much. Visualizing bounties of food, sanity, time escapes them. Laughing noisily, as other hotel guests arrive, the lateness of the hour, dawns on them. Once again, checking cell phones, anxiety about the cab arise.

Kat looks at her cell, "Ok, we're running out of time." "Damn, where's that cab? We've been 'ere a while an' we can't order pizza if we ged there too late." Chloe feeling impatient, tired, "Dang, we could have slept in another twenty minutes." Just as they were contemplating calling the cab again, a white hotel van drives past them, driving into the parking lot. A short, stocky, dark haired Hispanic man steps out, walks towards them.

"You girls part of *Idol-A-Try*?"

"Yeah, we're waitin' fer a cab." "Just finished my last round, could drive you over there." "Would you? We don't want to stay out here too long." "Yeah. Sure, just got back from there." Rita realizes this isn't a hotel service he's offering, "How much?" "Five dollars apiece, it's not far, it would be extra cash for me. Is that ok?" Nodding in agreement, they're game. Van man points to a white van in the parking lot. Cheerfully walking over to it, Van man gallantly slides the door open. "Get in."

All three climb in. He starts the engine, pulls out. As they drive out a taxi drives past them. Chloe takes the front passenger seat, "Hey where you from? You got a cute accent."

"Me-he-co, ever hear of it? Me-he-co. Senorita," "Yeah, like the way you say that. Me-he-co. That soft sound to it. But you live here now? You from around here? I mean do you live in Jersey? I don't. I've come up from Maryland. Around the DC area."

"Yeah, have a whole bunch of family here now. A couple of kids, been here twenty-five years. *Came here looking for a better life. God bless America!* Work for the Sheraton a while now. I manage the vans. It's a good job."

"You have any young kids?"

"Got a kid in college, one in the Army, one in high school. They're doing pretty good. They like this *Idol-A-Try* thing. They're excited it's here. I won't let them participate though. Better for them they study something serious. Something that gets them a job. Maybe become a teacher or an engineer. The Army will pay my son to learn engineering."

Kat's eyes meet his in the rear view mirror, "Some people love the arts. It's not for everyone. It's a calling."

"You sing? Trying out for the audition? I've driven a whole lot of people to the Izod Center. All day. People coming in. It's been busy." "Whole bunch of people out there now?" "Not as much as earlier today. But there are some people out there. Mostly the event people now. Don't know if you can be out there this early. Yeah, some people have lined up already."

"Yeah well, we want to be first in line. That way we don't lose out on the audition. Could, actually miss out on it, if you get there too late. Don't want to miss out."

"My mom and I came in from northern Virginia. They gave us reserved seats, numbered tickets." "Ged as close as yew can. We'll walk tha rest of tha way. We know tha path." "Ok, *senora* not a problem, we'll make sure you don't walk too far and you get there safely."

Me-he-co van man drives into the well, lit, Izod

Center. Heavily loaded down with equipment, *Idol-A-Try* staff walks hurriedly in the parking lot. Food tents, DJs are setting up under ramps of the large five storied garage. But, for the most part the area is devoid of contestant wannabees. And there had been thousands and thousands deep, lined up around the Izod Center, over the course of three days.

"Just look at this, *senoritas, oportunidad* all around you. *Buena suerte.* God Bless America, the land of dreams."

Land of *suenos*.

Mas.

Si hay mas.

Chapter 22

Back of the Bus

Timothy had done anything but sleep on the 164 back to the Port Authority. One would have thought they'd become the *Three Amigos* because of their bulwark highway journey and overnight open sky street fest. As it turned out, Chloe continued her aimless chatter from their last good bye and hug at the Izod Center to their arrival an hour later at the Port Authority.

As they walked to the 164 bus stop, panic ran through Tin Man's tired bones. It occurred, "Holy mother of Christ, the energizer Sista bunny might sit next to me." That thought played out over and over, as he stood on the bus line. Trying to end the nights' serendipitous act of punishments, he looked up and down, peering inside the bus when it approached. Counted seats, but he couldn't know who was a couple, who would skip a seat. There was no way of knowing how it would play out inside the bus.

Begging his exhausted mind to stop re-numerating seating possibilities, he thought of speaking to Jay about sitting together. But, he couldn't pull Jay aside privately. Jay seemed to be deep in thought. An aura of impregnatable wall enveloped. If anyone could ever embody other worldliness at this moment, it was Jay. Tim's mind raced, his body quivered and shriveled from exhaustion.

Chloe on the other hand was re-energize, engaging. Re-telling events, body movements gyrating,

Tin Man couldn't get a word in edge wise. Everyone was mesmerized. Jay continued to look uncomfortably away. Chloe played the damsel in distress to the hilt. Jiggling her ladies, swirling her booty, Timothy wondered why she hadn't tried reality television. "Act is, MTV winning."

Trying hard to become invisible, Jay was struggling with anguished thoughts.

All Jay wanted to do was sleep. Jay's mind raced. "Rest, sleep, rest, sleep, rest that's all I want," his mind said, loudly. Overwrought, exhausted, it addressed him in the third person, "Let's hurry up and get back home, to our dog, our porch, our bed. Our place in Jersey. Let's close the door and rest," it taunted. Resoundingly his mind wanted to announce his intentions to sit alone, apart.

"I don't mind, if 'we'sit next to Tin Man," continuing, "after all, it's a bus, we havta sit next to someone. But God, oh God, oh God, not the Sista. Sista needs to be still and shut-up." The third person conversation continued, "Not the Sista, 'we' need to sit elsewhere. Please God." Jay looked around for a chance encounter with someone other than his new wannabee Izod central family. He tried to muster up the last vestiges of his voice to speak to someone on line. But Chloe had sucked up the oxygen, everyone was engaged in her story.

Finally quieting his inner exhausted demon and having observed that during the long night on the concrete, Timothy had quickly fallen asleep, he appealed to a higher being, "Oh, please, God, oh please, please God, let it be Tin Man I sit next to," his mind taunted, silently in line.

Timothy let Chloe move ahead on the line, hoping "She'll find a seat, next to someone else and Sista will sit and sleep. Maybe someone keenly attractive, someone she'll get attached to." So, he hoped that a lucky straw would come his way and an empty seat would open up and Chloe would sit. "Next to someone else," his mind said. At this point he wasn't hoping she'd sit next to Jay, "But not next to Jay, I know my man's gotta be tired." Tin Man wasn't wishing his new friend further mental exhaustion, he could see the wear and tear on Jay's face.

But the bus was full, seats were taken and Chloe had her own plans. Jay, Timothy and Chloe walked to the back of the bus, squeezed in, three across.

It was just as Timothy and Jay had feared. Chloe took up as much of the seat as she could with her designer bag, constant squirming. Rummaging through it, finding Twinkies, money, lipstick, pictures of her baby, she showered unwanted attention onto her two captives.

Timothy exhausted from the long work hours, the night on the street, pretzeled his thin body somehow onto the seat pad. Before wedging his knapsack between the bathroom wall with its clanking door and his head, he pulled out his earphones, closed his eyes pretended to be comatose. In a way he was. The music engulfed his tired spirit, moved his soul to a calmer, quieter space.

God had only half answered Jay's prayer. Chloe sat between Timothy and Jay. Anguished, he prayed, "Fuck, fuck, fuck, mother of Christ, please let's get this ride over with quickly." Jay tried as he could, to not acknowledge Chloe. But passengers kept throwing him looks, as she re-played her electrocution. Jay finally took a cue from Timothy, pretending to fall asleep. Chloe continued with her antics, apparently not caring if her two seatmates participated in them or not.

After a while, Bus 164 arrived at its destination. No lip, no argument, no attitude from the bus driver. The three quietly gathered their items, were the last to walk down the aisle, this time they didn't land on a grey pebbly road in the middle of marshland, nowhere, off a highway.

Tim embraced Chloe and Jay, said goodbye, when they disembarked the 164. Each had another arduous commuter trek to hurdle. Travelling lightly, moving in and out of crowds easily, Tim made his way to the LIRR.

Finding a window seat on the commuter train, he put his small knap sack beside him. Wondering whether or not he'd still have a job, thinking that sometimes you have to sacrifice for your art. So maybe he'd lost his job. But here was a chance at the big time. Television, recording studio, producer, a real producer, a contract with a real salary at the end of it. Then puff, you're on your own to create your own music.

Idol-A-Try had given rise to a number of gifted musicians. Not all the finalists were gifted, but they individually found a niche in the ever surreal world called the entertainment business. And if you wanted to make it big, be-on-the-cover of every magazine, newspaper, internet operation, this was what could catapult you there, on the quick. No working lounge bars, hotels, cruise lines, noisy restaurants.

This could find you in front of an audience that wanted to hear you … your stuff, they'd listen, they'd murmur the words back to you. Cooing came to mind when he got the music right in his head. He'd heard a cooing. Something so pleasurable, so intense, so optically sensual, that it was like the quiet cooing of the two loves birds sitting in a nest near his bedroom window. Yes, cooing he thought. A room, or maybe an auditorium, full of people cooing.

It was soothing for him to think of it this way. The embrace he felt when he wrapped his tenor voice around the words. Classical was best for this, but then there are love songs of the do-wop era of the 50s, 60s. After an excursion away he'd come back to his first love. "Give me a Puccini opera," he thought. "How many ways to make love with your larynx?" Puccini thought of them all. "Embrace, embrace," Puccini said. Hug the notes emerging from the bottom of your diaphragm, call it up through your larynx, to the back of your tongue. Hold, curl, trill your note, let it loose and become that immortal sound called voice.

An excursion, *Idol-A-Try* was.

An expensive one for him at the moment. He knew it. His tall thin body, got thinner. His wardrobe, had to be mended, taken care of. All things he had taken from home, he took care of. This wasn't mom's or dad's identity, this was his own, and he wanted very badly to have it recognized. He wanted to succeed so he could calm their trepidation. But ultimately, he wanted to share his gift. The train rolled into the Long

Island City train station. Timothy gathered his things and caught a bus to his job.

His *suenos* would have to wait.

Dreamers.

Chapter 23

Gangplank, Asphalt, Oh My!

Realizing dreams … *realizando suenos,*

"Jesu Cristo!" Tanya exclaimed as the small banana boat vessel, *Platanos* passed the Statue of Liberty. *"Ni, el Capital,"* compared. If that wasn't enough, the majesty of New York's intricate shipping harbor and islands floated in cool dark green rippling waters. Tanya received '*La Senora marravillosa,*' arms wide open, knowing little of the Statue of Liberty immigrant promises and lore. Standing above board, along with other passengers, a quietness took hold as it passed.

The flag of *los Estados Unidos de America* flayed before them.

Humbled,
  hands raised to hearts.
Honoring,
  caps removed.
Eyes moistening.
Children stared,
  clasping hands,
  becoming quiet.

Si hay mas.

El Don had recounted travels through Mayan and Azteca ruins, but she understood them to be folkloric histories embellished by *mi querido papa*, for *Dona Dela*, *campesinos, peones,* and Tanya's *entretimiento* during evenings after a day's hard work on the *veranda*. Now she knew, *"Que si hay, estatuas"* and *"edificios que son la distancia de una isla,"* reaching, up to *el cielo*.

During weeks on the vessel, Tanya endured a sea sickness so profound few had the pleasure of her company, for days at a time. The voyage made her beg for land. Nor did the over bearing journeymen, heat, storms, windless days and sour tasteless food, help. She had finally arrived. Leaving everything familiar. Except for her original Spanish landed gentry *familia*, she was the first to cross along an *Americano* ocean in centuries. As the city skyline grew larger and piers approached, Tanya ran back to the cabin. The white lattice wooden door wasn't locked. Grabbing the rickety ivory door handle, pushing it open with a thrust of energy saved for athletics, she ran into the cabin room.

Gathering thoughts, Tanya searched through drawers for items to make herself presentable. Anticipating this day, every single day, over the course of her trip. Lifting clothing from a chair, pressed, starched the evening before, Tanya changed from everyday attire, dropping the slip to the floor. *El sueno de ella* was to please in the same manner she pleased *familia* during special events.

Stepping before the oval mirror, brushing softly curled hair, dexterous youthful finger tips rustled through a vanity drawer, for fine embellishments, one last voyager time. Finding, delicate filigree Honduran pure gold white shell barrettes *Dona Dela* designed, for this special occasion Tanya, remembered her brothers panning for gold nuggets on the Juticalpa riverbed.

Dona Dela saved the gold nuggets in a trunk storing family *reliquias*, portraits, *biblias* with birth, death and wedding dates. Loose opals, jade, cameos, emeralds saved in small bottles for later use. Yards of hand strung wedding pearls, highly polished pink coral pieces, thick gold and silver bracelets, earrings made of layers of delicately spun gold with hanging aquamarines.

Thick gold rings from marriages now laid to rest in the family crypt. Family documents leading back to the 1600s, land grant parchments with Spanish seals, political party testament to their founding days, ancestral baptismals, plates, trays, and cutlery pressed out of their silver for a table of fifty. A rich Honduran family's history filed under their high canopied matrimonial bed. *Moneda*, of gold and silver, *lempiras* stored in special trunks in the Capital bank of that era, carefully recorded and watched over by well paid guards.

Choosing a mother of pearl mirrored, silver powder case, knowing it had the lightest of powders, pressing fingers along cheek bones, stopping short of her hairline, thought better of adding the darker rose colored powder. Changing opinion, felt the other would be saved for late evening outings, and dinner parties. Satisfied with the effects, closed the ebony clasped, searched for a small hand crafted finally embossed leather cosmetic luggage case, placing the ivory and silver brush inside.

Checking her countenance one last time, adjusting three long strands of pearls, with matching tiered pearl earrings, finally adjusting the hemline of the finely hand embroidered cotton white dress with a red satin waist sash, then making sure the lightly starched crinoline slip didn't show, satisfied, twirling, looking about, one last time in the mirror she was set to go. Anxious spirits ran high.

Tanya sparkled. *La Matrona* would be happy to host such a fine example of a *Hondurena*, to be introduced to *la sociedad.*

Hurriedly, quietly, moving towards the door, grabbing the ivory handle, squeezing it in nimble fingers, turning it down to loosen the latch, opening then closing the door, she squeezed through the lower deck hall, briskly running past opened doors and stacked luggage. Remembering a childhood game; inhaling deeply, filling lungs to capacity, holding a breath, gained steam and ran up the long stairwell narrow wooden stairs, once standing on deck, exhaling, pausing, Tanya walked towards the gangplank. *Platanos* dwarfed by other ships slipped in.

Approaching the pier, shiphands, moved about shoring up its side, bumping slowly into the pier. Tanya watched crowds below as *Platanos* was tied and anchored. Buildings castle size, like pictures in history books of Europe, lined the harbor. Castles upon castles of brick buildings lined treeless streets. No green verdant *montanas*. Streets leveled, filled with people, cars, luggage, containers and push carts. An unharmonious noise rose from its streets. Where had the earth gone? Hoping to touch soil, feel it under foot, kiss it. *Mother Earth* was covered. Asphalt, hints of cobble stone, as far as the eye could see. Where was the iron rich black and red colored earth? Maybe *Americanos* had learned to do away with it. Would she miss *el lodo* too?

Tanya walked down, the gangplank to these United States of America. *Los Estados Unidos*. New York City. *La cuidad de Nueva York.* Landing at the pier, greeted by a man in his early twenty's dressed in uniform and cap. The dark black uniform, a curiosity. Drivers in *el Capital* wore ordinary clothing, and couldn't be distinguished in a crowd. Quietly laughing, thinking that maybe a uniform was a good idea. *Un chófer* wandered, and *desaparecio en la marqueta central.* A picture had been sent, ahead. *El chófer* stood in front of the large crowd waving a sign with her first and last name.

El chófer, approached, instructed, "*¡Quédate dónde estás y no te muevas*! Don't move! Stay here!" He found a porter to gather and pack the luggage into the car's trunk. Tanya, Rita's mother, was to be hosted by *sociedad* friends on the upper Riverside Drive. The woman, *la Matrona*, offered a welcome. With confidence *el Don, y Dona Dela*, sent their only daughter to *la Matrona's* twenty room Riverside Drive, Manhattan penthouse, unseen. Trusting in *la Matrona's* thin *sociedad* resume.

Tanya's ride from the pier frightened, so far away from beloved *familia*. This was all so different. There were no adobe pink or blue colored houses. No, French cake-like decorations surrounding windows. No roofs for as high as the eye could see. So foreign, she could not suppress excitement, overwhelming the Spanish speaking *chofer* with a relentless number of questions.

Wealth in the surrounding buildings became obvious. A fabled wealth *chistes*, rumors, spoke of, from travelled sophisticates, during *siesta café's* in interior exquisitely tiled patios, filled with trees, wing trimmed parrots, servants, silver tea sets, carefully coifed matrons, watching over gentile *joventud.* Chaperoned. In *el Capital.*

While *la familia* were of *una familia de sociedad,* they lived a simple life. The *hacienda rancho* and *el Capital* house were ample, but unimpressive. The compound in *la Mosquitia* even simpler, made more for rooming and feeding *peones* safely from temperamental rainforests. Theirs's was the way of old oligarch's, landed Spanish, English and German families. *Familia, religion y trabajar,* were their cultural values. Land, was king. And what was on that land, ruled. They were not an ostentatious people, these ranchers.

The ride wasn't long, but it was impressive. Following the Hudson River, on a road better than anything ever experienced, her senses overwhelmed. Wheels beneath, hummed, passing cityscape more impressive than anything imagined. Succumbing to insecurities, Tanya wanted to be comforted by *la Dona.* She wanted to see *las montanas,* rainforests and friends. She wanted to sit, and rest. Yearning for comfort, after such a long, difficult trip. Meeting her hosts was something dreamed about, but now apprehension, anxiousness emoted.

Finally, arriving, exiting the car, another suited man approached. Did everyone in this new country wear a suit? The doorman, with an unpronounceable name, introduced himself showing the way to something called an 'elevator.' Head, feet, feeling light, she leaned against the cold dark rich mahogany door.

"So this is where our *caoba* lands. *La madera nuestra.* Our wood." *El chofer* unlocked the penthouse door. Tanya was not greeted by *la familia*. No one from the family was home. Another uniformed young woman appeared. Politely touching her arm, the maid showed the way to a bed room, passing an opulent living and dining room.

Tanya not yet realizing that indeed she wasn't a guest, rejoiced at the expanse of the terrace, walked past the maid, French glass doors onto it, losing her breadth looking out at the bejeweled skyline that is New York City. The maid, cautiously pulled her into the living room, prompting Rita to hurry.

They reached a room down a long corridor, through, past the kitchen. Tanya's room. Small, with a single bed, whose bedding, too simple, signaled psychological alarm. Tanya's own bed, larger, covered in beautifully hand embroidered sheets, of birds, flowers, cherubs, trees, bordered with fine filigree lace. *Dona Dela* hired the town's best embroiderer to make pillow cases, bed sheets, coverlets, employing a lace maker in the nearby town to finish bed linens. On Tanya's rides through their *terreno*, Tanya collected fresh flowers, cutting, arranging, placing, them in each room. *Un abondancia de flores, de todo colores*. No welcoming *flores* here. The room was devoid of warmth, feminine touch, *un abrazo*. Tanya's bureau plain, a small lamp sitting atop a glass plate. A small square mirror rested near the door. The wall paper a greyish blue pebble, ordinary.

Quieted by the momentous realization of *su situacion*, sadness rose *del corazon*. Slowly eyes welled with tears, before she could hold back, they fell on the softly powdered, flushing hot cheeks. Hand raising to cheek, wiping tears away, the powder stained her white gloves. A caged bird in an ill-omened cage. She did not turn to face the maid. Quietly, *"Gracias, dejame aqui."* The maid understanding left. Tanya never turned, walking backwards, into the door. Quietly closing it, body falling against it, raising a hand to the latch, locked the door.

What was to follow so far away from beloved *familia, patria*? Wanting to run, panic entered *el corazon*. Frozen in the horror, movement became impossible, implausible. There was nowhere to go. Who would help? *Quien me ayudara?*

Late into the evening, *la Matrona*, arrived asking her maid to find Tanya. Tanya stayed in her small room, door locked for a week. Food pushed on a tray against the door. Tanya refused food, opening the door when no one was there, taking only tea, or milk. Thankfully the room had a connecting door to a bathroom, Tanya kept the doors locked.

After a week, key in hand, *la Matrona*, opened the door ordering Tanya to follow to the living room. Tanya followed, *la Matrona* remained, haughty, demanding, cold, businesslike. Snapping fingers, pointing to a penciled sheet of paper, *la Matrona* didn't share a seat, but ordered Tanya to stand, barking commands. Explaining needs, expectations, outlining chores, Tanya again realized why she had been brought over, at her parent's expense; it was to become *la Matrona's* personal servant.

The day for Tanya started at four am. *La Matrona*, demanded work 'round the clock.' Because of Tanya's white European looks and beauty, a jealous *Matronna*, made Tanya's world the smallest it had ever been. Prisoner, now. Freedom gone. Memories of horseback rides in rainforests, across rivers, would sustain. Remembering an unchaperoned life, freely wandering about *Tegoose*. Roaming, questioning everything. Searching through fields, sitting at rivers edge, in brush, looking out at *familias'* lands, every fiber, now longed for *el rancho* way of life.

La Matrona, a *café con leche meztijo*, remembered bitter cruelties of *La Ceiba, sociedad*, where color mattered. *La Matrona*, savvy and beautiful, kept company in *politico* and merchant mercantile parlors. Used by men, never to become a *senora de sociedad, la Matrona* was righting grievances.

Tanya's unsuspecting family became easy prey. Tanya's existence was to serve *la Matrona. La Matrona* punished Tanya for things wronged in a unforgiving past. Tanya, punished for inequities *la familia* had not executed, had to survive by her wits, hopes of exploring the world almost, now extinguished.

Mornings' *café y pan* was brought to *la Matrona's* bed, reading the Daily News, the Post, and the Tribune. Slowly learning to read and speak English. Night's while everyone slept, taking newspapers including *La Prensa* from the garbage Tanya quietly, poured over sullied pages. Life of all kinds popped out; city life, politics, stories of life left behind, life in sprawling New York City. Reading saved a fragile now damaged psyche, such was the level of cruelty.

Tanya spent nights anguished, crying into

pillows, putting towels at the door's base so comments wouldn't be made by passing servants *"Oye? Estas bien?"* Sitting, leaning against the door with cross and bible in hand, searching, through its pages asking *Jesu Cristo* for answers. None came. *"Dios mio adonde estas?"*

El mundo limited to the penthouse. After several months, servants created excuses, insisting they needed her help during street errands. Chaperoned, Tanya explored surrounding areas on these forays. Enduring jealousy, vengeance and beatings, watched by employees, paid to be vigil, there was no escaping.

A number of seasons passed. Arriving during summer, as trees changed from brilliant green, Tanya's eyes roved, with wonderment. Overnight one morning a patch work of orange, golden red, green and brown trees mystically appeared.

The slow morning sun, no longer provided warmth. One could now stare at its changing color, lighter yellows, bordering on white. Bright but not with its fiery golden aura, trees died in its coolness. Reflecting a heart pained with coolness by *soledad*. Yearning time and again for escape, but poorly clothed, no money, no connections, waiting was the answer. Waiting, with no hope. *Esperando a quien?* Waiting for who? Waiting for what? Days like her spirit, grew darker. Soulful spiritual warmth was escaping, in this new land. Tanya's heart was dying. *"Esto no es vida."* This is not life.

At the days end, putting her head on a pillow, finally giving way to exhaustion, Tanya remembered, one of those end of day quiet moments when *la familia* gathered on the large front *veranda*, after feeding field workers, *compesinos*, laundress', maids, cooks and putting the last *lena* embers of the *adobe fogon* out, quietly approaching *el Don*, who lumbered through a book. Tearfully recalling, pulling a chair towards him, sitting beside him. Hesitating. Eyes raised, for one last moment, towards an elegant, aging exhausted mother, rhythmically moving to and fro in *la hamaca*. *Mama's*, long thin exhausted body, resting. Tanya, now imprisoned, asked, "What have I done wrong? Why? *Dios mio, porque?"*

Letters, received, stolen and destroyed. Servants taking pity, checking mail, found and kept a letter, then another, then one more, carefully sneaking letters. In family letters they wondered why she hadn't written, "*No sabemos de ti. Porque no escribes*?" They questioned whether *la Matrona* was telling the truth and asked if she had run off with "*un amor de poca consequencia.* Did you run off with someone of little consequence?*" "Haci pasa en este paise, con joventud.* That's what happens with this youth in this country*" la Matrona* had written. Long days resumed.

"*Se me fue mi joventud.* I lost my childhood." Tanya would later share with Rita.

Chores started in the kitchen, which didn't have *lena,* at dawn, but were as much work, preparing meals, for scores of guests. Tanya after a time, didn't fight imprisonment, instead slowly earned confidences of fellow servants, finding ways to leave the apartment, although they couldn't themselves help an escape. Slowly, carefully given an opportunity to walk the family's three small dogs, Tanya discovered Central Park. Met other people in the park. Meeting dog people, who approached and shared dog stories. Slowly learning new words.

Spanish wasn't spoken in the Riverside *shtetl*. So she learned *Ladino* and *Yiddish*, first. English not needed. Chatting with other servants, washing, cleaning, ironing, preparing food, Tanya learned of factories, sweatshops, and jewelry shops in the Lower East side. There was hope. Freedom was a possibility. All it required was hard work, and hard work was all she knew. If that's all that was needed, Tanya would never fail in *these United States of America*.

Tanya wasn't unprepared, she sat with *la Dona* during merchant meetings, and *el Don*, plowing through accounting ledgers, noting money, mahogany, corn, sugar cane or land deals. Tanya helped *campesinos*, in tiny villages. Working side by side, *peones*, understanding physical labor.

Tanya wondered how *la Matrona* earned a penthouse lifestyle, knowing her *familia's* work ethic, she didn't see such a work ethic here.

La Matrona's familia wasn't of the oligarch families. In truth, there was less known of their business, and more assumed. Boasting about their cash crop, and political connections, Tanya realized she had landed in the lion's den. Starting small, in New Orleans, *la Matrona* found connections to illegal alcohol and prostitution syndicates. Becoming known to important illegal syndicates, *la Matrona* ran numbers, kept the cops at bay, proving trust worthy, was awarded with larger gambling spots to oversee.

After a number of years, *la Matrona*, moved

from New Orleans to New York, opening the penthouse; running numbers, marijuana, alcohol, gambling and prostitution. Needing more young women, *la Matrona* returned to *Honduras,* laundering money, exploiting unsuspecting immigrants looking for streets paved with *oro*. Tanya guarded her body *con mucho cuidado.*

Looking for opportunities, to escape, a door to open.

Tanya had dreams of escaping.

Suenos.

Chapter 24

Audition Night at Izod Center

So here they were, looking for opportunities, adventure, a door to open. Kat, Chloe, Jay, Timothy and Rita were thankful that first day, getting wristbands and tickets, by coming in early. Tonight, the dawn of the final most important day, seemed anti-climatic. Walking slowly on the asphalt street, getting bearings, they wondered where everyone had gone.

Kat receives a phone call. "Hello? Hey Jay. Over where?" "I'm waving," "Are you near the building stairs, ok, I'm looking." "I see you guys, I'm over here towards where all the cops and event crew are." "We'll come over there and join you. We just got here." "Yeah, saw you walking. But don't know if you can do that." "What do you mean?"

"Well we got here, I mean, I got here, there were a couple of people standing around trying to figure out where to sit and cops kept pushing us away. Finally, there were a bunch of people about seventy-five, the cops said we could stay, but they wouldn't let anyone in or out. They roped the area, so, now I can't leave, you can't come in here." "Ok, well, guess we'll have to deal with it."

"They don't want people here this early."

"That sucks, we're here, what are they gonna do with us?" "That's the big question, any how's, you can't sit here. Sorry, didn't know shit like that would happen. More shit served up, been that kinda Jersey day." "Ok, well we're sitting together inside, so we'll see you at the seats. Bye, Jay." "Talk to ya later. Bye!"

"Heard it. The conversation. Let's get closer anyway."

Even with the warning, they continued walking towards the abutting Izod Arena steps. Kat searching for space, "Let's walk over there. See if they'll let us up there." As Jay warned, they met harsh resistance from the *Idol-A-Try* staff. Approaching cell bearing police, speaking with superiors, receiving and executing orders to not let street campers settle, the police pushed back harshly, pointing them to an implausible high way road rendition.

A State Trooper, leers as they approach, "You're too early, you can't line up and," "I just spoke with a friend on my cell. They're near the area by the steps. You let them through. We just want to join them." Rita, Kat and Chloe, point to sitting contestants wannabees. An event person approaches, "No, you can't go over there." "Hey! Yew guys didn't put out notices! We wanna join that group." "Go over there, to the other side of the street. You're not supposed to be here this early."

Irritated, "I'm tired. We cudda slept in. This is *mishegas*. If they're gonna be this toxic, it wud of been better tew stay in bed, cudda slept more." Inner turmoil starts to surface. Annoyance Rita feels towards State Troopers and event people gets redirected. A small argument erupts between mother and daughter. Kat directs Rita, "Ask that guy over there, that event person" pointing, standing next to a barricade across the street in the parking lot. "If, we can stand there."

Testily, frustrated, "Yew do, it, yew aesk. It's something yew wannna kno', yew, go ... aesk."

"Why are you angry? You're standing closer to him. What's the problem?"

Bothered, "Well yew, go over tew that attractive, young staffer an' aesk 'im."

"Mom! Just find out if we can stand there. They're telling us to go away. We can't go back to the hotel, there's no way of getting back there. He might think you're an authority figure ... I don't know, just try!" "No, sorry, won't work, yew go ova tew that guy and aesk 'im. Yew!! Aesk him, if we can stand there."

Chloe concerned, "Why are you getting so angry, why are you so upset?" "Kat always aesks me ta dew somethin'. And I always deliver, but damn she cud do this herself! He'd like tew smile on 'er circumstance," "I don't understand your anger, Miss Rita, I mean it's no big deal to ask that guy." "Then dew it! Jist dew it! Yew gals are pretty. He'll like tawking ta yew. I got tew many tear drops on my crows,"

"What? What the hell does that mean? Mom?"

"It means, yew go ovea there an' *schmooze* with that young guy. Yew dew it. He's not gonna give me tha same answer he gives yew. I've got experience being a middle aged woman" "Oh, come on, Miss Rita. I don't like the meanness." Angrily, "Yeah, please, please go away." Walking away in the opposite direction, "Aesk him. Tawk ta him, yew do it." Adamantly, "Jist dew it."

Although the discussion seemed to have no grounds of rational thought, Rita walks off leaving the girls alone. For the first time in three days, Rita and Kat separate. It could have been fatigue, or disappointment, the rejection, it was anything, and nothing. She couldn't explain it to herself. Sullenness, irritability, stupidly arguing, knowing it wasn't based on anything of substance, irked even more. Pride on being rational, able to think on her feet. But the harsh taciturn vagueness, nothingness of the qualm, here, with which they were greeted by event *Idol-A-Try* staff, the trooper, other event people, made this journey a great deal harder, longer than patience could withstand.

Frustrations ruled, troubled, disharmonious thoughts began bubbling, surfacing, realizing this, she felt the need for privacy. Questioning her state of affairs, she remembered their love, abiding respect, mutual affection of one another, had recently become breached, but there was always an inner unspoken need to remain, even during the most arduous arguments, a hair's breadth of delicate longing to always, always stay the course.

Rita, the adult with wisdom, experience Kat lacked, worked arduously to repair terse times, remembering her mother's words, "Sometimes you have to dance left, even as you know right is best." Rita danced as best she could. Solemnly, walking away.

Walking along with Kat towards the event staffer, Chloe shrugs shoulders, "I don't get that. I don't like meanness. Well let's follow up, and talk to the guy. She wants to be alone."

Un-tranquil, engulfing memories, surfacing insecurities, thinking of the last three days made questions of all of it; her life, Kat's life. Having worked so hard at everything, never doubting Kat's talent, wondering, why were they here, in the middle of the night, the middle of nowhere, with complete strangers, striving for an implausible coveted top dog commercial pop music prize? Could Kat become the winner of *Idol-A-Try*? Could she land in the coveted ten finalist spots, Rita hoped for?

Prickly personnel, made the simple act of sitting, or just standing, in the dark, hard, unaccommodating concrete street, … impossible, and left her vexed. Shrugging shoulders, stopping a distance away from the girls, bearing down on a johnny horse more turmoil surfaced. Anchoring thoughts physically on unsteady wood, joining a group of Black girls applying make-up, dressed in elegant sequined mini dresses.

"Might, be a little tew early tew dew that. We've still got all night out on tha street." "It's for the camera, you never know." One of the girls' adjusts the mirrored compact, while standing under a street lamp, leaning against the johnny horse. "Filming goes on all night." "Oh, yu're right. Forgot. Dey film. What don't dey film?"

Looking around, shouting, "Going tew tha John, I'll be back." Walking away, alone, she recalls Kat's classical resume; years in the opera chorus, a child treated like an adult, the grueling hours, the exacted professional fortitude, two am drives from the Opera House in blizzards, after the last sung note. No big payout there.

She'd hope tireless efforts for the Hispanic community would open doors, push buttons, whisper Kat's name to successful artists. But they did nothing. What's the joke about Latino crabs in a pot? She couldn't remember the joke, but she remembered the punch line, the one about how they all pull one another down. "Lawd, what are we doin' here?" Walking towards bathroom stalls Rita hoped to regain a sense of calm. Negotiating a song, near the Johns stood two tall thin Black women, vocalizing.

"Hi, yew girls gonna use tha John?" "Oh, we'll go in one stall together." "Using this side?" "We're gonna use tha stall on this side," "Is tha other side available?" "Go ahed, nobody's using it. We'll go in on this side. We're gonna practice in 'ere." "Hey, okay, t'anks."

Entering, accommodating her body, overhearing both girls entering the stall. With palms pressed hard against the toilet rim, so her bottom uncomfortably hovers, not touching, Rita, listens amusedly to their coke induced conversation and rungs.

"Cum on. Squeeze past. Gurl, yur bags' too big! Git yur damn booty past me an' ova to tha side." "Yew got it? Dang, this is a small space. And, oh Lord ... can barely see." "Yeah, I got tha stuff. Where's yur mirror? Yew need a steady hand. Hey don't sit down, tha seat's disgusting. Yew don't know who's been in 'ere."

"It's tight in 'ere, and its foul, yew hold it. Don't let tha paper slip outta yur hand." "Don't drop, shit man, be careful, yew go first. Let's do some rungs." Teasing her throat with a few notes. "Hey, watch yur dress, don't lean on that. Don't put your bag down. Who knows what's on tha floor. From tha smell in 'ere I cud only imagine. My shoes are stickin' to tha floor." "Yeah, mine too. Ok, let's practice." Adds her sound, "This ain't tha Apollo, but tha acoustics are gud." "Check it out. Woooo hoooo! We're it! Idol-A-Try! We're it! Hey, be careful." "Yeah, I'll take another hit. Leave some for later, we've got all night. Save some of it for later."

Thoughts crystallized in the small, odiferous, skanky dark space for Rita. Negative images of the pop do-anything to make it-wannabe diva world came through loud and clear from the next stall. Their raunchy sexually explicit songs and drugs made Rita re-examine this vinyl Mecca jaunt. Kat wanted to be a lady, but the pop world wanted a hoe.

Suddenly, feeling that being there might be wrong after all, Rita wondered, "Whose dream was this?"

Leaving the stall, walking past Johns, steady, strong vibrato notes escape the tin pan alley enclosures making way into the night air. "Pretty good." Rejoining the make-up girls, Rita leans hard against the johnny horse.

Subconsciously, now resenting those who escorted Kat at events she produced. The men did so, just to massage their egos. At twelve, sixteen or twenty Kat turned heads. Kat was accustomed to the fine accoutrements that high powered national events provided; hotel suites, limousines, opera houses, concert halls. This young beauty with a lyrical soprano voice was perhaps at the wrong Mecca.

"Are we paying homage by this trek to the wrong vinyl god?" Rita asked herself.

Minutes pass, eyes roving into the parking lot, where 'her girls' were last seen. Comfort finally embraces, finding their silhouettes in the distance. Smiling, pointing towards the base of the steps leading to the Izod Center entrance.

Kat shouting, "The event person said, they'll let us line up over there. He asked his supervisor. We asked him to look into it." "Hmm, wonder if he'd done me that fava. Don't think sew." Speaking to the make-up girls, "Hey, gurls they're gonna let people start linin' up ova dere."

Shouting directions from the other side of the street, an *Idol-A-Try* staffer, catches their attention. Crossing hurriedly, following his lead, walking one block away from the front stairs leading to the entrance, entering a guarded opening, doubling back through the labyrinth of yellow and black tape to the head of the area at the buttressing steps, reaching the front, once again, bags are rested.

Rita silently hands Kat the corner of the faded, thin blue blanket, it's placed on the hard concrete floor. The area starts to fill quickly. Jay's group which had been separated is escorted to the head of the line. Shouting into a megaphone an *Idol-A-Try* crew, "Everyone, move a little further back. Gotta make room for this group. They were here first."

Unsurprisingly, this particular order met resistance, grunting, groans, grumbling. After all, these contestants had complied with every flagrant, exhausting request and requirement. Hesitantly, lifting marker possessions everyone is forced to move fifty feet back. But, once settled, the mood regains its upbeat composure, as the area becomes filled with hundreds of wrist-band proven *Idol-A-Try* wannabe's.

Checking the time, Kat, punches in the telephone number of Amalfi's pizza. "Yeah, want one large pizza, pepperoni, onions, ground beef, pineapple, all double cheese, ham, sausage, black olives, bacon, green peppers, thin crusted. And sodas, yeah, Sunkist, Coke, iced tea. Coke, six ounces, yeah, all of them. Yeah, ok, we're at the Izod Center. The Meadowlands. The guy said you would deliver. You sure we can still put the order in? Uhhh, ok, hold on. Chloe, go check to see what the street name is."

Chloe runs across the street to see if there's a sign, shouting, "No street name. But we can wait for him in front of this area. Over, here at the entrance to the parking garage. We'll wait for him where the ramp is to get onto to it. Tell him to come down the main street. I don't see a street name, though."

Kat continues with the order, "Ok, in front of the sign, at the entrance to the parking garage. Over by where the DJ and food tent is. When, you first drive down the entrance to the Izod Center, the main road, we'll be in the street waiting for you. Call when you start driving down the main road. Yep, ok, we'll get out there and wave you down. CALL Us, on this number. Great! Thirty minutes, (closes the cell phone) OK, food's on its way! Finally, real food and lots of it."

Feeling relief that their hunger pangs are going to quiet, all three offer up, high-fives. "Oh my God ... PIZZAAAA, I wasn't sure they would take my order. But we're getting pizza, yes, yes, yes, we ordered Pizzzzzzza. We did it. We're getting it delivered here! Woooo .... hoooooooo."

Hands in the air, above her shoulders, Chloe can't contain herself, "WOOOO, HHHHHOOOO. OH MY GOD." Hips jigging, swaying, "WE got PIZZA!" Shouting, dancing. "Pizzzzzaaa, and We're not sharin' with ya all!" Pointing to no one in particular. "We got pizza! You all! WE Got Pizza! Pizza! Honey, Yes!!! That's right." Wriggling. "Pizza delivered right here!!! YOU." Pointing and looking around. With arms raised over her head at no one in particular Chloe shouts, ever so loudly, "You, hear me! I AM hungry. We're not sharing!"

Applauding, laughter ensues. Visions of one large hot double cheese, pepperoni, pineapple, ground beef, sausage, black olives, ham, green peppers, bacon, thin crusted pizza comforted their tired famished bodies.

Images of a pizza cab driving down towards the elusive night emptiness of the Izod Center, Meadowlands, in the middle of electrified marshland, electrified asphalt, electrified toll gates, electrified bridges, electrified bulwarks, and electrifried twelve foot high chained linked fences, in nowhere electri-fried, New Jersey felt surreal.

Feeling diva-like, powerful, chattering and laughing, suspended perceptions. Suddenly without noticing, the area had gotten crowded. Happily, casually, familiar faces start to pop up. The ambiance becomes, warm, boisterous, joyful, friendly and spontaneous. Makings of an all night fabulous musical, tailgate parking lot party takes hold.

Noticing an old friend, Chloe waves, "Hey Spicy, over here! Yea! Over, here! Come on over here!" Spicy starts towards Chloe. "How you doing? Spicy!" Rita looks up, "Hey! Hey!" Spicy hugs Chloe, "How you guys doing? Hanging in there? Sexy lady, how ya doing?" "Good, babe, we're doing great. Hey Spicy, what's that on your shirt?"

"Producers gave me a tag. I'm in." A red rectangular sticky badge rests on his shirt. "Made it through the first round."

"Whadda ya mean you're in? Spicy? Yew got auditioned already?" "No, but that piece I put together, you know when I performed the other night for the camera, well its making the cut on the show." Kat standing to take a closer look, "Hey that's cool." "I made it past this round to the next." "Really Spicy, what happened after I saw my sexy man?" "They interviewed me, after we picked up the wristbands." "Boy you sure got your game going on." "That's why I stood out on the street, I separated myself from the crowd."

Leaning in, Chloe nods approvingly, "Spicy, I need some of that."

"Hey, I told you, sexy lady, you gotta do something which makes them notice." Flirting, "Do you think you could give me some of that? Really!

Whatever it is?" "You can't just sing, hell they've got thousands of singers. You gotta perform, something different. Bring your game." Chloe raises her arms, grabs hold of Spicy "Can I rub up against you, I need it."

"Make them remember, you, sexy lady. That's what I planned, to be out there in front way early. That's what you gotta do! Baby gurl."

"Hey, they're calling you over there, they're singing." Spicy looks towards another familiar face, "Remember, do something different. Something that gets you noticed. That's what'll get you on. Go for it sexy lady!" Spicy, stokes baby gurl, starts singing, walks towards the front of the line.

As Spicy walks, tightly nestled contestants crouched on knapsacks turn their chins upward, taking note. News of his fame spreads like wild fire. Spicy walks proudly over squatting wannabees, nodding to his 'wannabee' red medal of 'oh you made it' sticker acknowledgement. Spicy in more ways than one, reached his destination. Harmonizing, Spicy holds court with his guitar. Enjoying the moment, singing, strutting, leading the song, or being led by air spun vibes.

Congratulatory ooo's are heard as the producer's red sticker is noticed. Fingers point, questions asked, answered, fist bumps, high-fives, hugs. Man chest bumps, cell phone camera's click, click, click. Mock interviews go on, as these momentary brushes with fame are noted with 140 characters or less on Twitter. Spicy, Instagram, Facebooked, YOUTUBE'd on and on, has become a viral wannabe vinyl celebrity.

Celebrating the plausibility of fame comes to this corner of the neon wannabee castle, everyone basks in its kinetic energy. This amicably rotund small town Twenty-something talent from suburban northern Virginia has succeeded to penetrate the vast empire that is, *Idol-A-Try*. As in all auditions, there is camaraderie, friendly competition, but eventually these contestants step up to the plate alone at the end of four days.

Spicy made it through on smarts and merits, earlier than most. Thru practiced exposure, to reality show TV land, he learned the nuances of the game, one audition at a time, and now cut to the head of the line. His turn was coming. Mega fame, or mega blitz into the pantheons of *Idol-A-Try*, re-run clips. Whatever! He was basking and proud.

Nearby, voices could be heard, pitchy, or in tune. Good voices, some not. But that was the fun. Everybody there believed they had 'it,' whatever *Idol-A-Try* 'it' was. On a national television program such as *Idol-A-Try*, produced not only for talent, but for entertainment, their own personal 'it' might be their voice, their look, their ego. Spicy practiced what he preached, it was as he'd said to Chloe, 'You gotta do something different, you gotta stand out."

Chloe asks, "Is it me, or does everybody seem more awake tonight? There's more singing and dancing tonight. But they don't care about the dancing so much. I remember when they changed the format on *Idol-A-Try*." "Last season there wuz this amazing singer, dancer. Had a great *shtick,* shudda gone all the way but tha judges, shot 'im down early on. Shudda been headlinin' on Broadway. Loved his voice."

One of the many questions invading a wannabee's mental space was whether or not one had to be, 'a triple threat.' How would you know if you were wasting the producers and A-list judges air time? But in truth, at this stage of the game, it didn't matter, the hours spent on line, on the street, were part of the show, so nobody lost. They'd become cast fodder whose shouts, taunts might land on the cutting room floor, or might not. Video producers, throughout the night recorded tens of thousands free, and free roaming cast. The Meadowlands became an open air music festival being readied for prime time television. Everyone was willingly suckered in.

"It don't matter none tonight. Everybody's just jived up. You could hear it all around us. Look, look over there."

Turning the heat up a notch in the triple threat department, a small group of Black males pulsates upwards from the concrete sidewalk and uncomfortable knap-sack pillows. Hands clapping, head bobbing lips singing, "uh, uh, uh," full bodied pelvis thrusts, feet, hips, fluid agile legs, they lead the crowd through a synchronistic rendition of Beyoncé's, 'Single Lady.'

Wild applauding nods approval. Like the harmonic do-wops of another generation, continuing effortlessly, their physical musicality, body movement's wraps, engages, hugs, those watching, a communal hyper dance fervor spreads. Finished the crowd applauds.

A few feet away a lithe, angular, Asian dressed

in a short pleated skirt, catholic school girl drab sweater with black fish net tights, pump ankle boots, shortly cropped straight bangs, painted red, pink, yellow and purple strands. Moving into a small pocket of space, launches into a crump.

Initially, greeted with sneers, and snickers, steadfastly confident, she continues. A row of young Blacks not feeling the moment, make a statement by turning away. A microcosm of America plays out. Black vs. Asian, suburban vs. city, gangsta vs. crump, folk vs. rock, crooners vs. hard ass rap, played out throughout the night. This wannabee ghetto Asian girl took the grueling concrete sidewalk stage and owned it.

Her movements proved to be sharp, hard, spot on. Much to the cynical young Black male observers' eyes and surprise, the Asian eases through the edgy movements with practiced precision. Enthusiastically, she's joined by two white boys. Erotic tricky bumps, pumps, erotic grinds climax. Her small platform for dance turns out to be none too small. Boisterous, hysterical applauding, breaks loose. Joyously, joining in are the Blacks who sneered, as are entranced white boys, and finally everyone, together is finding their groove in the hot nasal beats of her voice and physicality. A call comes thru to Kat.

Kat's cell rings, "Hello? Oh, sure, yeah we see you. We're not that far. Ok, I understand they won't let you all the way through. We'll be right there. Pizzzzza! Pizza!" Chloe jumps up, "Pizza, I'll get it. I see him. Tell him it's a pretty Black girl that's gonna get the pizza." Steps carefully through the crowd, "Tell him I have long hair, I'll be there in thirty seconds flat. Tell'em I'm waving to him."

On the phone with the pizza man, "Yeah, stay there. A pretty Black girl, her name is Chloe, she's going towards the van now. Yeah, yeah, that's her. Ok. She's got the money. She just has to get there. Yeah, ok, great, I can't wait. Thank you, thank you so much for coming out here. I really hope you got a lot of business tonight! Bye!"

Looking towards Chloe, who is dodging street traffic. "Real food, thank God. Let's eat, I'm ready! Let's make room. We got a large? Right?" Chloe returns, "Ok, here it is! Wait, I'm not putting it down yet. HEY, hey everybody, everybody listen up, I ... I got PIZZAAAA. You hear, hey you, listen up. Yeah I'm talking to you. Look, I got PIZZAAA!"

Chloe, dances with the pizza raised over her head. "Pizzzaaa, you all understand." Sways her hips sexually, twirling back and forth, dancing in one spot on top of the blue blanket. Moving the pizza close to her breast, "Hmmm and I'm gonna make love to this pizzzaaaa, not any of you fellers." Moving her hips erotically, "but I'm making love to my pizzzzaaaa!" Continues to sway her hips back and forth with the pizza over her head, then down back and forth by her pelvis.

Continues, "Making love, here, to this PIZZZAAAA! And fuck, I'm not sharing! Thank you! Thank you, you all can stand by and just watch now!" Chloe's pizza dance goes on for three or more minutes, enjoying the attention. Riveted by the sexually charged dance, everyone's eyes are transfixed. Laughter, applause erupts from every corner. Chloe, finally puts the pizza down.

Kat and Rita, watching, laughing hysterically wait their turn to engulf the pizza. Hungrily opening the box, slices are split, eating begins. Its fifteen minutes after 3 am. The pizza man kept his promise. He delivered. Engorged their attention turned to a handsome young man walking through the crowd.

"Hey, hav yew noticed that really gud lookin' guy?" "Miss Rita, you're too funny, you're checking out the bods?" "Mom! You're staring too hard, he's coming over." "He's been lukin' ova this way. I jist noticed, that's all." Climbing over bags, blankets, he makes a bee line for them. Suddenly, he's standing over them. Looking at Rita, "Hey, I'm Cliff, I was wondering if my mother could join you." Looking back past herself, "Yeah, sure."

"Mom, come on over here." Cliff motions to his mother to move. Thankfully there was a small space. The mom a fiftyish woman, crawls carefully, pulling her blanket over beside them. "Finally an adult I can speak to here." Openly laughing, "Hi, I'm Rita." "Joan, hi, nice to meet you. Cliffs walking around. He likes talking to people. I've been left to sit alone. And, you are?" "Chloe." "Kat." "Kat, my daughter and Chloe is now a family. It's been a long three days. Been together for all three in one way or 'nother, if not physically, cell-phonically!"

Laughing, "We met one another at tha bus 164 from the New Yawk City Port Authority, an' now we're tied at tha hip."

"Cliff and I drove in from Rochester. We crashed at the hotel after the seven hour drive. I've got

237

frequent flyer miles, so we went wherever that was accepted. This could get expensive if you're from out of town." "It's costing us. I'm not workin' right now. Thought this wuz worth a try. Came in from DC, three days ago, without a reservation. But Kat was able to find a room tha night we slept out 'ere."

The tall, broad, muscular twenty year old Cliff, with Ricky Martin good looks is on his way to a drama school in New York City, Joan mentions. Rita wished him luck. They talked about their desire to see their children succeed and laughed at the *Idol-A-Try* journey, but both took it seriously.

"Well this is a long shot. We don't know anyone who has won, I mean made it past this audition. Do you?"

No one had any real exposure to someone who had won, so they talked about song choices and what their kids had already accomplished. Talking easily, as experienced older women could, time passed more easily. Each felt this to be a journey of plausibility's, possibilities. "Cliff has a beautiful voice. I know everyone has boasted. He needs to have someone like David Foster hear him. My Cliff is as good as Groban."

Rita nodded, approvingly, not knowing what Cliff sounded like. But sure, why not, she understood where Joan was coming from. "He's modeling now. I'm really proud of him." "He's gorgeous," Rita concurs. "I can see why he wud. He shuld be successful in tha City."

"He's going to drama school in October. The

school's right behind Lincoln Center. The location is amazing. I think he'll do great." "Musical theater?" "Yeah, but that's not what he really wants. He wants a recording artist deal. Cliff's done some of Foster's songs on video. Hey Cliff, over here." "Wow, I love Groban, really, wit' his luks, he shud dew really well in musical theater."

"Well, he's determined. Cliff, let her listen to you on your Ipod." Cliff walks over, finds a song. Kat, listens in first. "Oh, mom, listen to this, his voice is amazing." Kat listens with her classically trained ear. "You don't warble like Groban does your voice is purer." Handing the Ipod to Rita, "You should record." "Oh wow! Yur right. He's incredible! He shud ged in. He shud make it."

"Let me listen," handing it to Chloe. "Wow!!! And honey you got it going on too!" "I'm here to get a recording contract. I can sing anything. Did *Idol-A-Try* two years ago. This is my second try, my voice has matured. Didn't really know back then that I wanted a recording contract, I do now." "Hey, can yew sing somethin', anything. It wud be great tew hear yew live." "Sure." When he sings, area quiets, everyone listens. Smiling, feeling the moment, Cliff stops, there's resounding applause. "Better than Groban!" reassures Kat.

"Thanks! Look, over there. I think they've got a TV crew. Come on." Noticing news vans lined up, Cliff walked away to a gathering group pressed into the yellow and black tape. Almost on cue, the crowd became quiet as reporters paced through their scripts. Large flood lights bathed the entire area. "Come on Kat, let's get over there. Hurry!" Kat, and Chloe rushed away and squeezed through the crowd to the front of the line joining Cliff. Kat stood protectively behind Chloe and Cliff.

An attractive news reporter from a local station walks towards Cliff. Tall, slender, double-D, dressed in a short skirt, bare legs and high heels, motions towards contestants, standing behind the yellow tape. Counting down, walking a little closer to the crowd, facing the camera she speaks.

"We're here, reporting from the Meadowlands, *where Idol-A-Try* hopefuls are lining up this season. Thousands register, then, take a spot in line. Many waiting for hours." Pushing, shoving the crowd screams. "Why?" Walking closer to the crowd she asks Cliff, shoving the mike into his face, up against well shaped lips. "Why? ARE you here?"

"I'm here because I want this more than anything in my entire life. I've been up here for more than eighty hours. This is my third season, my third season trying out. I'm the next *Idol-A-Try!*"

The buxom reporter moves mike away, "There's plenty of anticipation to see if they're the next winner. This is Mox News channel, from the Meadowlands."

Wrapping the story, the camera pans the screaming crowd. Moving above their heads, hands wave furiously. Lights are turned off, the crews collect wires, flood lights, and finally quietness surfaces. Cliff rushes over to his mother and hugs her. Kat and Chloe aren't too far behind. An explosion of singing erupts behind Kat and Rita's blanket. A group of ten or twelve, who had been playing cards start singing songs from the 80's. Cliff walks over joining in.

"I don't think Spicy should be singing any longer, his voice is getting hoarse." "Oh sexy man has it in the bag, he's not worried, Kat." "Yeah, but the others should be. They're not gonna have a voice in the morning. You can't sing all night in the open cold air expecting to sound good." Speaking to Cliff's mother, suggesting, "Maybe Cliff should take a break." "He's like you, he's got training, so he knows when to quit."

Throughout the night Cliff nervously walks from singing group to singing group. Some he listens in, others he sings a few stanzas. Repeatedly questioning, assessing the competition, nervously walking back to his mother, crouching, whispering. Everyone everywhere is pitching in with their own rendition of a 70's, or an 80's song. A song here, a festive beat there.

Clapping, singing, laughing, the festivities continue through the night. Flashes of talent take their turn. Finally, towards 5 am, it's quiet, most everyone is slumbering, if not lying down, resting.

Chapter 25

Shtetl, which kind?

Tanya mirrored the inhabitants of the late 1920s, 30s, upper Riverside Drive *shtetl*. No square peg in round hole. After enclosed apartment living, alabaster creamy *color de leche* skin re-emerged. Dark amber eyes, red highlights, gentle fine wavy hair, fitting squarely with a superficial quixotic, ideal of their very own. No one was suspect. Tanya learned her looks helped, in this world where people looked eternally pallid, "*No cojen sol. Se parecen enfermo, y las mujeres no comen aqui.*" she wrote *mama, papa y tias* in imaginery letters.

> Visually cohesive.
> *En punto.*
> Superficially.
> *Como siempre.*
> In these United States of America.
> *America-na.*
> Immigrant.
> *Judeos.*
> American.
> *Ladinos.*
> Riverside Drive.
> *Shtetl.*

And where ever it was, neighbors hailed from, there were worldly cruelties. Cruelties, by whole tribes, to the likes of which Tanya had known nothing. *Mother Nature,* en *la Mosquitia* wasn't as evil. One had to be *humano* to be so cruel.

Pogroms.
Destruction.
Starvation.
Demigods.
Wars.

They didn't suspect *third worldliness*, 'til uttering a consonant. Little by little she learned their languages. Speaking, thoughtfully, obligingly, slowly, deliberately. English not needed here, in this predominantly German Jewish *shtetl*. English came third to her, after *Ladino* and *Yiddish*.

Walls.
Boundaries.

Her world, wasn't outside, it was cloistered by walls. Brick, thick, tall, papered, plastered wainscoted walls. Interiors, vast apartment buildings, covering whole blocks. *Bubbe's y senoras' de edad*, took notice in elevators, laundry-rooms, basements, hallways and corner shops. *Ladino* came easiest. *Ancianos*, Sephardic *Judeos* warmed first. Tanya became a maid whose *delicades, cultura, inteligencia* came through. So while adult children were away, seeking a subterfuge from loneliness, *las viejitas* sought her, sending lovely handwritten invitations, asking for her company. Knocking on *la Matrona's* door, *la Matrona* not wanting to raise eyebrows of illicit enterprises occurring in secret walled rooms, said nothing of the invitations, pretending not to notice, allowing the neighborly visits to *ancianas*.

Las viejitas, knew there were profound sad stirrings of things knowingly buried, in those amber colored eyes. Tanya wanted to speak of humiliation at the hands of *la Matrona*. But the humiliation proved to be too great. Understanding her position, worried she might over step, and land on a park bench in Central Park before she was prepared to leave, Tanya stilled words.

Accepting these tea visits, she gave up trying to find a way out of indentured servitude. Perhaps her problems weren't so bad, after listening to their stories of loss. On a superficial level, they connected. "Ah, yes," she thought, "damaged. Injured. *Lloro con lagrimas, los cuentos de ellos son tan duros.*"

Tanya's vulnerabilities were carefully wrapped away beneath layers of sublime psyche curative gauze. Coming to these United States of America, "*Un innocente. No sabiendo de la vida.*" Individually, every emotional physical wound formed a scab, in her soul. Tanya's heart developed a protective wall. Hiding, the harm.

Las viejitas understood, suffering, guilt, pain, sorrow of their own. Coming to this land for refuge. Finding it. Tanya was a recent open wound looking soulfully for bandages and refuge. Tanya, left safety and found cruelty, '*un crueldad no sostenible.*'

Cruelties.
Bingo.

Early 20th century Tanya wounds ushered in a greater resolve to survive.

Survival.
Endurance.
Escape.

Caged bird wanting
   to fly.
Dreaming of freedom.

These trespassing ephemeral afternoons, were
reminiscent of *el Don's parlas*. Different stories, yes.
To *entender y apprender* listening to *anciana's* more
carefully than *Papa* would be schooling. Absorbing
words. Hearing differences between *Ladino* and
Espanol caused pleading nightly grievances voiced to
Jesu Cristo.

Haunting was her
   beloved *Espano*l.
Not wanting to lose it.
Because of its absence,
   her mind cried
Espanol.
Voices spoke
   in the middle of the night
her
   parents,
   brothers.
   Kindred people.
Speaking *Espanol*.
She cried.
Sobbing, a*donde estas*.
Familia.
No te conocere,
   hamas.
Distancia.
Mi,
   fogon apagado?
Por favor Dios, deja
   me, mi Espanol.

After a time, it didn't matter where she was from. Immigrants, all. These *shtetl* buildings full of people from somewhere else. Not speaking English, but German, Yiddish, Ladino. All learning the subtle inner woven threads of these *United States of America* on a small island called Manhattan. Over time, Tanya mastered various languages.

Yes, *si, ja, si, yo.*
No, *nein, no, neyn.*
Please, *per favore, bitte, por favor, zayt azoy gut.*
Thank you, *grazie, danke, gracias, A dank.*
Thank you very much, *molte grazie, vielen dank, muchas gracias, A dank.*
Please, *Prego! Bitte, por favor, zayt azoy gut.*
Excuse me, *mi scusi, entschuldigung! Perdoname, zayt zhe moykhl!*

Time passed. Navigating the dark world of illicit alcohol, marijuana, gambling, numbers rackets, and *senoritas* for hire, Tanya, learned it best to hide in simple maids' clothing, and remain in dark corners of the penthouse during business hours. Enclosed in her small, plain room when not needed. Not wanting to encourage the wrath of *la Matrona*, whose jealous diatribe scorched earth, Tanya fearfully stayed in the background.

The penthouse was opened as a speakeasy Tuesday through Sunday. Private rooms, for special paying customers. No time for *Dios* in these corners. But as human nature would have it, Tanya was talking less to *Jesu Cristo* these days, no longer looking to visiting his house on Sunday, or for that matter, any other day. Then, one late evening, after *la Matrona* pleasantly marijuana high and drunk, bid a last farewell to guests, forgetting other business duties of the night, weaving down the hallway to a bedroom, rustled to bed earlier than usual.

Waiting for a signal from head staff to start the cleanup, Tanya stood against the hallway wall. Orders passed down to each staff member after *la Matrona* slipped unconsciously under covers allowed Tanya to prepare cleaning tools in the kitchen. It had been a long day for Tanya, but better than most, *la Matrona* was sweetly high.

Tanya waited, gathered everything walking onto the expansive balcony. The Hudson River view, stars above always took her breadth away. The galaxy above stretched out to Honduras. The Manhattan blue aurora shared expanses, reaching beloved *Mosquitia.* Sure of this, Tanya was always content to be outside, after closing hours. Short lived as they were, these hours on the *veranda* offered up *Mother Earth.* Alone, Tanya engaged *Mother Earth* in conversation. Speaking to old friends, sure, anguished soulful whispers would be carried back by southern winds, carrying a wounded heart, soul to *la Mosquitia,* looking for healing. It made sense her words engage *Mother Earth* where they originally conversed. Hadn't she always spoken to *Mother Earth*? Wasn't it always in *la Mosquitia* where there was a space the daily noises of humanity didn't interfere. Wasn't *la Mosquitia, Mother Earth,* central? Her Cathedral? Hadn't *Mother Earth,* always answered back questioning doubts. Making Tanya more curious. Making her less restive?

Now on this man made cathedral of heights, Tanya hoped her words to *Mother Earth,* would be carried over Manhattan skyscraper caverns, past *la Senora Maravillosa*, to the open ocean, over small sea faring vessels like *Platanos*, past waves touching hot sands, warmly covering mango colored children, reaching out and up *las montanas*, to puff dragon clouds, passing *la familias' rancho*, past *cerritos*, to the majestic, secretive ocelot king of *la Mosquitia* who reigned over night. *El ocelote rey* would recognize her voice, hearing cries, carried by sonorous winds. *El viento* would send a message to parrots, parakeets flying overhead. Their chattering reaching, down below to river banks she sat beside, dipping her naked body into its warm undulating river, waist high, reaching below to fish she never caught, but watched as time, light, breezes passed.

Watching, harming nothing.

Tanya was sure there was more than one language for inhabitants of *Mother Earth*. Sure, her soulful lament would reach above, remembering her voice, sending out a prayer to the universe, hearing her pleas for freedom. Tanya in Manhattan darkness, was sure her prayers would be heard and answered. When? Well she also knew the Universe had its own schedule, she would have to wait.

Tanya was at wits end, needing to escape after so many beatings, starvation. Giving up hope, life would end, her heart would die first. Her soul second, she assured *Mother Earth* and Gods of the Universe, every weekend, having given up on *Jesus Cristo*. Which was worse, soul first, heart first? "Please tell me Mother Earth?" This time on the balcony, a secret lament nearly pulled the pulsating heart out of it cavity.

Tanya waited for a bird to fly overhead to pluck its freedom.

Transfixed for a time, regaining composure, after soulful pleadings Tanya, regrouped. The penthouse had become hotter, the air filled with the sweet smell of marijuana, stale Cuban cigars and cigarettes. Settling a bucket, mop, brush and pail in one corner, Tanya's eyes looked over the expanse of the large elegantly furnished balcony. Furniture moved, things disheveled, legions of ash trays scattered on table tops, seats, floors, food piled on plates, drinks and glasses strewn in every corner. Clean-up would take time, leaving only an hour of sleep before sunrise. On sweet marijuana nights like these, the drugged *Matrona* slept in, so Tanya hurried, wanting to catch some early morning rest before *la Matron* rustled.

Concentrating on work at hand, Tanya went about cleaning not noticing a slumbering elegant handsome, lithe older figure in a dark corner sitting on a chaise lounge chair, behind French doors. Clattering, china movement woke him. Waking, watching someone, quietly, removing ash trays, chairs, cleaning plates, hers was a world devoted to making things cleanly right. "Young, too young, to be in this illicit bistro." Realizing he might deeply startle this young being, deciding to gently move an index finger around a crystal glass rim, creating a reverberating sound he knew as a musician she would hear. Waiting, looking towards the solitary figure for reaction.

Startled, eyes search the dark area, an accented, "Hello?"

Cautiously, a response, "Hello." Like a deer in headlights, Tanya stood still for what seemed an eternity. Waiting for a first move, minutes passed. Frozen, not knowing whether to run towards the living room, slam the door shut, or stay put. The flush hot air deflated as if escaping from a balloon, quickly a chill enveloped, unifying them in one purposeful instant. The outline of a thin body, small, delicate, shivering. Drawn to her fear, his eyes fixated. What he saw was a frightened teenager. The elegant conjunto orchestra leader, stiffening, feeling pity, stood still. He noticed a fright, running so deeply, rising, he walked carefully, slowly. "I'm sorry, I've freighted you." "No, *perdone senor*," Tanya continued in heavily accented English, "I'm sorry." "*Hablas espanol?*" he asked. "Ahh, *si*," with such a resounding sound of relief, he laughed.

Slumbering, left behind to handle *la Matrona*, the conjunto orchestra leader became salvation.

Papi.

Papi, recounting the story to Rita, "*Me salvo*." Tanya lapsed into tales of being so loved, she understood why *Jesu Cristo*, brought her to *these United States of America*. God Bless America.

Papi understanding Tanya's dangerous predicament moved her to church *familia*. Then, cautiously, their friendship started. But in truth they loved one another that moment when the chill on the balcony enveloped them. They didn't need a long courtship. *Mother Earth* and the sublime language of *la Mosquitia* made it happen. The wind carried her prayer to friends, and they prayed in unison to an all encompassing God. Prayers, answered, delivered.

Tanya and *Papi* moved to Spanish Harlem, *El Barrio*. Noised filled, tenement buildings. Crowded tenement buildings. Not the sweltering Lower East Side. Not Red Hook. Not filled with sweat shops, jewelry factories, ship yards, Irish, Italian, German and Jewish gangs. Not Riverside Drive by any stretch of the imagination. But working class. Immigrant, Southern migrant working classes. Tree lined. Street benches. Wide open paved streets.

Harlem, where urban America met. Harlem Blacks, Harlem Italians, Harlem Jews, Harlem Spanish. Everyone walked over the same coagulated fish smelling sawdust floors *en La Marqueta*. Sat at its wooden, knife carved, rustic tables, underneath the '*El*' and between buildings. Families, huddled under the '*El*,' organizing brown paper shopping bags, gathering multitudes of noisy children. Shifting groceries between bags, to make things lighter for everyone. Children carried their weight in bags, down streets to three storied townhouses or five story tenements.

This was life she thought

Filled with loud laughing, screaming, crying children, playing captain against brick walls, marbles on streets. Women moving laundry between buildings, stretching bras, diapers, panties, undershirts, napkins, pants, socks, sheets, table clothes on clothes lines.

This was life she thought

Men crouching over dies, engulfed in smelly cheap cigar short brown stokes rising above them adding a sweet layer to their sweaty shirts, palms and hair. Old men playing, joking, arguing over dominoes in small parks. Hop scotch, double dutch. Captain. Large squared off marks with numbers 1, 2, 3, … chalk enumerated on concrete sidewalks. Recent immigrants, first generation families sitting, squeezing themselves across, stoops, benches, cooling hot bodies after work at factories, ship yards, sweatshops, offices, schools.

This was life, she thought.

Blowing a whistle a policeman, with city boy swagger, asking neighbors to move the few cars in the neighborhood, "Yeah, like I sed, keep gawing. Get 'em parked ova dere fellas," so he could open fire hydrants, spraying, cooling over heated bodies in sweltering New York City summers. Heat wave ripples rose five feet, from the asphalt. Fully dressed women holding small children, walked towards the pouring cold water, exposing the outlines of their womanly shapes.

This was life she thought.

Italian *gelato* push carts filled with ice, scrappers, blue, red, green syrup. Vegetable carts filled with bananas, lettuce, tomatoes, fruits. One, two, three bedroom apartments. Private bathrooms. Kitchens with stoves, refrigerators. Hot running water. Radiators in each room. Icemen, milkmen making stoop stops, singsonging their arrival from the cobble stone streets. Superintendents, landlords sweeping sidewalks. Cars squeezed between sign posts.

Musicians, lawyers, doctors, accountants, teachers, professors, publicists, writers, painters, publishers, newsmen, lived here amongst the immigrants who manually ran Manhattan. Subway engineers, nurses, construction workers, salesmen, City workers and a Council Member or two could be found walking home, towards three story brownstones.

This was life, she thought.

The '*El*' passing overhead. Underneath, *La Marqueta*, the most famous open air market running the length of Harlem and the width of the '*El*.' *La Marqueta central* of Tegoose, came to mind during visits. "*Las lagrimas, me salieron.*" What didn't they buy to slaughter, butcher, cook, smoke, cure to feed *los trabajadores, peones y campesinos*?

This was life she thought.

Under the '*El*' in heatless green *La Marqueta* buildings, she found smokehouses filled with hanging hams, sides of beef, poultry. Chips, sawdust, three inches deep clung to shoes or boots. Corrugated three storied metal warehouse type buildings, filled with sausages freshly made by butchers cranking grinders, pushing pork, using stuffing tubes, filling sausage casings, combining vinegar, salt, blood, black pepper.

This was life she thought.

Live chickens whose necks were broken for your liking, feathers plucked, quartered, fish scaled, meat carved, hacked and sliced. An open air market filled to the rafters with teaming immigrant and American urban street life. No English needed here. Here Manhattan found fresh cut tripe, gizzards, freshly caught striped bass, bluefish, porgy, flounder, oysters, crab, lobsters, lamb, open fire pits cooked meats, hung from the ceiling on metal hooks.
This was life, she thought.

On any given day workers made Harlem thrive. Bustling, hustling, energetic combustible street movements. Brickmen. Carpenters hoisting, boxes filled with hammers, screwdrivers, nails, saws, and wrenches. Milkmen delivering bottleneck glass bottles. Newspaper boys loudly regaling sales. Postal workers, carrying bags filled with news. Visiting, stoops, sharing news of one immigrant family's good fortune, or notices of death in the old country. Ice men delivering blocks in square refrigerator trucks. Garbage men, street cleaners, hauling, sweeping debris into gutters and onto push carts. Teachers, speaking casually to mothers enveloped by extended family and school children.

This was life, she thought.

El Barrio teamed with life. The entire City inhabitants met here. Its' fishmongers, deli's, clothing vendors, teachers, mothers with six or seven babies, teenagers, *abuelas, bubbe's,* truck drivers. Shop life owned by its residents.

This was life, she knew.
La vida.
El Barrio.

Gentrification was generations away. White people were still immigrants speaking another language. They hadn't become that white yet. No *Ingles* needed here. Italian, yes. Yiddish, yes. German, yes. And, Jazz, yes.

Chapter 26

Please Step Forward

A hubbub of sounds and activity started at dawn. Wannabee central was awakening. It is, finally, the day of reckoning. It couldn't come fast enough, and too fast it came. *Idol-A-Try* mega-phoned staff channeled orders into the ears of limp, tired, exhausted youthful and not so youthful bodies, bringing them to their feet.

"Ok, we're going to start lining up at 7, its 6:20 now. Our camera is going to pan over you and we are going to have chants that we want you to say, here. Then we are going to move you to the stairs in front of the arena. We're going to line up as many people as possible on the stairs. There will be helicopters going overhead. Read the cards that we put up. We'll practice once we get up there. Don't do anything until we give you a signal."

Kat, Rita and Chloe start gathering belongings. Cliff and Joan fold their blanket. The surrounding group closes in, walks towards the front of the crowd. Rushed from behind, they found themselves walking upstairs, feeling as if being lifted. Locking hands, fearing separation, somehow their feet find the stairs, while being pushed, their feet barely touching the ground. At some point Cliff and Joan disappeared, swallowed by the aggressive multitude.

Reaching the top of the stairs, not following the crowd to large broad steps in front of the arena, to be filmed by hovering helicopters, they stay at the Izod

Center's entrance. Swarmed by impatient, aggressive rushing bodies, they're pinched against the johnny horse barricades, event staff stretched across the length of the entrance doors. Wave, after wave of wannabee's pass, walking towards the television cameras to take their place amongst tens of thousands hopefuls, gleefully shouting placard cues hoping for their nano Instagram hall of fame shot.

Repeatedly, under the direction of the event crew and producers, chants are screamed. Prompting and responding goes on for more than two hours. Weathering exhaustion, Rita, Chloe and Kat, don't care to chant, are beyond caring if a camera panned their way. Overhead whirring helicopters, nearly drown out the chants. All three stood at the barricaded doors. It was difficult to keep their spots. Tugs, waves of bodies repeatedly hit them.

Overwhelming exhaustion made the shoving, anticipation, excitement, eclipse the experience for them. An ending to this exercise, was hopefully being orchestrated by the crew. Wanting it all to end. Soon. Now. Individually, quietly started asking God for help. A plea to end this nonsense came from them, and everyone their bodies hugged.

"Chloe has Timothy called you. I haven't heard from Tim in a while now. I know he caught the first 164 from the Port Authority this morning. But he hasn't called since then." "Well, we're 'ere. We'll see 'im inside. Let's jist hold our places 'ere. Which is really hard tew dew, tha pushin' and shovin' is gettin' tew me. Nuthin we can dew about 'im." "Oh God Miss Rita. I'm getting pushed hard from behind. Some guy parked his knees into me. I wish they'd open the doors already. I'm tired." "I know, I'm short. I've had more elbows in my face in these last twenty minutes, than my entire life before this."

Finally a call came through. *"Schlemiel* , ladies!"

Kat relieved, *"Schlimazel, hasenpfeffer incorporated*! Where are you? Still on the 164?" "I'm here." "Here where? You mean the Izod, by saying here, right? Can you make it over to the entrance steps?" "Okay, I can meet you." "We're at the front of the arena." "I'll get there." "I don't know how, there are thousands of people standing all around us, and on top of us, I might add."

"Don't worry, Kat, you're talkin' to the Tin Man remember? Keep your composure." "But, I doubt they'll let you through. I mean it's really thick with people. We can hardly breathe, there's no room." "Ok, so where exactly are you, just tell me that. Like give me an idea. Down the steps? Over by the," "We're standing at the barricades in front of the doors to the arena. Let's just say that I'm riding a Johnny Horse, it's so tight up against me."

"I hear your pain. I feel your pain, I just ended a 12 hour shift to make up for the other day." "You can't see us, because we're right in front of the doors and there are tons of people all around us."

"Ok, but is there a sign, like what entrance sign? I can see way above the crowd. You up by that sign. Like tell me," "Let me see, yeah well it says Welcome *Idol-A-Try*." "Are you under the Welcome or the *Idol-A-Try*? It's a pretty big sign." "*Idol-A-Try*. Over towards the word the right side, near," "Ok, I think I know where you are I," "You might know where we are, but I doubt you can make it up here. It's wall to wall people. Sardines, have it better. And, we're not all in a good mood. I mean the crowd is tired, and," "Ok, ok, I see you."

Giddily, Chloe asks, "He sees us? How can he be doing that? He's got to be nearby." Kat replies, "How can you see us, where are you? Its way too crowded. And we're way too short for you to see us from the street. I mean, I know you can make out the sign." "Look to your right, over where the bushes are, the hedges." "Along the steps, by the bushes? But I don't know if they'll let you through, its too, crowded. People are downright mean right now. Those people aren't gonna let you walk up the steps and get past them. They'll beat you up! If you go along the steps stay to your far right, along the handrail. We're," "Yeah, I see you. I don't see Rita."

Laughing, "Oh, hey nobody can ever pick my mother out in a crowd." "But I see you and Chloe." Looking to the right along the large hedges and lawn.

"Oh, oh my God, I see you! He's, he's there, look, he's over there. He's not on the stairs, he's on the grassy area near the wall. Yeah, I see you. You'll have to climb over the hedge and people. Hope they don't get pissed off." "Ok, just help me out when I get there. You know I can squeeze my skinny Tin Man body through anything." "Over here, I can see you. Put your hands up. Look over against the building on the grassy knoll."

A narrow space of green grass was available

for walking. Timothy walks towards them.

"Timothy! Grab his arms. It's not a bulwark this time, but you still gotta climb over." Chloe reaches out, "Oh my God, how did you do that?" Grabbing his arms, they help him climb over the hedge and over the barricade. Without hesitation, having heard their conversation, others standing around them make room. He lands on their side of the barrier. Excitedly they hug. Another journeyman has joined their group.

"Christ, I didn't think yew were gonna make it. We decided tew stay up 'ere sew we cud git in first." Looking at the people he got past Rita turns, "Thanks for letting 'im in. He waited with us on tha street tha other night. But, he had tew take tha 164 back into tha City, thank you!" Laughing, "It's so good seeing you. Wasn't sure I was going to make it. I left Long Island City like four am this morning. Got on the train, took the fabulous 164. Bus stopped here this time! Didn't have to deal with that lady driver. You know the line is thrice wrapped around the building."

An exhausted Kat offers, "Hoping they wrap THIS, up soon. Crew has been filming forever, I'd like to get inside and just sit down. Don't give a damn about their filming. People are tired." "Know you're tired. Had to call in sick today, after the twelve hour shift to make up for the other day. My boss was pissed. Had me in the stock room, overnight. But God, there was no way I was giving up my spot. My wristband, (holding up his wrist) cudda made money on E-Bay!" Laughing, "I earned this."

Small talk starts, then the event staff standing, six abreast, at the front doors, ask for their attention.

"Attention, Hello! Ok, Listen folks, DO NOT, rush the barricades. Everyone will get in. There is no need to push. We know you're feeling tired, impatient, but you're almost there. Ok. Stay calm!"

"Finally," their brains feeling fried, begged for a quick entre. Anticipation was thick in the air. Like a tightly closed water spigot, the event crew, twisted, twisted, turning tightly the crowd's emotions, energy. At last, the event crew pushed the barricades out of the way, opening the metal doors. Pent up frustration, pushed everyone forward. Bus 164 wannabees, were at last in the bowel of their vinyl Mecca.

Nervously, "GO! Tew tha ladies room. Git changed, I'll meet yew at tha seats, jist make sure yew hav' yur tickets. Timothy, I'll see yew downstairs. Seats shud be on tha lower level, somewhere. Chloe, Kat try stayin' ta-gether."   "Kat, let's get to the bathroom, quick. Have to put my face on. Get cleaned up. Timothy, we'll meet you later, at the seats."

As the group separates, Rita finds herself alone searching for the reserved seat numbers in the arena hall.

The bathroom fills rapidly, becoming a large dressing room. Bags, shoes, costumes, pants, bras spill out onto the floor. Makeshift squatter rights rule. All the stalls are occupied, lines form for the mirrors, its ten fold deep with humanity. Once in the bathroom Kat finds a clean corner, drops the designer bag onto the floor, pulls a dress out, strips the blouse off, tugs the dress down over head and works the lipstick. Chloe coyly squeezes past bodies towards a large mirror. Darting hands, heads, quickly paints her lips, brows, cheeks, tassels the hair, adjusts the girlfriends and calls it a day.

Finished dressing, worried, about the audition time, they find their tickets running to the arena first floor. Carefully walking down the stairs are Kat and Chloe.   Rita has found her seat, seated beside Jay and Timothy. "Oh, I see 'em. I'll move ova so yew guys can sit ta-gether." Rita starts to move. Jay leans in whispers, "Rita, stay between us, I don't want to deal with Chloe. On the bus the other day there was too much drama. I've got enough of it going on without having to deal with her. I'm really tense and tired."

Tin Man chimes in, "Oh, yeah, there was drama. But thank God, I hooked my music in and fell asleep. You know I can contort this skinny Black ass into any space, I can sleep anywhere." Jay responds, "Well, after a certain point I pretended, but she put me through shit before I decided to ignore her." "What happened? Hurry, up, they're cummin' down tha stairs." "Oh she pretended she was having a, some sort of panic attack, or convulsions."

"What?"

Tin Man continues, "Well I started laughing, don't know if she was playing or not, all I could do was laugh. You know she's a drama queen. When she started contorting, you know, I closed my eyes. She was pulling our leg."

Jay interrupts, "Yeah, well I didn't close my eyes, we were sitting in the back.   It was uncomfortable. People were looking. They could hear her making moaning sounds. Shit, it almost sounded like we were fucking back there. And, hey, that's not what I'm about." "Acted like she was having an epileptic fit. Don't know, maybe because of the electric jolt. Hadda be bullshit. Didn't pay her no mind after a while. I closed my eyes, prayed she'd stop." "Rita, please, stay there, in between us, like I said, I can't deal. Don't want to be near her. It was embarrassing." They all rise, Rita points, suggesting they climb over.

Watching the Arena fill steadily for the next two hours, Jay, Timothy, Rita, Kat and Chloe are finally sitting in a row beside one another, just as they'd anxiously imagined when they'd gotten the wristbands.

To Chloe, Timothy observes, "You look good, I see you brought the ladies out." "Gotta use all the weapons, I know how to use these." Leaning over past Rita, "Hey, Kat, I love that dress. Designer? Love that designer." A blonde male auditioner sitting next to Chloe asks Timothy, "Hey! I like what you have going on with your hair. You do that?

Smiling, "Yeah, thanks. I penciled it in. It stays on, if you're wondering."

Chapter 27

Bryan Earcrestful, the Idol-A-Try God Arrives

Although the Arena was the hub of activity, a hurry up and wait feeling surfaces. Sitting fairly close to the Arena floor, they could comfortably view ongoing activity. Behind them were rows filled with forty thousand, then fifty-thousand, certainly more contestants. Camera crews carried, set up cameras on the floor while contestants milled about, crossing the staging area. Suddenly a producer grabbed a mike, gave everyone a welcome, then got into the business of show business reciting a long list of directions for the crowd.

"Ok, the camera is going to pan overhead. We're going to start on my right, this section will raise their hands when you see the camera over you. Then, the next, and so on. I know you all have done this before, so let's start." With cameras panning in and out, several rounds of waves, and chants were executed for filming.

Chloe, "Okay, here it comes."
They raise their hands overhead, and stand,
They do the wave,
Kat, "It's coming around again,"
They repeat the wave,
Chloe, "One more time, around again,"
They repeat the wave,
Jay, "Who the fuck wants to see this many waves?"
They repeat the wave,
Timothy, "Lord have mercy,"

They repeat the wave,
Rita, "Damn it, I'm not standin' again. I don't
 give a flying hoot.
Timothy, "They need to end this NOW! I mean
this better be the last of the wave.
Rita, does not stand, but her section does.

Producer, "Ok, folks, get quiet now. We've got
a surprise for you. The great Host of *Idol-A-Try* is here
and we're going to do a few shots of him greeting you
all, working this side of the auditorium. Ok? I'm gonna
pull some people down from these rows. Once I get
that set, he'll come in, we'll work together. Stay
patient!"

At long last, the Host enters, greeted by a
roaring crowd. "Welcome everyone, as you might
know, I'm," crowd roars, "happy to see you folks at the
Izod Center in The Meadowlands." Crowd roars, "Can
we do one more WAVE?"

Jay, "Shit! Fuck 'im, I hate this. I'm not
standing!"

Crowd does the wave.

"I'd like to introduce a former winner of *Idol-
A-Try*. Give him a hand." Host chatter, camera pans,
continuing for the next twenty minutes.

Guest *Idol-A-Try* Idol, "Hello, everybody, I'm
gonna do a little song you might know." Song, "Come
see me on Broadway! And good luck! Thank you, The
Meadowlands. Good luck!" "I'd like to thank you all
for coming. Give yourselves a hand! Good luck!"

Relieved by the Hosts' exit, the group sits up becoming laser focused on the producer walking towards the center of the stage. Audition business, finally, they could sense, all the waiting, staging was finally going to be over. You could feel combined exhaustion, energy in the air.

"We will call you down, in an orderly fashion, no one is to rush." They'd heard it before. At this point, this was all old hat, their patience had worn thin. "You are going to be signaled by an usher to rise. Have your paperwork ready, all of it. You can't return to your seats. No one will be seen without the paperwork once they come down here. If you need anything, please raise your hands, we will have someone come over to you and help you." Thousands of hands rise. "Ok, please," Ushers pass out the paper needed, "please," Again, tens of thousands of hands reach out, forms are passed around.

"Ok, here's what you are going to do once you come down to this level. There will be tables across the arena floor, there will be two producers who will ask you to sing. Stand forward when you are called upon. Please be ready."

"This is your chance, this is your one and only chance for now. Remember to do better, than your best. This is it, there is no turning back. We want to hear what you have to offer. When you are finished, please step back. The next person will step forward upon a signal and sing. Another will follow, so on and so forth. Once all of you have sung. The producers will speak to each auditioner and tell them whether or not they have made it, then will go to the next round."

"If you've made it you will go to the entrance to the right of the producers where you will be greeted by someone. If you haven't made it through, this is the end of the line, you will go to your left, proceed quietly. Remember, you can't argue with their decision. If you've made it we will follow up with you on the right side. Right side, everybody understand. Right side if you've made it. Ok, thanks everyone! Give it your all."

He motions to the ushers. They ask the first rows of wannabees to stand and go downstairs. Rita looks right and left. Nerves are raw. Kat is biting her lip. Chloe sits nervously chattering with the blonde. Jay and Timothy smile. They'd been through this before, all the pain for much awaited gain.

"Well, finally. I'm feeling it. I've done plenty of auditions. Show Choir, stuff, but this is really, audience size is huge. Here goes. See you later mom." At last an usher signals to their row to step down. Rita leans over and places a kiss on her hand, presses it against each of what have become fellow journeymen, extended family.

Looking fondly, lovingly to this new brood, Rita offers, "Don't know if yur ready. We've spent some damn ghastly, exhausting, hour's t'gether since stepping off the 164. Well, this is it. *Besos*!" Looks left then right again, softly, "Gud luck, I luv yew guys." Timothy looks, surprised. Shyly, "Thank you, thank you so much." Grabbing a hand, "You've been kind, I really appreciate it."

Rita remained seated wondering where the other friends made where. Hoping to see them again, less exhausted, her mind chased disconsonant and melodic memories of those four days. Wondering if others, stretching larynx, vocal cords throughout the night, would they make it? Would their voices reflect their exhaustion? Who would win? The voice, or the exhaustion?

Eyes focused on wannabee hopefuls walking down stairs, wondering if she'd witness their audition for posterity. Sitting as an audience member, but really more than that, Rita was part of an exclusive club who survived exceptional circumstances to be at this Mecca. Bus 164 voyagers, were now a unique extended *familia*. Anxiously, turning towards the stage floor, hoping for the best, waiting for them to appear before seated producers, anxiety crept into her heart.

In the distance, bounding down steep steps, Jay loudly sings, mustering up much needed *chutzpah*.

Chapter 28

Border Crossings

"Chutzpah ..."

Puerto Ricans migrated to *Nuevo York*, running from distressed economic conditions, hurricanes stripping vegetation, vanquishing sugar cane plantations, destroying coffee crops, creating famine, killing hundreds, decimating hundreds of thousands of homes. The late 19th Century and early 20th Century were foreboding years for *los Estados Unidos* and its relationship with the Spanish Caribbean islands. Looking to live, survive, *Caribenos* left once lush, verdant mountainous lands, *verde esmeralda islas con,* pristine white, pink and black sands doting vast churling *mar Caribe,* warm trade wind waters. A resilient desperate people struggling to survive, embarked on a *diaspora a los Estados Unidos.*

But as the Great Depression appeared on the horizon, Puerto Ricans arriving in the City competed with other ethnicities, filling jobs for unskilled labor. Considered 'cheap labor,' willingly working for substandard non-union wages, replacing more expensive older unionized immigrants, tension rose between unemployed Jews and Puerto Ricans. Older immigrants, Italians and Irish began attacking Puerto Ricans. Destruction of Puerto Rican owned *El Barrio* businesses escalated. Puerto Rican tenants living in overcrowded, substandard buildings, owned by Jews, were evicted. Their leases broken, evicted onto Harlem streets led to the *Harlem Riots of 1926.*

Spanish immigrants like *Papi's* family wended their way from Spain through the Canary Islands, Cuba, Puerto Rico, *las Islas Virgenes*, the coast of South America, finally landing around the 1870s. So small the numbers no one took note. That migration, barely perceptible, rooted themselves in Brooklyn, or Manhattan not giving pause or concern to undulating waves of Germans, Italians, Irish, Polish, and the largest Jewish populace outside of Europe. By 1910 two million Jews immigrated to New York City.

Tanya, arriving at *la Matrona's* illicit penthouse bistro, learning toney Riverside Drive Jewish traditions understood her Harlem Jewish neighbors well. Speaking Yiddish, or Ladino, when needed made life noncorrosive. *Papi* and *Tanya* quietly moved into Harlem after the riots when Puerto Ricans demanded civil rights, and the Mayor's Office took note. Italian Harlem shared *El Barrio*. Continuing ethnic, racial tensions saw the beginnings of flight to the Bronx. Settled Spanish immigrants, remained. Italians moving further north, left for the Bronx for better apartments and schools. Second generation Jews, wealthier than their immigrant parents also moved, buying buildings creating newer *shtetls*. Earlier Irish and Italian immigrants who made their money by smuggling illegal whiskey, moved up in the economic world. Their speakeasies replaced with new housing. The Bronx was seeing a building renaissance.

Tanya, *Papi*, nestled comfortably, working, raising a family during the Great Depression. But, *El Barrio*, was not forever. The overcrowded public schools wouldn't do. The Bronx called to them. Moving was a reality, a necessity for the betterment of their brood. Now years into *America*, Tanya knew 'the

269

Spanish,' were red-lined out of broad tree lined avenues, private beach clubs, pools, sometimes doorman northern Bronx *shtetls*. Friends moved north, how north determined by religion, skin color, ethnicity, the City, the gateway of America, had top tier, top shelf categories for immigrant humanity. While Tanya came legal, above board and *Papi* a second generation native, they remained 'lower shelf,' to Jewish landlords' Bronx housing. Native born citizenship was of no consequence for 'the Spanish' in northern Bronx *shtetls*. Recent immigrants from Eastern Europe moved in unquestioned, but third generation Spanish Americans or citizen Puerto Ricans, suffered discriminate redlining.

World War II intruded before their move. Regardless of ethnicity or color, bodies were needed for the War. The country went into over drive. Women replaced men in factories. Life changed on a dime. Tanya out of necessity became economically independent during *Papi's* War years. Taking care of family, with very little income from the Army, realizing meager income from painstaking factory jewelry work, wouldn't do, Tanya decided to become a business woman. Consulting friendly Harlem shop owners, who suggested looking north to where small shop rental space was cheaper. Everything pointed to the Morrisinia area of the Bronx. Brandishing a map, crossing the bridge, riding the *El* to Third Avenue and 148th in the Bronx, walking through its expansive commercial center, vibrant, ethnically mixed, Tanya thought, "*perfectamundo.*"

Tanya spoke further with store vendors and after a time found a two story shop on Third Avenue, whose down payment she could handle. For this new *adventura*, Tanya understood she'd have to part with cherished *familia* tokens. Tanya asked *las ninas* to the small kitchen table, reassuring it was best to move. *La familia* agreed to pull up stakes. The shop had an apartment upstairs, an *El* stop and trolley cars within walking distance, *las ninas* would be in better schools. This would be what *Papi* wanted.

Suenos, coming true.

So, Tanya pulled a locked hand hammered leather *baul* out from under a husbandless matrimonial bed. Never having a need before to part with beloved momentos of a former *vida*, the trunk gathered dust. Except when her feet brushed against it, mostly forgotten. *Las ninas* watched as their mother's finger tips traced raised silver nailheads family initials, retelling *la historia nuestra*. Its contents individually wrapped in gauze, parchment, silk materials. One delicate piece after another, Tanya shared with *las ninas*. Stored were photos, family papers, strings of pearls, gold, silver, gold filigree earrings, emeralds, silver cosmetic boxes, embellished hair pins, bracelets, nuggets of *puro oro*, *la familia* collected at *Olancho* pebbled riverbeds. Holding family treasures in her small calloused hand caused great distress. Sorrowfully, Tanya decided she could not yet part with everything. Tanya wondered if *mis padres* would understand the parting of such unused luxuries. After much soul searching, anguished with grief, Tanya accepted parting ways with her material heritage and push forward. In the end Tanya knew, *la Dona,* the business woman, understood this sacrifice.

Tanya carefully wrapped the most valuable items in small pouches, removed the lining of an oversized jacket, sewed pouches into the lining, covering the lining with another cloth. The next day rising earlier, walked her daughters to school, where she placed a *beso* on their foreheads, then made her way directly to the Diamond District. Tanya took the gems and gold to trust worthy jewelers. Exchanging jewelry for cash, Tanya cemented a rental contract moving weeks later. These were war years. Tanya entered the second hand furniture business. Times being tough, families brought items in exchange for hard needed cash. Tanya bartered, bought, sold items of consequence from other peoples' rich family history. *El Don's* lessons at bookkeeping, recordkeeping, served well. Tanya succeeded in supporting *la familia*, hired a driver and bought mobility. They had arrived.

> *Suenos,*
>   dreams,
> *Si se puede.*

La familia received letters in the beginning, during *Papi's* training. Once overseas, letters became intermittent. Tanya never knew his battalions' movements. Tanya learned to speak to *Dios* again, praying nightly with '*mis hijas.*' Then one day, the War came to an end, and a deafening silence became the norm for weeks, then months, then a year. No news of *Papi's* whereabouts. Not hearing anything was almost worse than knowing the War was ongoing. During their father's absence, the girls became young women.

Tanya turned to the Veterans Administration. A search turned up nothing. Tanya insisted *Papi* was still alive, continuing with inquiries until a notice came. Found. *Papi* was injured, convalescing in a French hospital. Finally, *Papi* left France, returning home.

Tanya was thankful for insightful favors given by God. Tanya thanked *Dios* for this home with no other tenants, after closings, no one nearby. *Papi's* searing cries in the night, terrified. Resolute *la familia*, accepted *Papi*, as he was. Tanya spoke to her girls, "God brought him back. *Dios lo salvo.* He's ours to take care." Consoling *las hijas*, "*Paciencia, por favor*, patience, please." *Las lagrimas salieron.* *Papi* had in that illicit Manhattan bistro brought her salvation. Tanya understood she would never leave. Anger might surface, impatience certainly, but Tanya would stay. Till death do us part. Yes, till death do us part.

La familia worked through the same pain most World War II, veteran families worked through. God spares no one during wars. *Papi* returned. *Their Papi* had not returned. Damaged, wounded in need of … well of what, time would tell. But returned from a War so egregious, millions upon millions died. Millions turned into refugees. Millions lost everything. They prayed for his safe return. And, here he was.

Enduring, knowing his sacrifice Tanya, worked through the nightmares, the deep anguish, the silence, the distance. They could not share his Normandy landing experiences. They could not share his wading through ocean water, beaches turned red from mortal wounds, injuries, death. At times *Papi* became silent, mute, shuttering his memories.

Sacrificious.

This time it wasn't for music.
No not for art, either.
This time it was for country.
There was a purple heart in there.

Somewhere.
A trunk.
Un baul.
Somewhere.
He received it.
She put it away.
Somewhere.
He never spoke of the War.
He put those memories,
  away somewhere.
No one had to tell him what he sacrificed.
His *suenos* were done.
His *suenos* now terrified him.
Papi's suenos died at some point on D-Day.
As he picked bodies, American bodies
  from the red European ocean.

Time passed. Their girls attended distinguished high schools, independently easing in and out of Manhattan, the Bronx. Exquisite music finally returned to *Papi's* memory, emoting through gifted elegant instrumental fingers. During the War, musically dexterous memory was replaced by nimble fingers of a Medic, suturing, bandaging, mending.

Feeling restive *Papi* formed a small orchestra with old *amigos*. Giving private lessons, no one noticed his internal mental wounds. Fits and starts. Fits and starts. Old gifts of musical intellect returned. Tanya embraced this.

Life's former normal rhythms found its way back. *Las ninas*, looked to move away. Tanya and Papi were becoming empty nesters. *Tanya* and *Papi*, started another family. So after comfortable years, south of the red-lined border, Tanya offered, "*Tenemos que buscar*

mejores escuelas. We have to look for better schools."
"*Y como lo hacemos*." "How will we do it?" "They will never rent to us."

> *Never understanding 'no,' not on this level.*
> *Understanding 'no' if you were asking for peas,*
> *while passing butter, but in the big scheme of*
> *things, 'no, you can't live here.' 'No you can't*
> *go to school here.' 'No your kids won't go to*
> *college,' was only an invitation to engage,*
> *break barriers.*

Having time, *Papi*, y *Tanya* planned the move. Deciding to trump the *chutzpah* card, having mastered English, *Yiddish,* and *Ladino*, Tanya *schmoozed* landlords. *Papi* searched apartment notices. Spinning *spiels*, using *Yiddish, Ladino* and English, Tanya, visits. Using *Papi's* stage name, then, based on amber colored eyes, auburn wavy hair, milky white pearls and skin, Tanya got *them*, in. With an established business, Tanya was able to secure a rental. Quietly after the lease was signed, ever so quietly, *la familia moved in,* using their truck, hiring friends, moving in darkness.

> *Invisible.*
> Being quieter.
> *Invisible.*
> To live there.
> *Invisible.*
> In this free land, home of the brave.
> *Invisible.*
> These United States of America.
> *Invisible.*

In yes, but neighbors privately repeatedly, *kibitzed*, each, every year Rita's family lived in this exclusive *shtetl*, "*So* exactly, how did *that* family sneak in?" Repeatedly, asked by one or another canasta street gamer, privately. Their consternation never eased. Never openly confronted, rumors whispered by dyed platinum blonde bee-hive well-coiffed, *yentas* in mink coats, stilettos, pushing carts, in cold air conditioned grocery stores reached their ears. Polite hellos exchanged, but Rita's dark auburn unruly long hair was always jostled, by be-jeweled, red nail lacquered fingers, questioned. "Imagine having to listen to this. Sometimes, in a verbally cautious nuanced *Yiddish or Ladino*, only I can hear," she thought.

Bigotry, perceived, unseen, nuanced, real. Egos intact, they survived.

Neighbors knew there was a crack in the damn. And the damn wall would break one day. Tanya's keen understanding of injustice, in this *Americano* land of opportunity, made her the original tiger mom. If in coveting the best schools, she had to *finagle* a spot in this coveted segregated community, she would and did.

Rita had ring side seats to her parent's comfortable older years, after her father opened a studio, teaching every frickin' kid in the 'hood. Rita took her parent's lessons in *exceptionalism*; discipline, artistry, and ran with it. Carved out a life independent, stridently, uniquely her own, a '60s child. Passionate about civil rights, feminism, the Vietnam War, the Great Society and bigotry, Rita escaped the City during its worse years to liberal Governor Rockefeller's, newly constructed upstate marble university while 'da Bronx' burned.

The melting pot pockets in *these United States*

of America, was starting to look more like them. An exodus of major proportions began to Long Island using Robert Moses highways.

White flight.

The City defaulting, class warfare ongoing, red-lined former potato, duck farms with single family subdivisions got filled with former 'white' City dwellers.

Progresso, no.

[This land was made for you and me.]

Was a high wall there that tried to stop me
A sign was painted said: Private Property,
But on the back side it didn't say nothing

[This land was made for you and me.] *
*Woody Guthrie

Rita became part of the great Bronx diaspora. Jewish landlords hired arsonists burning, hundreds of their own buildings. Using insurance money to buy homes, create businesses further out on the Island, not wanting to live amongst Puerto Ricans and Blacks, paying rents in their tenement buildings, for which in return they got no repairs.

Invisible
wall up.

"This land is your land, this land is my land,

from the New York Island."

'Da Bronx' became a black and white photographers' dream. A token brown man's Dresden. Written about. Denigrated. Presidents visiting to observe the decimation in person. The Third World, looked better.

Flames,
  cinders,
  ghosts.
The City,
  warring,
  itself.

A undeclared Civil Cultural War.

Block by block tenement buildings once housing generations of stable families, became void. Whether Puerto Rican, Spanish, Italian, Black, *Caribeano* ... Creeping shadows entered the corridors, where children once played on roller skates. Drug addict squatters, gasping their last breath in a declining life, found refuge from the temperamental elements of *Mother Earth*.

Sans heat,
Sans Dignidad,
Invisible.

Sans water,
Sans Dignidad,
Invisible.

Sans gas,
Sans Dignidad,

Invisible.

Sans windows,
Sans Dignidad,
Invisible.

Sans garbage pick-up,
Sans Dignidad,
Invisible.

Sans law and order,
Sans Dignidad.

Invisible.

Rats over-ran floor mattresses, beer cans, soiled clothing, used heroine needles, squalor, human waste and food bins. This was a brown man's addiction, not a white man's disease. The Federal government looked away.

The Italian Mob moved unto the top floor of her building, to better control the heroine market. On visits home from University, Rita felt safer, reaching the bottom subway tile steps, greeting a pistol armed Mob guard. The Black Harlem drug cartel moved uptown, past that once impenetrable red-lined barrier. Drug money welcoming, recruiting eleven year olds. Color, no longer a barrier. Light a match if you like. Burn a building. Help a landlord move to Long Island. Pockets lined with insurance monies. Who would care? Who would notice the ordinary disintegrating lives of brown people?

Well, the people who had no place other than this as home, would. Crime became the new fashion. If you wanted to lose, or buy a stolen car, this was the hood you came to. It was no longer 'Da Bronx.' Now it was the South Bronx.

> *All of it.*
> *Chutzpah y la familia's* exceptionalism served her well.
> *Vida, la Vida.*
> Rita honed that Bronx *chutzpah.*
> *L'Chaim.*

Like Lot's wife, Rita, packed her parents belongings,
   sent them south to Miami Beach.

She returned to the safety of the marble ivory tower university.

Rita never looked back.

Chapter 29

Auditions

Not looking back, speaking to Chloe, "Damn, I've been to plenty auditions, but look at this place, its huge, it's a cattle call. There must be fifty thousand people." Jay and Timothy are no longer visible. Perhaps Jay had pulled Timothy away from the girls, perhaps not.

The producers sit two to a table. There are ten tables across the arena staging area. A long line of contestants emerged from an entrance Rita couldn't see. Finally, a production crew member walked Kat and Chloe, and two others, across the length of the arena floor to a table.

Rita stopped searching. She would miss Kat's audition if lingering too long in the search. Even if she couldn't hear the audition, she could see it. Eyes razor focused, she returned to watching Kat walk across the arena. Rita prayed. The tables separated by white curtained dividers, four contestants faced two producers.

As Kat and Chloe walked towards the producers, Kat turned to Chloe. Kat had become nervous at the very last. Not because of the actual audition, but because of the size of the audience.

Showing Chloe, pointing upwards, "Look, it's their logo, you know the one you see on TV." Stopping for a moment Chloe looked up. Kat's eyes panned up towards the last row of the arena. Pointing. "Tiny dots, tens of thousands of tiny dots, all the way up to the roof top. Come on let's walk." "Well you look good girl. You got it going on, ha! Worked it in the bathroom!" "Thanks, I love this dress." "Tight, nice. Shows off your body. Yes, I see. I just got my girls going for me." "Well then let's hope we get guy producers."

The stage crew member leading the way stopped. Rita could see they had reached the table. Watching intently, wishing to be closer, to hear them sing. Feeling cheated, waiting in anticipation for this moment for days, and now she couldn't hear them. Kat first in line. Chloe, second and two others to their right.

"Your first, Kat, please go ahead. We're ready."

Kat steps forward. Knowing this song well, gives it all. A disciplined musician, she'd practice even though singing it throughout childhood at school events, galas, White House events. Feeling comfortable, belting making sure the distant first row could hear. Knowing from operatic songs how to take every breadth with ease, Kat was confident. Her diaphragm was trained to inhale, then expanding, pushing out, through her esophagus long breaths making it possible to reach high notes with ease.

Soulful soprano notes emanated into the air. Emphasizing its melody, Kat finished, feeling right by the song, had been done. Stepping back, searching the producer's faces for reaction, but didn't notice any. Thanking her, Chloe was up next. Kat steps back.

Producers, "Chloe, please step forward." Chloe steps forward, two feet away from the line. Raising hands, as though, in prayer. Chloe looks down. Finger tips held closely to lips. Whispering, sings, raises hands up towards the rafters.

Rita can see movements and is concerned thinking Chloe has become ill. "Oh Gawd, she's sick! What tha fuck is going on?" Suddenly Chloe drops on knees, lowers hands as though pleading, pulls hands towards her body, placing them down over her face. Chloe head lowers, lips, into hands, continues on with the song.

Chloe does this for what seems an eternity to Kat, who wasn't sure what to make of it. Kat, stands there hoping to finally hear Chloe's voice, but can't. She heard Timothy and Jay. But Chloe always said she was saving her voice.

Now here, waiting in anticipation, Chloe's voice is but a whisper. Chloe continues singing softly, with conviction, into her hands, Kat, concentrating on Chloe's performance, still can't hear her. But Chloe, finally stands, places her hands to her side and steps back. Apparently done, the others take their turn singing.

All four contestants audition. Kat felt there were contenders, although perplexed by Chloe's performance. Kat heard everyone but Chloe. Kat thought her own performance fared well, and was comfortable. Then the interminable wait for the producers as they take a moment to consult one another. Waiting anxiously, Kat and Chloe shared sideway glances.

"Kat, please step forward." Kat steps forward.

"You're not going on. Thank you."

"But I've got another song, if, you give me a second,"
"No, thank you. You didn't sing it strong enough, it needed to be louder."

Suddenly from the audience sitting yards away in the first row Kat hears, "NO, no way, she belted! Booo!" Kat, leaves to the left towards the exit, walking past the producers. Walks out of the area. Hesitating a moment at the exit door, turns around, lingering at the exit waiting for Chloe.

An interminable amount of time seems to pass, waiting in the hallway of the exit door she hears,

"Chloe, please step forward."   Chloe steps forward.

"You've made it through to the next round. Please go to the right."

Chapter 30

An Ending, Fit For An Opera

Kat was not terminally unsettled by the abrupt unequivocal decision of the judges, after all this wasn't a first audition. The sheer number of contestants, made this a cattle call, unlike anything most artists would ever experience in their life time. Kat nodded, walked past the judges. The first audience row sitting behind the judges, twenty feet away cheered, shouted, "Luved you." Another, "We heard you." Smiling, she continued upwards into a long corridor towards the exit doors.

Rejection is always abrupt, she knew. One's metabolic heart rhythm would speed up, thump, thump, thump, then swoosh, drop. A breadth caught mid-throttle. Palms suddenly sweat, rapidly dry up. Not for the weak kneed. Competition at its most personal. One wasn't really competing against someone else. A singer was competing against herself, in efforts to get it perfect. Get it beyond perfection.

For the jokers in the room, the clowns who were there just for the fun of it, the hook-up, the all night festivities, they knew none of that. They didn't understand the voice was the finest instrument God had given man. A beautiful voice, with vibrato, tonality, quality, distinction took time to craft. Some like Kat were born with the 'gift.' But still she honed it. Understanding, it was a privilege to carry about this 'gift' enclosed in its protective human skeleton. Kat protected it from invasions of strep, over-use, physical exhaustion and fevers from that same exhaustion.

Honey teas, warm salted waters, vapo-rubs, humidifiers, neck towels, hats, coats anything was worn to keep it well, and lubricated. Soft whispers, days of silence, mentally taunting it. Practicing scales, mentally. Pulsating beats, counting, notes, reading, taunting the interior of her psyche.

It required the same understanding of sound that a fine violin or string maker would understand. Etching, molding, stretching the so called strings of a larynx. Pushing the air through, then trilling it into shape from the back of the tonsils bringing it forward. Each voice a unique instrument. Those that practiced this art form, were in it for the long hall. They were practitioners of inflection, patience and perfection.

What did these fools know of voice? It didn't matter, she was teasing her vocal cords to satisfy herself. To watch the faces in the audience. Kat knew when they heard the best, or something beautiful. Kat looked to them for approval. These front line judges, were part of, what?

One of the many questions invading a wannabee's mental space was whether or not one had to be, 'a triple threat.' How would you know if you were wasting the producers and A-list judges air time? But in truth, at this stage of the game, it didn't matter, the hours spent on line, on the street, were part of the show, so nobody lost. They'd become cast fodder whose shouts and taunts might land on the cutting room floor, or might not. Video producers, throughout the night recorded tens of thousands free, and free roaming cast. The Meadowlands became an open air music festival being readied for prime time television. And everyone was willingly suckered in.

Kat knew no judge or critic ever sat there and languished over their decision. It's business as usual for them. In this particular group of judges, how were they picking? Her experience was that sometimes you get to sing a whole song, other times, three stanzas. Usually they smile politely, some won't look up from their notes, but, they'll mumble something about "you'll hear from us, at some point in the distant future."

"That is always a death sentence."

"It would be nice every now and then to see a judge play out a Pagliacci." Cosmic humor, inspired by a love of Opera, chuckling, Kat continues this train of thought, "Maybe the death scene. Yes, the clown scene. The judge plays Canio, the clown." Imagining herself as Nedda, Canio's wife who is giving the best performance of her life, to save herself. Nedda sings to the rafters. Heard to the upper recesses of the opera house balcony trying to save herself. "Well I thought I belted. No, I know I belted, the judges lied." The audience concurred. Kat's ego received a boost.

Thoughts return to Canio whose mind is made up, and wants to dole out judgement. He delivers his judgement. Kat continues to walk up the hallway, further away from the arena. Nedda pleads to Canio, using her own words, "but I've got one more song." Metaphorically, like a knife, his dismissal stabs her heart. The words wound deeply, Nedda dies. For some *Idol-A-Try* contestants, rejection would wound mortally. It would be the end of a journey.

Continuing up the hallway, "Nothing grander

than opera," Kat thinks, "Opera is exceptional. Stage craft at its best. It lifts, it makes you cry. It elevates that only instrument the human body has. The voice." Kat stops, looks behind wondering where Chloe is. Then slowly she realizes *Chloe has made it.*

"Well, isn't this a silly tela-novella street carnival playing itself out? Isn't it tugging at our hearts?" Kat reviewing its optics, "It's staged in front of more than any opera house of any caliber. Possibly millions?" Continuing, "Oh, what could be worse? Failing in front a few hundred classically nuanced appreciative seats? Or, millions of 'she didn't belt' audience members?"

Sanguine after so much exhaustion, "Well, I won't have to worry about the millions."

Checked it off, "Been here, done this."

Bucket list, done. Well at least her mother's bucket list.

Professionally trained, with years of experience Kat's mind quickly reviews, retraces every syllable, fluctuation, notation in her voice. Kat shrugs off the false twisted fate she was just handed. This wasn't about her. It wasn't about her talent. This was about video sub-plots, producers needing to get ahead, television ratings. She wasn't rating material. She didn't trick, or game, or plead. Wasn't going to, she knew that going in. Still a thought lingers, "Well, what did just happen?" It may have been her largest publically viewed audition, but it certainly was not her last.

Kat wondered about Chloe. Vexed, "On what points did she win a chance to the next audition?" she asked the impervious Gods of this vinyl Mecca. There was an injustice here. A confusing one, at that.

Chloe certainly couldn't be heard. Kat wanted Chloe and she to win a spot at the next level. It would be easier for them to travel forward, together they could comfort one another. Auditions rattled. Kat knew there were several auditions involved to get to the television audition in front of the A-list celebrity judges. She'd read about that in the *Idol-A-Try* blogs.

Thinking of possibilities, knowing Rita needed to return to work, Chloe, Timothy, or Jay could offer one another support. Kat was that sure Timothy and Jay could sing their way out of a bag. Wondering where Timothy and Jay were, Kat tried calling, their phones were turned off. She'd have to wait till later to learn of their outcome. Realizing she didn't have to worry about her mother's circumstance Kat continued up the hallway, passing other rejected candidates. Finally reaching the heavy metal doors, she pushed with athletic strength and opened them.

Rita stood to the left of the doors. Kat met a surprised Rita up at the exit, embracing her mother. Relieved, "Well, mom that was interesting." "I saw yew both, but I cudn't hear yew or Chloe, so,"

"I couldn't hear Chloe either, mom, and I was standing right next to her, wondering when am I gonna hear her?" "Wait, yew cudn't hear her either?"

"No, I waited to hear something, when she started. I looked forward to it. We'd all sung something during this past week, except Chloe. I badly wanted to hear her voice. I thought finally, I'm gonna hear her. You know you always want to hear what the competition is like."

"But, ah, yeah well, just a whisper came out. That was it. A whisper."

"That's too odd. I cud see yew all, from my seat. I watched closely, an' moved closer. I lost sight of Timothy and Jay. Thought she wuz convulsing, an' maybe havin' a reaction to tha electric shock. Wuz watchin' 'er an' thought, dear Lord it luks like she's in pain. Why isn't anyone helping?"

"No, nothing like that. It was just a whisper. A dramatic whisper, but a whisper nonetheless. I was underwhelmed by it. Left me, confused when she didn't come out the door right behind me. What an adventure mom. Really, the next time you think one up, don't include me. I won't be doing the likes of this any time soon."

"I hear ya darlin', let's ged on tha 164 an' go home. Hopefully, Sista Soulja, Guardian of Mid-night hotel lobbies, and thieving Hispanics won't be driving. I'm tew tired tew hear her nonsense."

Kat and Rita returned to their routine in northern Virginia and finally, four weeks later, the phone rang. Lifting the receiver, Kat answers, "Chloe, hey! How you been? I tried calling, left a message a few times, I lost Timothy's number. Jay must not want to be talking to me, because I've left messages, he doesn't call back. We wanted to know how things were going. Mom, says hi!" Rita moves near Kat on the sofa to hear Chloe on the speaker.

"Hey Miss Rita. Missed you both. Oh Kat, honey they've run me ragged. Timothy got a pass, so he and I hung together. Wish you had been with us. Don't know what happened to Jay. Timothy says they got separated somewhere along the line. Well you know he wasn't in a good mood. Guess that night out on the street with his dog, took away his sense of humor."

"He was pretty exhausted by that whole episode. I know he was worried. He was becoming homeless, don't forget."

"Kat, I don't understand why they didn't pass you. You've got an amazing voice."

"Hey thanks. I thought I should have at least gotten to the first round, but it wasn't meant to be. I had to get back to work anyway. I supposed if I had moved up one more station, my boss would have been happy for me, cut me some slack, but what the hey, there's always another audition down the road, isn't there? It was one heck of a trip wasn't it? So what happened after I left the audition?"

"Well they told us to wait in a room and fill out more forms. They formed us up the ying, yang. Then told us to come back in four days. We met at some hotel in Manhattan. They had hordes of us in big empty ballrooms. We were told to check in, leave our things in our rooms, to hurry up and meet in a ballroom. Well they got us all signed up. You know the way we did on the first day, then we got to sit down and wait forever."

"Bryan Earcrestful show up again."

"No this was more of those high school producers roaming around. They video everything. I mean everything. If you're havin' a fuckin' nervous breakdown from the tension, they're in your face. So, it got a little exhausting because they held us locked up in those rooms waiting for announcements."

"Damn Chloe, that's annoying. How long did that go on for.?"

"Well that was a day. All the paper work was done, we went to our rooms, the next day we had to compete again. We had to do the whole damn thing over."

Quizzically Kat asks, "Over, the same thing?"

"Yeah well that's what they told me. Do what you did the last time. Well, I thought I'm game. It's exactly what Spicy had said, 'you have to have your game on. Do something different.' Got me to the next round didn't it? So I did the song the same way."

"Exactly the same way? Chloe? I mean you bowed, and whispered?"

"Yeah, exactly the same way. I got to the next round, Timothy was still with me."

"Oh gosh Chloe. But you had a song prepared."

"Yes, I did, but they said do what you did at the Izod Center."

"No shit. That's really odd."

"You betcha honey, then they said, again, the same way."

"What, are you kidding Chloe?"

"No, not kidding."

"Were you and Timothy still in Manhattan, or did they take you someplace else?" "No we stayed holed up in the room for ten days, couldn't go anywhere. We didn't know when we were gonna be called." "That sucks, Chloe, you would have loved walking around Manhattan above ground."

"Don't you know that gurl. Here I got a paid hotel, food, in mid-town Manhattan no less, and this gurl has to keep her booty indoors. Looked interesting enough out my window. It didn't look like the Bronx. Well I got to the next round of judges, I started to sing the song the way it's supposed to be sung. You know, full voice, not how I did it first, or second, or third. Well one of the producers, says 'hey I got notes here, I've seen the video, you did that song a certain way. Well that's what I want to hear.'"

"I asked him. Don't you want to hear my real voice?" He said, 'no, we like it just the way you did it. If you wanna go through to the next round, see the celebrity judges, we want you to do it exactly that way here and then, in front of them.'"

Kat breaks in, "Oh Chloe, you didn't. That's part of those look foolish parts on the show. What did you do?"

"Well I said, I'm here to sing, that wasn't singing." "Oh God Chloe, I'm so sorry." "Well I thought of my baby, my family, I thought, I'm not gonna have some video go viral on YOUTUBE for him to see me making a fool of myself."

"Good for you Chloe. What happened next?" "Well they showed me the door."

Silence fell between the friends for a few minutes, then Kat suggests, "Let's do some auditions down the road. We can go in together. Take the Chinatown bus from DC. We can avoid Bus 164 altogether now. I have to get back into the game. Even if it's just to practice. I'm getting my vocals ready for Conservatory. You interested Chloe?"

"Don't havta ask me. Let's do it gurl!"

"Good Chloe. Maybe we'll meet up with the Tin Man. We'll find the South Carolina Jersey boy."

Suenos

dreaming the
dream.

Dreamers.

GLOSSARY

Phrases; Spanish and Yiddish

'Adobe fogon': Adobe stove.
'Anos de las cosas politico': Years of things politic.
'Campesinos, trabajando duro, siempre': Peasant workers, working hard, always.
'Con assesino, hombres borachos, hombres crudos': With assassins, drunken, crude men.
'Con humilidad': With humility.
'Con pelo de indios': With hair like Indians.
'De su consequencia': Of her status.
'Deja que la gente te pasan, por favor': Please let the people pass.
'El color': The color.
'El hombresito': Young male child.
'El momento': That moment of time.
'El mundo Hondureano no era tan pequeno': The Honduran world wasn't so small.
'Er Toig nit': No good, worthless.
'Eran poderoso': They were powerful.
'Fogon lena': Wood burning stove.
'Gefilte fish': Ashkenazi Jewish dish made from a poached mixture of ground deboned fish, such as carp, whitefish, or pike, which is typically eaten as an appetizer.
'Hija honrada kultur': Honorable daughter (derogatory) culture.
'Hija honrada': Honorable daughter.
'Hombres duro, bruto, pistoleros': Hard, brutish pistol packing men.
'La familia nuestra': Our family.
'La familias' rancho': The families ranch.
La frontera: The frontier.
'La hija querida': The beloved daughter.

'La misma Mama': Exactly like her mother.

La Marqueta: Marketplace under the elevated Metro North railway tracks between 111th Street and 116th Street on Park Avenue in East Harlem in Manhattan, New York City. In its heyday over 500 vendors operated out of La Marqueta, and it was an important social and economic venue for Hispanic New York.

La Mosquitia: Eastern most part of Honduras along the Coast. A region of tropical rainforest, pine savannah, and marsh accessible primarily by water and air. Its population includes indigenous and ethnic groups such as the Miskito, Pech. The largest wilderness area in Central America, consisting of mangrove swamps, lagoons, rivers, savannas and tropical rain forests.

'La nina esperada': The longed for child.

'La otra persona': The other person.

'La vida que tenian': The life they had.

'Las estrellas': The stars.

'Las lagrimas': The tears.

'Lo prometo': I promise.

'Los chavos': Money, change.

'Los partidos': The political parties.

'Mama's pello': Mother's hair.

'Mas pacifico': More peacefully.

'Muy querida': Beloved.

'No andas con esos ninos': Don't run around with those kids.

'No cosino de latas' : I don't cook from cans.

'No puedo': I can't

'Oi gevalt' Oy gevalt: Exclamation of surprise, incredulity, or simply used to emphasize a statement. often used when kvetching.

'Para la mama y el nino': For the Mama and the child.

'Peones, hermanos y el Don': Laborers, brothers and the Don.

'Por Favor': Please.

'Que me dicen mis amigos': What are you saying to me, my friends?

'Quien mas': Who else?

'Schlemiel! Schlimazel! Hasenpfeffer Incorporated': At the start of each episode, Laverne and Shirley are skipping down the street, reciting a Yiddish-American chant: '1, 2, 3, 4, 5, 6, 7, 8 Schlemiel! Schlimazel! Hasenpfeffer Incorporated!' Leads into the series' theme song, 'Making Our Dreams Come True' performed by Cyndi Grecco.

'Seas respectosa': Be respectful.
'Seguro que todo esta bien': Sure that everything is well.
'Spanish Harlem': East Harlem, also known as El Barrio, is a neighborhood of Upper Manhattan, New York City roughly encompassing the area north of the Upper East Side and East 96th Street up to roughly East 142nd Street east of Fifth Avenue to the East and Harlem Rivers.
'Su amor': Her love.
'Su pais, su amor': Her country, her love.
'Tacita de café': Small cup of coffee, affectionately.
'Tanta gente': So many people.
'The El': The IRT Third Avenue Line, commonly known as the Third Avenue El, and the Bronx El, was an elevated railway in Manhattan and the Bronx, New York City.
'Un abrazo': A hug.
'Una nina querida': A much loved daughter.
'Una senorita elegante y Hermosa': A young lady of elegance and beauty.

Words; Spanish, Yiddish

Abuela: Grandmother.
Abuelita(o): Grandma, grandpa.
Abuelos: Grandparents.
Adagio: A slow passage, movement, or work.
Adventura: Adventure.
Americano: American. (Male)
Amor: Love.
Andante: to describe a relatively slow, moderately paced tune.
Arroz: Rice.
Assesinos: Assassins.
Aya: There.
Azul: Blue.
Babka: Eastern European coffee cake flavored with orange rind, rum, almonds, and raisins.
Bandera: Flag.
Banderas: Flags.
Bendicion: Blessings.
Bendiciones: Blessings.
Blanco: White.

Bopkis: Nonsense or nothing.
Borsht circuit: Theaters, nightclubs associated with Jewish summer resorts in the Catskills.
Bubbe: Grandmother, grandfather.
Bubbleh, bubbale: Alternative Spellings. bubele, bobale, bubala, bubale, bubbaleh, bubeleh. Definitions; sweetie, darling [term of endearment].
Bubkes: The least amount.
Bupkis: Emphatically nothing.
Caballos: Horses.
Café: Coffee.
Cafecito: 'A little coffee' but it's not necessarily referred to the size of the coffee.
Campesino: Peasant farmer.
Caoba: Mahogany.
Capital: Capital.
Carribeno: Person from the Caribbean.
Casa: House.
Cenotes: A cenote is a natural pit, or sinkhole, resulting from the collapse of limestone bedrock that exposes groundwater underneath.
Cerritos: Little hills.
Chica: Girl or young woman.
Chisme: Gossip.
Chutzpah: Shameless audacity; impudence.
Cojones: Testicles, in profane slang; Courage or boldness.
Comida: Food.
Compesinos: Farm worker.
Con: With.
Conjunto: Small musical group or band.
Danken: Thank you.
De: Of.
Déjà vu: The feeling that the situation currently being experienced has already been experienced in the past.
Dignidad: Dignity.
Diminuendo: Gradual reduction of force or loudness.
Dios: God.
Dolce: Sweet.
Dominicana: Dominican.
Don: Title given to men of high social status through respect.
Dona: Title given to women of high social status through respect.

Dreck: Filth, dregs.

Dulce: Sweet.

Doctor: Doctor.

El Barrio: Spanish Harlem, a neighborhood in New York City.

Empresas: Businesses.

Espana: Spain.

Espanoles: Spanairds.

Espera: Wait.

Familia: Family.

Fershtay: Do you understand?

Finagle: Obtain (something) by devious or dishonest means.

Frijoles: Beans.

Gaelic: Celtic language of Scotland.

Ganado: Earned.

Gavalt: Exclamation of alarm.

Gelato: Italian or Italian-style ice cream.

Gestapo: German state secret police during the Nazi regime, organized in 1933, notorious for its brutal methods.

Goy: Used pejoratively to refer to a non-Jewish person.

Gracia: Thanks.

Grazie: Thanks.

Hacienda: Hacienda, in the colonies of the Spanish Empire, is an estate, similar in form to a Roman villa. Some haciendas were plantations. The term hacienda refers to landed estates of significant size.

Haggadah: Legend, parable, or anecdote used to illustrate a point of Law in the Talmud.

Hasanpfeffer: Hasenpfeffer (also spelled hasenfeffer) a traditional German stew of marinated rabbit or hare.

Hija: Daughter.

Humilidad: Humility.

Isla: Island.

Italianos: Italians.

Jesu Cristo: Jesus Christ.

Judeos: Jews.

Klutzy: Clumsy, awkward, or foolish.

Kulture: Culture emphasizing practical efficiency and individual subordination to the state.

Kulture: German civilization, culture (derogatorily suggests elements of racism, authoritarianism, or militarism).

Kvetch: Person who complains a great deal.

Kvetshing: Complain.

La: The.

Ladino:
Romance language, descended from medieval Spanish, spoken by Sephardic Jews.

Lavanderas: Laundress.

Leche: Milk.

Lempira: Honduran currency.

Lena: Wood.

Libertinas: Libertine. Loose female.

Llego: Arrived.

Lo: The.

Machetes: A machete is a broad blade used either as an implement like an axe, or in combat like a short sword.

Machismo: Strong or aggressive masculine pride.

Maize: Corn.

Mami: Affectionate term for mother, mama.

Mansanas: Apples.

Mantilla: Lace or silk scarf worn by women over the hair and shoulders, especially in Spain.

Matrona: Female head figure.

Mesa: The Table.

Meshugaas: Mad, crazy.

Meshugenah: Crazy person.

Mestizo: Person of mixed race, one having Spanish and indigenous descent. (Latin America)

Mishpocheh, mishpocha, mishpachah: Entire family network of relatives by blood or marriage (and sometimes close friends), 'she invited the whole mishpocha'.

Momento: Moment.

Montanas: Mountains.

Mucho: Much.

Mundo: World.

Musica: Music.

Naturalez: Nature.

Nina: Female child.

Nosh: Eat food enthusiastically or greedily.

Nudnik: Pestering, nagging, or irritating person; a bore.

Nunca: Never.

Nuvo-Spanglish: Miuxture of Spanish and English.

Nuyorican: Term used by Boricuas (Puerto Ricans from Puerto Rico) to differentiate those of Puerto Rican descent from the Puerto Rico-born. Nuyorican is also used to refer to the Spanish spoken by New York Puerto Ricans.

Oro: Gold.

Orquestras: Orchestra

Pajarito: Small bird.

Pan: Bread.

Papa: Father.

Papi: Daddy, extended as a general term of endearment.

Pavos: Turkey(s).

Peones: Laborer, cowhand.

Perfectamundo: Psuedo-street slang signifying something is exceptional or it is perfect.

Periodicos: Newspapers.

Perniel: Pork.

Pescado: Fish.

Pianissimo: Very softly. Used as a direction in music.

Pistolas: Guns.

Platanos: Plantains.

Pogroms: Organized massacre of a particular ethnic group, in particular that of Jews in Russia or eastern Europe.

Pollos: Chickens.

Pon: Put.

Presto: Immediately. Rapid tempo.

Pueblitos: Villages.

Putz: Fool; an idiot. 2. Vulgar Slang; penis. intr.v. putzed, **putz**·ing, **putz**·es. Slang; To putter.

Radio: Radio.

Rancho: Ranch.

Rendezvous: Place appointed for assembling or meeting.

Rios: Rivers.

Sacrificious: Sacrifices.

Sapodilla: Fruit tree.

Schlemiel: a stupid, awkward, or unlucky person.

Schlep: Carrying, dragging.

Schleping: Haul or carry (something heavy or awkward).

Schmeer: Anything that can be spread.

Schmilt: Made-up rhyming word ('shmilt') is a way of emphatically rejecting the idea that the first word ('guilt') applies.

Schmo or schmoe: Schmoes, also shmoes Slang. A stupid or obnoxious person.

Schmo: A stupid or obnoxious person.

Schmooz: Talk intimately and cozily; gossip.

Schmuck: Clumsy or stupid person; an oaf. Yiddish; shmok, penis, fool.

Seguro: Sure.

Senora: Mrs.

Senorita: Miss.

Shikker: Drunk

Shiksa: Disparaging term for a non-Jewish woman.

Shlimazel: a very unlucky or inept person who fails at everything.

Shtelt: Small Jewish town or village in eastern Europe.

Shtik: Comic theme or gimmick , in stand-up comedy a near equivalent term is a 'bit'.

Si: Yes.

Siempre: Always.

Sociedad: Society.

Spics: Derogatory term for peoples of Spanish heritage.

Staccato: Music. With each sound or note sharply detached or separated from the others.

Suenos: Dreams.

Tchotchke: Small decorative object; a trinket.

Tegoose calles: (Slang: Tegoose.) Streets of Tegucigalpa.

Tejanos: Mexican Americans from Texas.

Terenos: Land.

Todo: All.

Tokhes, tokhis: Buttocks, rear end.

Trabajando: Working.

Tuches: Buttocks.

Turistas: Tourists.

Un hombre: A man.

Vi: See.

Vida: Life.

Visabuelos: Great grandparents.

Y: And.

Ya: Already.

Yarmulke: Skullcap.

Yenta: Woman who is a gossip or busybody.

Yeshiva: Jewish institution focusing on the study of traditional religious texts; the Talmud and the Torah.

Yiddish: German dialect with words from Hebrew.
Yuchnat: 1. Coarse, loud-mouthed, boorish woman; 2. Fish wife.
Zapatos: Shoes.